"I chased you off," Emaline said quietly.

"I'm sorry about that."

"I have no intention of giving you an interview," Brett replied.

"I can see that," she said. "Again, I'm sorry."

"If it were just you and me," Brett said, his dark gaze latching on to hers, "I might enjoy the game of keeping my privacy and you trying to dig it up. But my nephew won't know how to deal with this kind of thing. So if you bring him up in a story in any way—that's crossing the line. I might be fair game but he isn't. He's a *kid*."

And Damian was just a kid...but he was also the center of some serious questions about the Rockwells. Senator Rockwell ran his campaigns on family values, and this little boy was a tough addition to the family for the Rockwells to explain. In fact, no one had explained him. Ever.

"I agree," Emaline replied, all the same.

Dear Reader,

I hope you have had as much fun with this
The Butternut Amish B&B miniseries as I have!
If you love books with lots of heart, cute kids and
strong families, then maybe you'll enjoy some
of the other books I've written. Come find me
online at patriciajohns.com for a complete list.

If you enjoyed this story, I'd love it if you posted
a review! Reviews help other readers to find
my books, and I'm eternally grateful for every
single one.

I also really enjoy hearing from my readers.
Feel free to find me on my website or on social
media. I'd love to hear from you!

Patricia

HEARTWARMING

A Boy's Amish Christmas

—

Patricia Johns

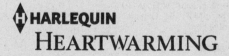

HARLEQUIN
HEARTWARMING

HARLEQUIN®
HEARTWARMING™

ISBN-13: 978-1-335-47550-3

A Boy's Amish Christmas

Copyright © 2023 by Patricia Johns

For questions and comments about the quality of this book, please contact us at CustomerService@Harlequin.com.

Harlequin Enterprises ULC
22 Adelaide St. West, 41st Floor
Toronto, Ontario M5H 4E3, Canada
www.Harlequin.com

Printed in U.S.A.

Patricia Johns is a *Publishers Weekly* bestselling author who writes from Alberta, Canada, where she lives with her husband and son. She writes Amish romances that will leave you yearning for a simpler life. You can find her at patriciajohns.com and on social media, where she loves to connect with her readers. Drop by her website and you might find your next read!

Books by Patricia Johns

Harlequin Heartwarming

The Butternut Amish B&B

Her Amish Country Valentine
A Single Dad in Amish Country

Amish Country Haven

A Deputy in Amish Country
A Cowboy in Amish Country

The Second Chance Club

Their Mountain Reunion
Mountain Mistletoe Christmas
Rocky Mountain Baby
Snowbound with Her Mountain Cowboy

Love Inspired

Amish Country Matches

The Amish Matchmaking Dilemma
Their Amish Secret
The Amish Marriage Arrangement

Visit the Author Profile page
at Harlequin.com for more titles.

To my husband and son
—you are my everything!

CHAPTER ONE

BRETT ROCKWELL GLANCED over his shoulder at the back seat of his Ford F-150, where his nephew sat. The five-year-old's hair was pushed up in tufts around his noise-canceling headphones. Brett had been warned that he wouldn't take them off for anything. The headphones helped with his aversion to noise, Brett's brother told him. Damian was a sensitive kid.

Snow spun from the sky in a heavy veil, and Brett leaned forward trying to peer past the whipping flakes. His ranch was still a good two hours away. He didn't like the prospect of driving through a blizzard at night, especially not on these narrow roads this far into the country. Even the two-lane highway was narrow.

It was a good thing that Brett knew the area. The Butternut Amish Bed and Breakfast wasn't too far from here, and if they stopped for the night there, they could carry on to Brett's ranch in the morning. Brett was pretty sure the kid would enjoy seeing horses and buggies out here in Pennsylvania's Amish Country, but the Amish weren't out this evening.

Brett was looking forward to a couple of weeks with his nephew while his brother and sister-in-law were traveling for the campaign. Dean Rockwell was a senator with an election coming up, and he'd agreed to some pre-Christmas appearances. They'd all meet up at Brett's ranch for Christmas Day. Dean and Bobbie's teenage children were skiing with friends over the holiday, and Brett was getting some quality time with five-year-old Damian. That was what the Rockwells did, especially during election time—they pulled together.

His GPS prompted him to turn at Butternut Drive. The pickup truck's tires crunched onto snowy gravel, and Damian roused in the back seat. Brett glanced in the mirror again to see the boy pull off his headphones momentarily.

"Are we there yet?" Damian asked.

"Change of plans," Brett said. "We aren't going to make it to my ranch tonight. We're going to try and stop at a little Amish bed-and-breakfast that I know about out here."

"What's that?"

"It's a place with a warm bed," Brett said. "I've eaten there before a couple of times, but I didn't stay the night. The lady who owns it is very nice."

"How long until we get *there*, then?"

"The GPS says three minutes."

Brett was almost on top of the white wooden sign before he spotted the dark green letters that read Butternut Amish Bed and Breakfast through the snowfall. He glanced into the rearview mirror and watched as Damian put his headphones over his ears.

"You might find it quiet enough to take the headphones off more, Damian," he said. "I know you hate too much noise, but out here, it's pretty quiet. These are Amish people. No radio or TV or YouTube or anything like that. These are the quietest people around."

Damian didn't touch the headphones, and maybe he hadn't even heard. Brett knew that the headphones were more than a comfort for the kid—they were a necessity a lot of the time. He had some symptoms of autism spectrum disorder, and those headphones helped him to filter out all the extra noise and distraction that he couldn't handle.

Brett slowed and turned into the drive. For the first few yards, it was all trees, and then they emerged into a wide-open yard, covered in snow, surrounding a large white two-story farmhouse with a broad veranda out front. The veranda looked like it had been recently swept clear of snow, and a broom was propped next to the front door. A whisper of smoke crept up from the chimney. They were one week from Christmas, but the only decorations he could see were some evergreen fronds bound together with twine and tied to the front of every third veranda rail.

There was a hatchback car parked in the drive next to a buggy that wasn't hitched up, its shafts resting in the snow. To the side he could see a small fenced field with a large bale of bright fresh hay sitting in a feeder in the center. A quarter horse was munching on the feed, not seeming to mind the falling snow one bit, and a long-eared donkey stood doggedly next to him.

"Hey, look out there," Brett said. He'd been trying to get Damian to engage with something—anything—ever since they'd left Pittsburgh. Brett wasn't sure if he was missing his mom and dad or his nanny the most. Brett had drawn the line at bringing the nanny with them. It was almost Christmas, and he got to hang out with this kid for the next week and a half and celebrate with him and his family, and he was determined to make the holiday as wholesome and filled with the Christmas spirit as possible. And in his books, dragging a nanny along with them wouldn't fit the bill. But he wondered now if he'd been too idealistic when he made that call.

Brett parked next to the hatchback and turned off the engine. Damian unbuckled his seat belt, and he opened his own door at the same time that Brett did. Damian jumped down onto the snowy ground.

The side door to the big white house opened, and an elderly Amish woman in a dark red dress with a white apron appeared in the doorway. She wore her white hair pulled back under a *kapp*, and her eyes sparkled behind a pair of rimless glasses. Her name was Belinda Wickey, and she was well known in this area for being both an Amish matchmaker and the owner of an in-demand bed-and-breakfast.

"She looks like Mrs. Claus," Damian said thoughtfully.

"Don't tell her that," Brett said with a chuckle. "She's Amish. I'm pretty sure they don't do Santa here. But she's a great cook and the nicest lady you could ever meet."

"Santa skips them?" Damian asked.

Okay, this had just taken the wrong turn. "Uh… No, he doesn't skip them, exactly, but he's sneakier out here. And they don't believe in Santa, so… Don't worry about it, Damian. Santa will make it to the ranch, okay? I know for a fact!"

"And you know that lady?" Damian asked.

"A little bit." This bed-and-breakfast was pretty well known.

Damian accepted that, and fell into silence.

"Hi, Belinda!" Brett called. "I don't know if you remember me, but I'm Brett Rockwell. I came out here for your Amish feast last spring?"

"Of course, Brett! I wouldn't forget you that easily." Belinda smiled warmly. "It's good to see you. How is your ankle?"

Right. He'd been nursing a sprained ankle his last visit. Just an accident at the ranch that was taking its time to heal up. It was impressive that she'd remembered.

"Much better, thanks," he said. "I'm sorry to just arrive with no reservation, but the roads are pretty bad, and I was hoping you might have a room for us."

"Of course," she replied. "I have another guest, but there is a free room. You're very welcome to it."

"Thank you." And he meant it from the bottom of his heart. "I really appreciate it."

"I'm just glad you made it this far, and I'm thrilled you'll get to experience a proper stay here. Come on in and get warm. This little fellow could probably use a cookie. Are there any allergies? My cookies are all nut free, and while I don't have gluten-free cookies, I do have some gluten-free apple crisp."

"No, no allergies. And that all sounds wonderful. I think you'll find us pretty easy to please." But as the words came out, he wasn't so sure that it was true. Damian found a change of plans difficult.

He went around to the back of the truck and pulled out their bags, Damian watching closely.

Belinda stepped back to let him inside, and he glanced over his shoulder to see Damian looking up at her quizzically.

"And who is this?" Belinda asked, fixing Damian with a grandmotherly smile.

"I'm Damian," he said, then lowered his voice. "And if it matters, I've been very good this year. You know…if you wanted to pass that along."

Brett stifled a laugh. So the kid was playing it safe, was he?

"Have you?" Belinda didn't seem to follow what Damian was thinking. "I'm very happy to hear that. The world needs more young men like you who behave well. We really don't have half enough of boys like you."

"Do you bake the cookies?" Damian asked cautiously.

"Do I ever!" Belinda replied. "I have some cookies on the counter."

"Do you have reindeer?" the boy whispered.

"Reindeer? No, they aren't too common here in Pennsylvania, dear. I have a donkey, though!" she said with a twinkle in her eye. "His name is Eeyore. And next door, my neighbor has chickens and five cows."

Damian didn't seem to know what to make of that, so he put his headphones back on again without response.

Belinda gave Brett a curious look.

"They cancel the noise," Brett said. "He gets overwhelmed with too much going on around him."

"Oh...poor little man," Belinda tutted softly. "Maybe cookies will help."

Brett wiped his boots off and carried on through to the kitchen. It smelled like cinnamon and cloves, and he noticed a pretty woman sitting at the table, a steaming mug in front of her. She must be the other guest Belinda mentioned. She wasn't Amish—she wore a cowl-necked sweater and a pair of blue jeans. She was petite and blond, and she had a young look about her that was betrayed by the depth of her blue eyes, and she regarded him pointedly.

"Hi," he said.

"Hello." She put her hands around the mug, as if she were warming her fingers.

"This is our other guest this week," Belinda said, bustling up behind him. "Meet Emaline."

"I'm Brett," he said. "This is Damian. We're only passing through, so we shouldn't be in your way for too long."

Was there a husband or boyfriend with her? He instinctively looked at her ring finger and saw it was bare. That didn't tell him much, though. But her name sounded familiar—it wasn't a common one, and he was sure he'd come across it before...but where?

"It's no problem. I'm here for a few days for work," she said.

She nudged the plate of cookies that sat beside her toward Damian and gave him a welcoming smile. Damian pulled his headphones off and smiled back shyly. Yeah, all it took was a pretty woman, apparently.

"You want a cookie?" Emaline asked.

Damian took one and shoved it into his mouth.

"Good, huh?" Emaline asked.

Damian nodded.

"I also have cinnamon buns, blackberry cobbler, apple crisp and three kinds of pie," Belinda said. "But don't fill up too much, because tonight's dinner is going to be roast beef, and I expect with that blowing snow, everyone is going to want to eat hearty."

This was just what Brett and Damian needed—a little break from the hustle and bustle of the city. Damian had gone to kindergarten for the first time that year, and Brett had been told that it wasn't a raving success. He had a support teacher who helped him to navigate school, but it hadn't really been enough. With twenty-five other kids in the class, he'd been permanently overwhelmed. That broke Brett's heart just a little bit.

The sound of boots echoed on the step, and the door opened without a knock. A moment later an old Amish man appeared in the doorway, accompanied by a black dog with a crust of snow on its back. Snow dusted the shoulders of the man's black woolen coat, and his woolen hat was covered in snow, too. His ears were bright red from the cold, and he looked a little different. It took Brett a moment to realize that this was the first old Amish man he'd ever seen with a shaved face. Beards meant a man was married—Brett knew that much. Did that make this old guy a bachelor?

"Oh, Eli, you're here," Belinda said. "These are my newest guests, Brett and Damian. And this is Eli, my neighbor, and his dog is named Hund."

Brett gave him a nod, and then the two old people broke off into a conversation in Pennsylvania Dutch. The old man brushed the snow off the dog's back, and then Hund sauntered over to the wood stove and lay down in front of it.

Damian put his headphones back on and helped himself to another cookie. Brett took a cookie, too. He met Emaline's gaze as he took a bite. Emaline…the name still nagged at his mind as familiar. Where had he heard it?

The cookie was shortbread with some gingerbread spice added in. Delicious. Emaline cocked her head to one side, regarding him thoughtfully as he ate.

"You're Brett Rockwell," she said.

So she recognized him, too. Maybe this would clear up the mystery.

"Guilty as charged," he said, attempting to joke.

"You look taller in person," she said.

"Do I?" He shrugged. "I don't normally hear that."

She didn't elaborate, and Brett felt his optimism start to wane. He liked getting out and doing things with real people, but every once in a while, he was reminded that families like his didn't get that luxury too often. Their combination of wealth and social standing made them the center of a lot of public interest.

"I feel at a disadvantage here," he said. "You seem to know quite a bit about me."

"From the news," she said.

He chuckled uncomfortably. "Don't always believe what you see in the news." The news stories about him hadn't been flattering, and not all of them were true.

She smiled, then lifted her mug and took a sip. The old Amish couple were still discussing something animatedly. They had moved over to the window and were peering outside.

"I suppose it's possible to get things wrong," she said. "That's what retractions are for."

Yeah, he had a lot of strong opinions about the press and their ability to plaster a story on the front page, then print a retraction on page six. The Rockwells had decided years ago to keep a cordial relationship with the press. It was easier than trying to fight them off at every turn. His senator brother was the one who had to tangle with them most often, not Brett. Unfortunately, there had been a few news stories about Brett that had centered around some drunken parties, a rather loud scene at a restaurant, a fistfight at a bar and an ex-girlfriend who sold her story to the press about how he was a hopeless alcoholic. All of *that* had been true.

"What brings you out to Amish Country a week before Christmas?" he asked, attempting to change the subject.

"I'm an influencer," she said.

"Yeah?" That didn't narrow it down at all.

"I'm a travel vlogger—I do stories on Pennsylvania tourist attractions, mostly. Though I'd like to branch out to do stories in other states."

"Right. I knew I recognized your name. You do those TikTok videos about packing light and airport drama."

"You've heard of me!"

"Yeah. I enjoy your stories. I come across them on social media a lot. You do a lot for Pennsylvania tourism."

"Thank you," she said. "I actually went to journalism school."

"Really?" That did surprise him. Maybe it shouldn't. Everyone had interesting backgrounds if you took time to ask. That was something his brother had taught him.

"Yep. It's tough to break in, though, and this pays pretty well if you have a knack for the tech side."

"Which you seem to."

"I definitely do." She cast him a smile. "But this is some extraordinary luck meeting you here… I'd love to do some short clips about a Rockwell in Amish Country. People would click on that, for sure."

"No, thanks."

"You're photogenic. I'm thinking of some snowy background and that cowboy hat on your head. My viewers would gobble you up."

"Yeah, that's the fear," he said with a bitter laugh. "No, thanks. I'm keeping out of the public eye these days."

"Don't you ever want to put out the real story about you?" she asked.

"Who says the one already out there is wrong?" He was getting irritated now.

She shrugged. "Because the stories I've seen about you were obviously just for drama and intrigue. No one is that interesting, Brett Rockwell. Including you."

He had to laugh at that. She was right—he'd turned things around, and he'd quit drinking. The reporters never got it right, and never handled his life fairly. They went for the story, not for the balanced truth. But who said he wanted every last bit of "truth" about him out there for public consumption? Something could be true and also private. Besides, this wasn't just about him—Damian deserved a proper Christmas. And he wasn't about to let anyone target Damian for a news story.

"Nope," Brett said with a shake of his head. "Not interested."

He just wanted a quiet evening and a rustic good time for his nephew, but it didn't look like that was going to be possible with an online influencer under the same roof who was looking for content. There was no way that they could spend the night here. Blowing snow or not, he and Damian would have to drive through.

"Damian, we're not going to stay," he said. "We'll head out to the ranch tonight."

AND AS QUICKLY as that, she'd chased him off. Emaline mentally kicked herself. She was obviously out of practice with actual people who made it to the news. All she wanted was some social media content that would pique interest. She had to keep the likes, clicks and shares up if she wanted to keep growing, and in this business, if she wasn't growing, she was dropping off the map. Pure and simple.

She put down her mug of tea and leaned her elbows onto the table. Brett hustled Damian away, but the boy looked longingly back at the plate of cookies.

"You could contribute to Pennsylvania tourism," she said, raising her voice.

"I don't need to contribute to tourism. I already contribute beef to people's tables," he said. "I run a twenty-five-hectare ranch."

"Good!" She leaned back. "So let's tell people that. You're not some rich, out-of-touch part of Pennsylvania royalty, you're a rancher."

"I don't need to announce it to the state for my own personal satisfaction," he said curtly. "I do what I do."

Brett headed over to the window where Belinda and Eli stood. The wind whisked the snow past the window in a blinding blur, then slowed again.

"I don't think we'll be staying tonight, after all," Brett said to Belinda. "I'll pay for my stay, but we'll head out now."

"What?" Belinda's eyes widened. "We have enough bedrooms for everyone. I'm sorry if I wasn't clear about that. Maybe we had a miscommunication?"

"It's okay," Brett said with a softened smile. "It's not your fault. It's a bit complicated, though."

Emaline wished she'd kept her mouth shut and said nothing—at least for the time being. But the damage was done. And she couldn't help but think that if she'd gotten a job in journalism like she'd wanted to, this would have been a plum opportunity standing right in front of her with a little boy in noise-canceling headphones in tow.

Brett scooped up his bags and looked back at the boy. "Come on, Damian. We're going to drive through, okay? You'll see the ranch tonight after all."

"We can't stay here?" Damian had sidled over to the warmth of the wood stove.

"Come on," Brett said curtly.

Damian did as he was told and followed his uncle out the door. Belinda and Eli watched them through the window, murmuring quietly in a mix of English and Pennsylvania Dutch.

"I don't think he'll make it in that storm," Eli said, his voice low.

"No, I don't think so," Belinda agreed.

"I'll have to go put the animals in the stable to weather this storm," Eli said. "I'll take care of yours, too."

"Mighty kind of you, Eli," Belinda said. *"Danke."*

Eli headed for the door. He whistled softly, and the dog looked up from his spot by the fire, then slowly rose to his feet and plodded over to the door. From what Emaline had seen of the pooch, he was loyal to Eli. The old man and his dog headed out, and Belinda stood in silence for a moment until the door slammed shut behind him.

"Men are stubborn creatures," Belinda said, turning around. "If I tried to stop Eli from taking care of my horse and donkey, too, he'd only argue with me. So I'll include him in that roast beef supper tonight to thank him for his trouble."

"He seems like a nice man," Emaline said.

"*Yah*, he's a very nice man," Belinda agreed. "He's a bit on the odd side, but nice."

"How is he odd?"

"He's stopped doing it now, but he used to have all sorts of animals in his house. Hens, a calf, and once a full-grown sheep!"

"I'd like to see that!" Emaline smiled, and her mind skipped forward to potential video topics, as it often did. "That would make an interesting human interest vlog."

"What's a vlog?"

"A video blog." That didn't seem to help. "It's a video where I talk about something and I post it online, and hopefully it gets shared and commented on, and..."

Still, this wasn't helping. Emaline let it go. "But you were saying about the farm animals in his house?"

"Oh, he doesn't do it anymore," Belinda said.

"Why not?"

"Because…" Belinda smiled faintly. "Because of me, I think."

"You sorted him out, did you?" Emaline said with a short laugh.

"I believe I did." Belinda leaned toward the window again. "And it looks like Brett isn't getting too far. I can just see his taillights. He's stopped."

Emaline got up and joined Belinda at the window. Eli's black silhouette was barely visible as he disappeared into the stable. She could just make out the red dots of Brett's taillights through the snow in the opposite direction. For a moment, nothing happened, and then the vehicle started to reverse. Ever so slowly, it came back up the drive.

"Just as well," Belinda said, moving away from the window. "It's cold out there and the roads will be terrible. That's the kind of weather where people end up in accidents. Everyone is safer and warmer indoors with a fire going."

The kitchen certainly was inviting, with the dry heat pumping out of the black potbellied stove and the soft glow of polished wood from the cupboards and the big table that dominated one side of the room. Outside, the wind whistled, and Emaline shivered.

She hoped Brett really was coming back.

Maybe it was the wannabe journalist inside of her, but he seemed like he'd be an interesting guy. There were a lot of stories about his playboy days a few years back, and then he just disappeared. Started ranching. Total about-face. What caused that kind of change in a man? She'd really like to know.

Belinda went back into the kitchen and pulled a big white enameled teapot off the stove. She filled it up at the sink and returned it to the stovetop with a hiss of cold water against hot iron. Then she turned toward the door and was halfway there before they heard the knock. Belinda shot Emaline a knowing little smile and disappeared into the mudroom.

"Come back inside." Belinda's voice was motherly. "I knew you wouldn't get far. It's just too miserable to drive in that snow. The weather is bigger than all of us, and all we can do is accept it. I have a fire stoked up, and I just put water on the stove for some tea, or some hot chocolate for you, Damian."

Damian came into the kitchen first and beelined for that plate of cookies. Brett stood in the doorway, his lips pressed together. He was of average height but tall compared to Emaline. He pulled his gloves off and tucked them into a pocket, his irritable expression firmly in place. That was because of her.

She stood and straightened her shoulders, then crossed the room.

"I chased you off," Emaline said quietly. "I'm sorry about that."

"I have no intention of being part of your vlog."

"Got it. It's fine. I won't push the issue."

"If it were just you and me," Brett said, his dark gaze latching on to hers meaningfully, "I might even enjoy the game of keeping my privacy and you trying to dig it up. But this isn't just you and me. I've got my nephew here, and he's just a kid."

"I agree," Emaline replied. "Look, it was just an idea. I thought my viewers would enjoy getting a glimpse of Brett Rockwell, the senator's bad-boy brother. I remember you were pretty popular, even with the bad publicity." He gave her a flat look, and she put her hands up. "I'm sorry, I'll stick to Amish simple pleasures. That's why I'm here, anyway."

Brett had the Rockwell good looks—strong jaw, good bone structure, piercing eyes. The Rockwells were born to politics. Rockwell men looked good behind podiums and rolling up their shirtsleeves next to miners for a photo op. But up close, Brett had a cornered, vulnerable look in his eye, and she felt a flicker of pity.

"You're doing a vlog about the Amish Butternut B&B?" he asked.

"I am. It's such a cute place, especially this close to the holidays. I promised Belinda that I wouldn't film her, but she says I can do a whole piece on their Christmas decorations." He glanced around, and she chuckled. "They aren't up yet."

"Okay…" He smiled sheepishly. "Treat me like I'm Amish—no pictures, no video."

"You don't know me, but I'm a woman of my word," she said. "I can't say you don't interest me, though."

"*I* interest you?" he asked warily.

"The younger brother of the senator," she said. "How does a man go from party boy to serious rancher in five years' time? What changed inside of you? What realizations did you come to for that kind of transformation? That's what I want to know."

"That's no travel vlog curiosity," he said, but a smile touched his lips.

"No, it isn't." She shrugged. "It's personal curiosity. But if we're going to be stuck here together, I think it will be incredibly awkward if you're constantly running from me. There's not too far to go."

"True." He smiled faintly. "And Damian is off-limits. Completely."

"Absolutely," she agreed. Besides, Damian with his headphones and his hunger for cookies had captured her heart a little bit, too. She would leave Damian out of this.

Brett still didn't look like he believed her, but it was the best she could do for now.

"Is everything better now?" Belinda asked from the table. She had a knife and was cutting apart a pan of cinnamon buns.

"Uh—" Emaline looked from Belinda and up at Brett. "I think so. I think we can coexist here for a day or two."

"Coexist," Belinda muttered, shaking her head. "This is an Amish establishment, and we'll do a mite better than coexistence. We'll leave here friends."

"All right," Emaline said. "We'll even be friendly."

Brett cast her a boyish smile, his earlier tension seeming to dissipate, and a shiver ran up her arms. He was still a very good-looking guy. Being snowed in with a handsome single cowboy wasn't exactly punishment.

"Come sit down," Belinda said. "The snow will fall as long as it falls. Sometimes, all you can do is wait out the weather. And while we wait, we eat good food and we chat. It's our way."

Belinda smiled and gestured to the table.
Brett looked toward Emaline, and she shrugged.
Like Belinda said, there were some things, like
the weather, that were bigger than all of them.

CHAPTER TWO

"CHRISTMAS IN AN Amish community is probably different than you're used to," Belinda was saying as Brett and Damian took a seat at the table. "For one, we don't decorate in quite the same way the rest of you do. We keep things simple, and we mostly rely upon friends and family to provide the sparkle in a room. But there are a few little decorations we like to put up. Emaline offered to help me with it. She's going to do a… vlog? That's what you call it, *yah*?"

He glanced over at Emaline and she gave the old woman an indulgent smile. "Yes, a vlog. My viewers will love seeing how you decorate."

Brett accepted a mug of hot water from Belinda, and she nudged a basket of packaged teas and hot chocolates across the table toward him. Damian sat up on his knees on his chair, and Brett handed him a pack of hot chocolate mix.

"What will you do for Christmas this year?" Brett asked the old woman.

"My children who've moved to other communities will all be back," Belinda said with a smile. "I have one son, Jonah, who still lives in Danke. He's got a farm, and between the two of us, we'll host everyone. It will be wonderful to be all together again, and I'll have all the grandchildren with me at once. I can't wait."

"When are they coming?" Brett asked. There was only a week until Christmas now.

"For Second Christmas," Belinda said.

"What's that?" Damian asked.

"Well, we have two Christmases," Belinda said. "There's Christmas Day, and then the day after Christmas Day—Boxing Day, you all call it—we have Second Christmas. It's Christmas all over again, and it gives big families more time to visit each other."

Second Christmas…instead of wasting money on post-Christmas sales. That Amish tradition actually sounded rather nice, not having Christmas suddenly disintegrate into shopping mayhem the very next day.

"How many grandchildren do you have?" Emaline asked.

"It'll be thirty-three of them in March," Belinda said.

"Thirty-three…" Brett suppressed his surprise. "Do you buy gifts?"

"With that many people coming together, we don't do gifts the same way," Belinda replied. "Everyone brings one small useful or homemade gift, and we pass them out at random. The homemade gifts are everyone's favorite. I'm breaking the rules just a little bit, because I'm making one special cookie for each child with their initial on it."

"That's a neat idea," Emaline said with a smile.

"I do make some very good shortbread cookies." Belinda blushed a little. "That is prideful of me to say, and I shouldn't say it, but I want the children to have something from their *mammie*."

Brett had to agree that it was a rather sweet idea, and the simplicity was far from the extravagant Christmases that the Rockwells normally enjoyed. Providing a quality Christmas for Damian had been on Brett's mind this year. Normally, he just showed up at whatever Christmas festivities were planned at Dean's home, and Bobbie was in charge of making everything festive and perfect. She was great at dinner parties, decorating and planning gatherings that felt effortless.

"And what about you all?" Belinda asked. "What will you do for Christmas?"

Emaline looked over at him expectantly,

and he felt that wary sense that anything he said would be locked away in her head for future use.

"Everyone will be coming out to my ranch," Brett said. "But it's just me and Damian until then."

"Where is your *mamm* and *daet*?" Belinda asked Damian. "Your mom and dad, I should say."

"My daddy has to get elected again," Damian said, "so he's got to go shake hands and cut ribbons."

Emaline chuckled and Brett suppressed a grimace. There were better ways to put that—true as it might be.

"Dean is going to be handing out presents at an inner-city youth shelter and serving at a soup kitchen this week," Brett said. "He has a few other obligations squeezed in, and it'll be a really busy time. Damian gets overwhelmed with crowds and noise."

"Ah." Belinda nodded. "That's good work for the holiday season."

"I have headphones," Damian said, and he pulled them back up over his ears, then turned to blowing on his hot chocolate again.

"So, just the two of you until then?" Emaline asked Brett. "You don't have anyone else?"

And now he sounded pathetic. He had

plenty of people who'd welcome him to a Christmas party—even relatives with kids—but this Christmas was about something more. But Brett was being cautious, trying not to get his hopes up.

"I…I guess I could have rummaged up someone," Brett said. "But I wanted to do this with Damian. A bonding time, I guess."

Emaline nodded. "That's very nice. I bet he'll have great memories of this."

"I hope so."

"And you?" Belinda said, looking expectantly at Emaline.

"For Christmas?" Emaline smiled. "Every year I spend it with my brothers and my mother."

"What will you do with them?" Belinda asked.

"We go to a candlelight church service on Christmas Eve. It means a lot to Mom," Emaline said, "and then we come home and eat chocolates and catch up with each other. None of us have children yet, so we can sleep in Christmas morning, and when we get up, we open gifts."

"And your *daet*?" Belinda asked. "Has he passed away?"

"No, he's very much alive and, well…" Emaline's shoulders straightened, and her grip on her mug tightened. "He left us a long time ago. He has Christmas with his other family."

Other family. Those words fell heavy across the table. Emaline took a sip from her mug, her gaze momentarily clouded.

"Oh, my…" Belinda murmured. "I'm sorry, dear. Maybe I shouldn't have asked that."

"It's okay," Emaline said.

"What happened?" Brett asked.

"Not a story for little ears," Emaline replied, glancing at Damian.

With his headphones, he wouldn't hear anyway, but Brett let it go. Every family had their painful stories—the betrayals, the mistakes. His was no different—the Rockwells just had to be better at hiding theirs. It was a matter of political survival.

"Well, Christmas is a time for loving the ones we've got," Belinda said. "And we take that very seriously here in Amish Country."

The conversation turned to the surrounding area—Christmas-themed events going on, the pond where the Amish liked to go skating and a story Belinda told about her niece who'd met her husband here in her own bed-and-breakfast. It was just chitchat, and Brett sat back, letting the conversation roll over him as his mind took its own path.

This year, Brett had set up the faux Christmas tree and decorated it. The decorations were a little skimpy, but he figured he'd take Damian to the store and let him choose a few they could add before the rest of the family got there. He'd stocked his cupboards with cookies, crackers and Damian's favorite cereal, and a pile of wrapped gifts were waiting in his closet. While it was still just him and Damian, they'd watch Christmas movies and make homemade pizza, and Brett had even bought the Dr. Seuss Grinch book to read to Damian.

And it didn't feel like enough… What made that run up to Christmas sparkle when a kid couldn't be with his parents until Christmas Eve? What could Brett give that Damian would remember fondly? Belinda made up for it with thirty-three grandchildren. Brett couldn't do that.

Boots sounded on the step outside, and a cold finger of air whisked through the room as Brett heard the door open.

"Eli's back," Belinda said, and she rose to her feet and headed to the counter. She came back with a plated cinnamon bun and a steaming mug just as the old man came out of the mudroom in sock feet, his wiry gray hair standing up in a tangled nest around his bald spot. His black dog gave a good shake, spraying snow.

"It's cold out there, and it's blowing, all right," Eli said. He brightened at the sight of the plate and mug. "Belinda, you read my mind. That would hit the spot."

He sank into the empty seat at the end of the table and slapped his leg. The dog lay down next to him.

"The animals are all right?" Belinda asked.

"Yah, yah," he replied. "They've got feed and water, and everything is clean. I was a little worried about my hens. They're sensitive girls."

Belinda fixed the old man with a meaningful look. "That new coop is tight, and you know it."

"Yah, it is."

"And the hens will be warm."

"I checked and double-checked, and they're quite warm," Eli said with a nod.

The aged couple exchanged a long look, and Brett had the feeling there was an old, unspoken tension being played out in front of them. He looked over at Emaline. She was watching the old couple with a curious look on her face, her short blond hair tucked behind one ear. He might not want to be featured in her vlog, but he couldn't deny that she intrigued him. Emaline was pretty and seemed insightful, and if he'd met her under any other circumstances, he'd be trying to figure out how single she was.

"Belinda is worried I'll bring my chickens in the house to keep them warm," Eli said with a low chuckle.

Damian took his headphones off his head. "In the house? Chickens?"

So, he could hear past those headphones. Good to know. But Brett was starting to feel bad for old Eli. Ranching life had different rules, and he could identify.

"I brought a new calf into the house to warm it up last fall," Brett said. "Sometimes you do what you have to do in farming."

"*Yah*, that's true!" Eli said, nodding furiously.

"Eli had chickens set up on his kitchen table for the better part of eight years," Belinda said. "How long was the calf in your kitchen, Brett?"

"A couple of hours," Brett said weakly.

Belinda shot Eli a pointed look. "You see?"

"They got cold outside," Eli said. "And one year, I lost a really good layer, too. She was one of my favorites. She used to be the first one out of the coop to come see me when I fed them. She liked to get pet. So I told myself I wouldn't have that happen again. And to my credit, I never lost another hen to the cold or to coyotes."

Belinda regarded the old man silently. It was a look that Brett remembered from his own mother—it was a silent warning to a man who was wise enough to take it.

"But Belinda can rest easy," Eli went on, a little meeker. "I promised her that I won't do that anymore. I might be the kind of man who brings chickens in the house, but I'm not the kind of man who breaks his word."

"I certainly hope I can rest easy on that..." Belinda murmured. "It just isn't sanitary, Eli. And you know it. If every other farmer can keep his hens warm and dry all winter long without taking them into the house, then you can, too. And those hens aren't half so sensitive as you are!"

"Me?" Eli looked ready to take offense, then sighed. "Maybe I am. I won't do it, Belinda. I think they lay better in the kitchen, but I promised you, didn't I? They'll be fine where they are." He tore a piece from his cinnamon bun and pushed it into his mouth, the discussion over—at least as far as he seemed concerned. Belinda eyed him a moment longer, then heaved a sigh.

"Would you like to see your room, Brett and Damian?" Belinda asked, turning toward him.

"Sure. That would be nice."

"I already had fresh linens in that room. There's two beds—that actually used to be the room my own boys slept in when they were young. I used to have two sets of bunk beds in there. I only had three boys, but they'd have a cousin sleep over or someone visit, and the extra bed got used a lot of the time."

The old woman headed toward the staircase without looking back, and Brett stood up. He tapped the top of Damian's head to get his attention, and Damian looked around, then stood, too.

Brett glanced back once to see Emaline watching him with an evaluating look on her face. He knew that he'd caught her attention, and he wondered what she thought of him besides curiosity about the man she'd heard about in the news. She was coming to conclusions about him—he could feel it. Except there were five-year-old news stories to color her view of him.

"But don't worry," Belinda said, suddenly turning with a bright smile, "there are no longer bunk beds in that bedroom. You'll be very comfortable, I'm sure."

EMALINE WATCHED AS Brett and Damian disappeared up the stairs. She'd already spent one night in her own room—a bright space with a double bed, broad windows and a thick block quilt. She'd slept like a baby.

She let out a slow breath. She should have taken her mother's advice and gone for a real vacation, not a working one. Emaline took another sip of her apple cider. It was cooling off now and was easier to drink.

"Are you enjoying your stay?" Eli asked. The dog sighed happily from his spot on the floor at the old man's side.

"I really am," she said with a smile.

"What's the problem between you and the other *Englisher*?" Eli asked bluntly.

"Uh—" She chuckled uncomfortably. "His family is in the news a lot. And I'm a vlogger, kind of a freelance journalist? I'm always looking for stories to tell… We're at odds."

"Ah." Eli nodded. "That's too bad."

"How long have you farmed here?" she asked by way of changing the topic.

"I'm eighty this year," he said. "My twin brother and I inherited the farm together when we were in our twenties…you do the math."

"That's a long time," she said.

"*Yah*, a long time," he said. "And this is my last year of it. This spring, someone else will be working this land instead of me."

"Are you retiring?" she asked.

"You could call it that." He sighed. "I never married, you see. Normally, if you have *kinner*, you'd have a son or a son-in-law who'd take over and you step back. But I don't have either. There's a Mennonite old folks home, and I'm going to sell up and go there."

"Are you ready to stop farming?" Emaline asked.

Eli shook his head. "The problem with getting old is that you aren't as old in your head as you are in your body. Do I want to stop farming? No! But I'm a man on my own. I have to take care of my home and my animals and my land, and…it's a lot for these old bones."

"I'm sorry," she said. "That's tough."

"It happens to the best of us…" Eli shrugged. "Enjoy your youth while you have it. It passes faster than you think it will."

Damian came back down the stairs then, his headphones on, and his dark brown eyes scanning the room cautiously. Emaline could hear the rumble of Brett's voice through the floor, so it seemed he was busy up there. She fluttered her fingers in a wave, and the boy headed over to where she sat.

"Do you like your room?" Emaline asked.

Damian nodded and pulled his headphones off. "Yeah. It's nice. There's no TV, though."

"We have no TVs at all," Eli said.

"That's what Uncle Brett said. Why?" Damian asked.

"We're Amish." Eli took a bite from his cinnamon bun and chewed slowly.

Damian looked up at Emaline questioningly.

"It's a simple life," Emaline explained. "No TV, no electricity, but there's wood stoves, and horses and buggies."

"Belinda says there's a donkey out there," Damian said.

"His name is Eeyore," Eli supplied.

"Can I see him?" Damian asked.

"Maybe tomorrow," Eli said. "He's in the stable now. And it's blowing hard out there."

"I pet him yesterday," Emaline said. "He likes carrots."

"He's also incredibly naughty," Eli said. "He runs away. A lot."

"Where does he go?" Damian asked. "Because sometimes at school, I go hide in the bathroom."

That revelation made Emaline's heart stutter in her chest. Damian fiddled with one headphone absently, his little fingers working around the plastic.

"Why do you hide in the bathroom?" Emaline asked softly.

"Because it's quiet in there, and my class is noisy," Damian said. "The other kids talk loud, and they yell sometimes, and we have to sing a song, and I don't like the song."

"What song is it?" she asked.

"The welcome song. I hate it. It's got bells."

Right. The noise. This kid really didn't like noise, did he? That was part of an autism diagnosis, and while she didn't have any information on Damian's situation, she'd seen it often enough. She had a cousin with autism spectrum disorder who'd attended the same school she had growing up. Times had gotten a lot better for these kids with special needs.

"Do you have a special helper in the classroom?"

"Yeah. Miss Tanner."

"And she doesn't come with you outside the room when the song starts?"

"Sometimes. But I tell her I have to use the bathroom, and she can't go in there. It's cool in the bathroom. And quiet. And empty. I wear my headphones until the teacher comes and says the song is over," Damian said. "Then I go back."

Damian put his headphones up over his ears and reached for a cookie. Eli was thoughtfully watching the boy.

"You must have sensitive kids in your community, too," Emaline said.

"*Yah*, I'm sure we do."

"What do you do for them?" she asked.

"I don't have *kinner*," he said. "I'm an old bachelor. You'd be better off asking Belinda that. But I have noticed that some quiet boys who stay back from the group tend to be very good with horses."

"As therapy?" she asked.

"As a skill," he replied soberly. "As a talent. As a horse-boy relationship. It's a special connection. Like that donkey—he's a terrible, obstinate, no-good donkey. But I think if you put this boy with that donkey, they'd get along. Just a hunch."

"You think?" Emaline asked.

"*Yah*. A long time ago, I was a boy who didn't quite fit in, either."

Emaline looked at the weathered old man, his not quite properly shaven face and his kind eyes. What sort of a life had this old bachelor lived? How many people had misunderstood him over the years?

"And you get along with Eeyore?" she asked.

"Me?" He shook his head. "No, no. Eeyore sees me as competition. He loves Belinda, and any time she casts a smile my way, that donkey is plotting his revenge."

"Does he really?" Emaline chuckled.

"He's a smart donkey," Eli said, tapping the side of his head. "He lets himself out of that stable. You'd think he couldn't, but he finds a way. And I shut the doors firmly. You can't lock a stable—it's not safe. If there were ever a fire, no one could let the animals out without finding the key. And that donkey can turn a knob—I'm sure of it."

"He can turn a doorknob?" Damian pulled his headphones off again. "Really?"

"*Yah.* He must. He also undoes knots in rope. Because I don't know how else he gets out," Eli said. "And you know who gets blamed every time he wanders away?"

"Who?" Damian asked, wide-eyed.

"Me!" Eli shook his head. "Every time. That's because I help Belinda with the men's work, and that donkey knows it. He thinks he's the man of this place. And while I might not be the man of this home, I'm certainly more of a man than that donkey is. I think he laughs to himself every time Belinda there gets mad at me for letting him get away."

A smile tickled Damian's lips. "You should give him a time-out."

"I would if he wouldn't wander off in the middle of it," Eli retorted.

"That's what happens when Ivy pinches people," Damian said. "She gets a time-out. And when Michael B. breaks the crayons, too. And when I hide in the bathroom and don't tell Miss Tanner where I went."

"How come you don't tell Miss Tanner where you're going?" she asked.

"Because I want to be alone."

"You get time-outs for that?" Emaline asked.

"Yeah," Damian replied, and he leaned ever so slightly toward her, resting one arm against hers. Just a sweet little kid who wanted some contact. She leaned toward him, too, just a little bit, to show him it was okay.

It tugged at her heart to hear that he'd get punished at school. She could understand that he shouldn't be hiding from teachers, but Damian didn't seem like a boy who wanted to misbehave.

"Horses," Eli said meaningfully. "Mark my words."

But she was the wrong person to tell all of this to. Brett was Damian's uncle. She was just a stranger staying at the same B&B.

"Uncle Brett has horses," Damian said. "He's got a whole ranch. And there's horses and cows and dogs and cats and everything on Uncle Brett's ranch."

"Then I have one word of advice for you,

young man," Eli said. "When you get back to your Uncle Brett's ranch, you go look those horses over, and you find the one who's looking back at you just as hard as you're looking at him. And then you go over and say hello real polite like."

"Really?" Damian asked.

"*Yah.* Keeping a carrot in your pocket helps to smooth over the introductions, but the hello is the important part."

Belinda came down the creaking staircase, Brett behind her. Brett looked surprised when he saw Damian sitting next to Emaline. She expected Damian to move away then, but he didn't. He stayed right where he was, his headphones around his neck, and his feet kicking in the air beneath him.

"Having fun, Damian?" Brett asked.

"Yep."

Brett's eyebrows went up. Before, she'd been thinking that if they were snowed in together, Brett might soften up and consent to be interviewed on her vlog about some fluffy topic or other—the emotional life of cattle or something. But now, being snowed in didn't seem like it was so great for Damian. Maybe it was better to get this particular Rockwell back on his land and his nephew into the company of some horses he could form a relationship with.

The poor kid. It wasn't easy being five, was it?

CHAPTER THREE

DINNER THAT EVENING was roast beef and potatoes with creamed corn on the side and the most delicious dinner rolls Brett had ever tasted. He ate two full plates of food and watched as Damian did the same. If the kid was eating, Brett figured he was succeeding on some level.

Damian sidled up to Emaline after the meal was over, and he leaned on her leg and petted the dog. He couldn't exactly stop Damian. It would be rude, but more than that, Damian had his headphones off. He was comfortable with Emaline, and maybe that wasn't such a bad thing…so long as Damian didn't say anything that sparked the vlogger's interest.

And that was the worry, wasn't it? That she'd grab something and run with it, promises forgotten.

Maybe he should just stop worrying about his brother's career and the family reputation, and let the stories fall where they may. The media certainly hadn't been kind to Brett over the years. But this was different—Damian was smack-dab in the middle of this story.

At bedtime, Brett took Damian upstairs to the bedroom with a little kerosene lamp that Belinda gave him for the purpose. It threw a soft pool of light around them as they climbed the stairs together. It almost felt like camping. Brett helped Damian find the Christmas pajamas that his parents had bought him especially for this trip. They had Frosty the Snowman on the front of the shirt, and Damian seemed to like these pajamas a lot. Once he was dressed, Brett pulled back the thick white comforter on the twin-size bed by the window, and Damian crawled between the sheets. Everything was clean and smelled faintly of cloves and cinnamon, and with the soft glow of that little kerosene lamp, it was rather cozy.

"We've got to call your mom and dad, right?" Brett said.

"Yeah. Let's call them," Damian said. "I bet they miss me."

"I bet they do," Brett agreed, and he dialed the number on Damian's cell phone, put it on speaker, and handed it back. It only rang once before Dean picked up.

"Hey, buddy," Dean said. "How's it going? Mom's here, too."

"I'm good," Damian said.

"Are you having fun?" Bobbie asked. "I miss you, sweetie!"

"There's lots of snow," Damian said. "And there's a lady who's nice."

"A lady?" Bobbie sounded wary.

"The owner of the Amish B&B," Brett interjected. He'd texted them earlier to update them on the plan to stay at the B&B. "She's a really nice older lady who's an amazing cook. Belinda Wickey. It's quiet and rustic and just about perfect."

"Right, right..." Bobbie sounded flustered. "It's a nice place? Clean? Respectable?"

"She's nice, too, but I mean the other lady," Damian interjected. "The one who makes videos."

"Videos?" Dean's voice changed tone. "How many guests are there? I thought this was a small place—out of the way."

"Can I talk to your dad?" Brett asked, and he took the phone and took it off speaker. "Dean, this is going to sound worse than it is, but there is a vlogger staying here at the B&B tonight. Her name is Emaline Piper."

"Vlogger?" Bobbie's tone turned taut. "Look her up, Dean."

"Hold on...." Dean muttered. "Okay, I

googled her. She's a lifestyle and travel vlogger?"

"Something like that," Brett agreed.

"Let me see…" Bobbie was on the case now, too, and for a moment, there was silence. "I'm seeing a lot of social media activity— local tourism, a smattering of theater pieces, local artists… Nothing political. She shouldn't be too big of a worry."

"That's my thought," Brett agreed. "Still, I would have avoided this if I could. The weather didn't cooperate."

"Look, from what I know of vloggers, they are incredibly media savvy and can be very flexible. She can be a lifestyle vlogger until she pivots and turns to something else that is more popular," Dean said. "So be careful. We'd hate to give her a reason to turn her attention to politics."

"Agreed. I feel the same way," Brett replied. "Don't worry. I've already made it clear that I won't be part of any of her content."

"So, it occurred to her already." Bobbie didn't sound impressed.

"We'll do our best," Brett said. "That's all I can promise. But I think it'll be fine. She's here for the B&B, not for me. Trust me, this place is far more photogenic than I am."

"Brett, everyone has something to hide,"

Bobbie said, her voice quiet, level. "You remember that. We don't need any distracting attention while Dean is campaigning. The media grab anything and start pulling on strings. *Anything.* Including your cameo in some TikTok that goes viral."

He knew what she meant and the secrets she was referring to. Her warning wasn't wasted. "I know, Bobbie. I'm not new to this."

"Can you put Damian back on the line?" Dean asked.

"Sure." Brett handed the phone to Damian. "Your dad wants to talk to you again."

"Hi, Dad," Damian said. He switched the phone back onto speaker, but he looked worried now. "Did I do something wrong?"

"No, buddy, not at all," Dean said. "But you know that lady? The one who isn't Amish?"

"The pretty one?"

"Uh—yeah. Her."

"That's Emaline."

"Okay. Well, remember how we talked about what we say to journalists when they want to ask us questions?"

"We say, 'No comment,'" Damian said.

"Exactly. Emaline is kind of like a journalist. So if she asks you questions about anything, you say no comment, okay? And you stick close to your uncle."

"But she's really nice. And I like her."

"I bet she is," Dean said. "But her job is to find stories and tell them, and we don't want to be in those stories, remember? That's not good for Daddy's job."

"Yeah..."

"So don't tell her anything. You can be polite and say hello, and open doors and pass her the bread, but other than that, you stick with Uncle Brett. Got it?"

"Okay."

"And Brett?" Dean said.

"I'm here."

"Just..." Dean sighed. "You know what I'll say."

Don't let her get a story on you. Watch what you say. Don't let Damian get too comfortable with her...

"Yeah. I've got it under control. Don't worry about it," Brett reassured him.

"We miss you, sweetie," Bobbie said, her voice softening. "And we'll call you in the morning, okay?"

"Okay," Damian said.

"Good night, buddy," Dean said. "Sleep tight."

"Night night." Damian hung up the phone and looked down at it mournfully. For a couple of beats, he was silent, then he put his phone on the bedside table. "I want to go home now."

"Your mom and dad won't be there, though," Brett said. He picked up the cell phone and plugged it into a portable charger that Belinda had provided for their phones. "That's why you're with me. But don't worry, we'll have a good time. And you'll talk to your mom and dad in the morning. Right? They miss you, too."

"I don't want to go to your ranch anymore," Damian said softly.

"Hey…" This was not going in the right direction. "We'll have fun, remember?"

"I don't want to have fun."

"Who doesn't want to have fun? It'll be great. You'll see. I have a Christmas tree set up and waiting for you, and if you want, I'll let you open a present early."

"Santa won't bring them till Christmas Eve," Damian said.

"Yeah, but I got you something, too, so…" Brett smiled at him hopefully. "Santa gives gifts, and so do I."

Damian lay back down in the bed, tears welling in his eyes.

"Do you want a story?" Brett asked. "Maybe I can think of one."

"No."

That's right. A spontaneous story from Uncle Brett wasn't part of the routine. Bobbie had gone over this with him fifteen times. These routines were life for Damian.

"Do you want me to sing the night-night song?" he asked hesitantly.

"Yeah. And you have to do the thing on my hand, too." He thrust out a hand toward Brett. Brett sat down on the edge of the bed and took Damian's small palm in his. He drew a circle around Damian's palm slowly, and he started to sing. "You are my sunshine, my only sunshine…"

When the song was over, Damian heaved a long sigh.

"What's wrong?" Brett asked.

"It's not the same. Mommy does it better."

Brett chuckled. "I know she does. And I'm not even going to try and compete with her. But I think I do a pretty good job of it. Come on, kiddo. Give me some credit here."

A smile flickered at the corners of Damian's lips. "Okay… Can I watch YouTube?"

"Uh—what do you want to watch?"

"Joe and Buster."

A kids' show. That wouldn't be so bad—get the boy's mind off how lonely he was.

"Sure." Brett made sure the parental controls were toggled and handed him his phone.

"But leave it plugged in. Your phone's battery is pretty low."

"Okay…" Damian pulled his phone up to his face, the soft glow of the screen reflected off the tears in his eyes.

Brett stood there for a moment, unsure of what to do. Damian was special to Brett—really special—and he'd been "favorite Uncle Brett" for a long time. But Damian was no longer a solemn toddler. He'd gotten more complicated, and Brett wasn't the comfort he hoped he'd be.

"Uh…if you want, I can stay here with you," Brett said.

"You don't have to." The sound of the show's theme song started up.

Brett leaned forward and ruffled Damian's hair, then he sighed and moved toward the bedroom door. "Okay, well, I'm going to take this lamp with me, so I don't trip on the way down. You sure you're okay?"

"Yeah."

Come to think of it, leaving an open flame with a five-year-old wasn't smart, anyway. Brett wanted to gather the boy up into his arms and hug him, but Damian didn't look inclined toward that, and his tears were already dried.

"Okay, well, good night, Damian. I'll be

right downstairs. I'll come up in a while, okay? I'm going to be sleeping in that bed right over there, so you won't be on your own."

Damian didn't answer, and Brett stood there awkwardly for a moment, then turned for the door. Brett had jumped at the chance to have Christmas with Damian and his family at his own ranch, but now he was wondering if he'd been foolish to do that. Maybe he should have brought the nanny, after all. She understood his routines much better than Brett did. But Brett was more than childcare this Christmas, and he hadn't wanted to share this special time.

He headed back down the stairs, and when he emerged into the kitchen, he noticed that the older people were gone, and only Emaline remained.

"They're out doing chores," Emaline said.

"Oh, okay," he said. "In that storm? I feel bad letting them do it. I wonder if I should go help them."

"That's right, you're a rancher," she said. "You're used to this."

"Yeah." He went to the window and looked out. A lantern bobbed by the stable, barely visible through the falling snow.

"I offered to lend a hand. I was scoffed at by both of them," she said with a low laugh.

"Yeah, but—" He was going to say that she was petite and looked like the storm could carry her off, but he stopped when he saw her gaze sharpen.

"But?" she said softly. She had the same soft voice Bobbie had been using.

"But nothing," he said with a small smile. He looked out the window again. Another lantern appeared, coming out of the stable, and both came bobbing back toward the house. They were on their way back, it seemed. A blinding blast of snow obliterated his view of them, then the lights emerged again, and he could see their faces now. He headed over to the side door, and when they got close, he pushed it open.

"*Danke*, Brett," Belinda said, coming up the stairs first. She came inside, stamping her boots on the mat, and old Eli came inside after her. He banged the door shut.

"I'm telling you, Belinda, that donkey knows how to escape!" Eli said.

"I know, I know…"

"It wasn't me!"

"Did I blame you?"

"Not yet, but you will!" Eli retorted.

"I'm not blaming you, Eli." Belinda looked over at the old man sadly. "Eli, what will I do when you're living in that Mennonite old folks home?"

"You'll sell that donkey, is what you'll do," he muttered. "You can't go chasing after him on your own."

Brett hadn't realized that Amish men retired from farming.

"I won't sell Eeyore..." Belinda sighed, and they both looked at Brett and seemed to realize they'd said too much in front of him.

"The donkey is missing again," Eli said.

"What?" Emaline poked her head into the mudroom. "The escape artist donkey?"

"He's gone," Belinda said. "He got out of his stall—he has his ways—and he made it out the back sliding door of the stable, and the corral was open. That was my fault. I opened the gate to get the hose, and..." She sighed. "It's lucky we checked, or my horse would have frozen with that cold wind blowing in."

"That dumb donkey is going to freeze outside, too!" Eli said, and he shook his head furiously.

"What do you do now?" Emaline asked.

"Wait," Brett said before he could stop himself. She wasn't asking him, but this wasn't exactly new territory for him, either. "And hope for the best."

"There's nothing you can do to find him?"

Emaline asked, and she unconsciously reached toward Brett. His first instinct was to reach back, to hold her hand, tug her a bit closer... But he pushed that back and felt a little embarrassed at the magnetic draw he felt toward this woman. Emaline's hand dropped, and he couldn't help but feel like he'd missed an opportunity there.

"Not in a storm like this," Eli said. "Brett is right. We wait and see if he shows up. If he doesn't, well..."

They all fell silent for a moment. They knew what that meant. Brett cleared his throat.

"If I can help out at all, I want to," Brett said.

"I was just telling Eli that he should stay the night here," Belinda said. "He's checked his animals, and with the way the snow is coming down, we're all safer together."

Brett noticed Emaline look toward the window. They were definitely safer together, and seeing the snow coming down as thick as a blanket, he was glad to be here. With her. The old couple murmured together again in Pennsylvania Dutch.

"Did you want to bunk with us in our room, Eli?" Brett asked. "We guys can stick together."

"I don't want to intrude," Eli said. "I could stay down here in the kitchen or the sitting room..."

"It's no problem," Brett replied.

"I have a folding cot I can bring out of storage if you'll carry it for me," Belinda said.

"Of course," Brett replied.

"Uh, young man, she was talking to me," Eli said meaningfully. "Of course, Belinda. I'll carry it for you."

Brett had to hide a smile. It didn't matter how old a man got, he still had his pride, and there was obviously something special between Belinda and Eli.

"Sorry, Eli," Brett said. "Didn't mean to overstep."

Eli gave him a curt nod, and he followed Belinda into the house. Brett and Emaline went into the kitchen, and the old people's voices filtered down the hallway.

"Poor Eeyore," Emaline said softly. "I hope he's okay."

"There's lots of trees around here," Brett said, trying not to sound worried. "He'll find some shelter. Donkeys really are smart."

But he hoped the donkey would show up, too. They needed a win this holiday. It was Christmastime, after all. It was the season for miracles. And somehow, Belinda's B&B didn't seem complete without Eeyore.

EMALINE SAT BY the potbellied stove, watching the snow spin down next to the glass. She couldn't see far out the window—everything was incredibly dark. No moon, no stars, just falling snow and blackness. Everyone had gone to bed already, and the house was silent except for the ticking of the clock up on the kitchen wall, and clicks and pings from the heat going up the stovepipe to warm the bedrooms.

She had her laptop open on her lap, a blank screen with a flashing cursor taunting her. She'd gotten good at writing up a tight script about the beauty and unique attributes a location could offer to tourists, but she was coming up empty when it came to Danke and the Butternut Amish Bed and Breakfast. It was ironic—she'd never had such a dramatic stay anywhere before this, and maybe that was the problem.

She had her laptop's Wi-Fi tethered to her phone, and she googled Brett Rockwell. Pictures popped up immediately, and she pulled them up, one after another. They were all from well over five years ago—Brett with his brother, Brett coming out of a restaurant looking bleary-eyed and haggard. Brett with his nieces and nephews, Brett with some scantily clad woman on his arm… He looked younger in those photos—sleek and muscular, like he spent a lot of time in a gym. Still good-looking, but she liked the way he looked now better. He had a bit more weight on him, although still obviously muscular. And he seemed more accessible somehow, a little more like the rest of them. If that could be said about a Rockwell.

Emaline sighed and pulled out her phone. A few days ago, her friend George from journalism school had texted to touch base. She hadn't answered. George was writing for the *Chronicle*, and he was killing it. He had bylines in a lot of different news magazines and kept on proudly sending her the links. She was happy for him—really she was—but it was hard to see his career take off when she hadn't even gotten a foot in the door when it came to traditional journalism.

Emaline needed to stop being petty. So she texted him back.

Nice to hear from you, George. All is well. I'm doing a vlog about an Amish B&B this weekend. Lots of good food and no distracting tech.

It didn't take long for him to reply: Sounds fun. What I wouldn't give for a relaxing stay somewhere right about now!

Was that flirting? It could be hard to tell with George. So she added, Snowed in with a Rockwell. Not even joking.

Which one?

Brett.

You're serious?

Would she joke about that? She thought for a moment. Actually, she might. The ironic part was that she wasn't joking now.

Completely. He and his nephew (senator's youngest) are here, too.

If only she'd made it in journalism, she'd be in investigative heaven right now.

Listen to me. You're sitting on gold, he texted back. There are some big rumors going around about the parentage of the youngest Rockwell son. Look up Celia Jenkins.

She looked at her phone for a moment, then she opened her laptop again and entered the name Celia Jenkins into the search engine. A course of photos popped up, and the first picture caught Emaline's eye.

Celia Jenkins was Senator Rockwell's top aide, and in this photo, she was walking next to the senator, a binder held across her chest, her chin high and her expression stony.

An older picture with a visibly pregnant Celia Jenkins caught Emaline's eye, and she clicked on the picture to pull up the accompanying article. Celia had taken a short maternity leave, and a baby had appeared in the Rockwell household about the same time. The Rockwells introduced him as Damian a couple of months later.

She knew all this…she remembered the gossip rags running with all sorts of theories because no one had seen the then governor Rockwell's wife pregnant.

Was that just rumor? Emaline typed in a search for "Bobbie Rockwell pregnant"—searching for photos that might match. There were a couple of pictures where she looked quite slim, and gossip magazines were circling a flat belly, insisting a pregnancy baby bump was there. She didn't see it. The only other pictures were from fifteen years ago, when she was pregnant with her older children. Bobbie Rockwell had never been pregnant in the last decade, yet this child was raised as their own.

There definitely was a story here...for a journalist. Sure, it made her pulse speed up to think about getting into this story, but her viewers didn't want politics. They wanted an escape from all that.

Still...she could ask a few questions, couldn't she?

She picked up her phone and texted George: Am I right in thinking that Bobbie wasn't pregnant before Damian arrived?

His answer was swift: Bingo. There's lots of conjecture around who the bio mom is. If you got a hint—a confession, even!—that would be the story of the decade. You write it, and I'll give it to my editor.

Emaline's heart hammered to a stop. You'd do that for me?

If you crack the story, you deserve it. We've all tried and failed. It's cutthroat here. I'd love a friend on the team.

Good old George...he always had been a straight shooter, even when it was irritating. And if he said this was the story no one else had been able to break, it was the truth.

She thought about Damian. He definitely

looked like a Rockwell. Same chin, same eye color. Was it possible that Dean Rockwell had fathered Celia's child, and he and his wife were raising that child as their own? Maybe Celia's loyalty had gone so far as to act as a surrogate for the couple. That wouldn't be as dramatic, though. And there'd be no reason to keep that secret. A lot of wealthy couples who could afford it chose that route to parenthood. Maybe there'd been some fertility struggles.

Footsteps creaked on the stairs, and she startled and turned to see Brett coming down. He was dressed in jeans and the sweater from earlier. She closed her computer and waited until he spotted her. Her heart was hammering. A chance at a byline in the *Chronicle*... she loved the freedom in her career as a vlogger, but the chance to break into real journalism was so tempting it made her mouth water.

"Not in bed yet?" Brett asked.

"Apparently, you aren't, either," she replied, and her voice sounded all breathy.

"Yeah... Eli snores." He smiled ruefully.

Brett came down the rest of the way and into the kitchen. He was tall, and there were more lines in his face than she'd ever seen in the pictures online. There were a few gray hairs around his temples, too.

"It was nice of you to let him bunk in your room."

"What can you do? It's a major storm. I had to talk Damian down, though. He's not good with any changes to an established plan. But Damian finally crashed."

She stood up and put her computer on the table, then grabbed another piece of wood and opened the front of the stove. She nestled it into the embers of the fire inside, then shut the door.

"Getting some work done?" Brett asked, nodding toward her computer.

"Trying. You can pull up a chair. The fire's warm."

Brett hooked a kitchen chair and plunked it down next to her, then took a seat. "Damian really likes you."

She looked over in surprise. "Yeah?"

He nodded. "He's a sensitive kid, and he doesn't like a lot of people right away. In fact, he's got a learning assistant who he always gives the slip to. Drives them all crazy." Brett chuckled.

"Have they tested him for autism?" she asked.

Brett froze, then nodded. "I guess it's evident when you meet him, but that's private information."

If he thought she was judging, he was wrong.

"There's no shame in that," she said. "Everyone is different. Some of the most brilliant minds of our time have likely been on the spectrum. My cousin is autistic, and she was in my grade all through school. But back then, she wasn't diagnosed, she was just 'different.' She got diagnosed in her adult years, and it helped everything make sense. She's brilliant. Today, she's an actuary working for a big insurance company."

"Wow." Brett's shoulders relaxed a bit, and he leaned forward, resting his elbows on his knees. "That's the kind of future I want for Damian—we want. The future we want for Damian."

"Well, Nadine was similar when she was young. And Damian is a really sweet boy."

"The thing is, he doesn't normally warm up to new people that quickly," Brett said.

"No?" she asked.

"He had one nanny he couldn't seem to adjust to. She had credentials as long as my leg, and they had to let her go. So when he was so comfortable with you, I was surprised."

"I don't know what I did," she said. "But I'm honored."

Brett nodded slowly. "Damian is a good judge of people. Not that everyone he dislikes is a criminal or anything, but the ones he does like are solid."

She felt herself warm at the implied compliment. A little boy thought she was okay, and somehow that was the best news she'd heard all week.

"Can I confess something?" she asked.

"Sure." He looked over at her with a rueful smile.

"I was looking up pictures of you."

He chuckled, the sound low and deep. She got that shiver up her arm again. "And?"

"And...you look different now," she said.

"Older?" he asked.

"A bit." She wasn't going to lie. "Maybe a bit wiser, too."

He smirked, then straightened in his chair. "We all have to grow up sometime."

"I suppose so." She was still curious, though. "What made you want to ranch?"

"My grandfather managed the ranch, and I had good memories there growing up."

"That's it?"

He cocked his head to one side, considering. "It was available. My family owns a lot of land, a lot of companies, and the one thing that my brother and my mother didn't have their fingers in was that ranch. So I asked for it."

"Wow…" She turned her gaze toward the fire in the stove for a moment. "That's not the kind of experience most of us have. We don't just ask for a ranch."

"I know."

Did he, though? He'd obviously grown up differently than she had.

"So, you run it now?"

"Yup. My mother put it into my name and told me that it was my early inheritance. If I ran it into the ground, that would be it for me. So I had no choice but to make sure it stayed profitable."

"And how did you do that?" she asked.

"Why does this feel like an interview?" he asked, casting her a wary look.

She put her hands up. "I'm not recording anything! I'm just asking. I'm just curious. I like getting to know people. When I decided what I wanted to study, I got a student loan. I recently got loan forgiveness, and I'm not ashamed to say that I cried with relief."

"But you did study journalism," he said.

"I'm a travel vlogger. I didn't cut it in journalism."

"Yeah, but I can still hear it in you," he said. "It's there—deep down."

"Then that's the bitter irony." She shot him

a grin. "You don't ever want your side of the story to come out?"

"For who?" he asked. "For someone scanning through their newsfeed on social media or idly reading a newspaper? I mean, why would I want my personal life to be their entertainment?"

"It would be the truth about you," she said.

"I'd rather have my privacy. I don't really care what people think. The ones who know me know who I am and what I stand for. One thing I've learned over the last couple of years is that you don't have to answer every accusation. Sometimes it only does more harm. In my experience, time shakes out more truths than journalists dig up. Patience can be your best weapon."

Brett Rockwell was a deeper man than she'd given him credit for. And he was very much changed from the supposed playboy he'd once been. She eyed him for a moment. Was it Damian's presence here that made the difference? Or was he simply a better man than the public had been led to believe?

"I've got to find an angle for this vlog post," she said. "I'll leave you alone—I promised that already. It's just…my original idea was to do one about Eeyore. But if he's missing, I can't very well do a story about a donkey who tragically disappeared just before Christmas, can I?"

"Not the heartwarming story you're looking for," he agreed.

"So, what if I did a story about Amish Country and how it helped a sensitive boy take off his headphones?" she asked.

Brett was silent.

"No names," she went on, "No faces. Nothing that would identify him. Just the Amish world and a very real kid who I think a lot of other people will relate to. Would that be okay?"

"I said Damian is off-limits," he ground out. "If you include his son's name in anything, Dean will take that personally."

Was that a warning? A threat? When she looked over at him, he met her gaze evenly, giving no hint of which way she should take it.

"If I say no names, I mean it," she said. "Damian is a little boy. Whatever I think about your brother's politics, it is unconscionable to use a child in that arena. Anyway, my vlogs are about travel and human interest, not politics. I could refer to him as…Benjie. But there are a lot of families with kids just like Damian, just like Nadine, and while *you* might be avoiding the news, they long to feel seen. I think a story that gives some Christmas hope would be positive."

Brett didn't answer, and they both turned back toward the fire.

"Benjie, huh?" he said.

"Yes. What if I put together the piece and let you see everything I'm doing? You'll see there are no faces or anything identifying."

"Okay...maybe."

Emaline leaned back in her chair. That was close to a yes, and she didn't really need his permission to write a story without names that couldn't be traced back to Damian in any way. Still, she didn't want to surprise a Rockwell, either. They had too many lawyers on retainer for that to be smart.

"You aren't a fan of Dean, are you?" Brett asked, changing the subject.

"Travel vlogger." She pointed at herself.

"I know. But you don't like him."

This was what it came down to, and she sifted her words before she spoke.

"I think he's a man who holds a lot of power and should be held responsible for it," she replied. "Not that it's my job to do that, but I think someone should."

"That's a deft sidestep."

"It's the best I can do," she replied. "Did you vote for your brother?"

"Of course."

"If he weren't family, would you have voted for him?" she asked.

Brett caught her gaze and a smile tickled his lips. "If I ever get to know you better, maybe I'll answer that."

She couldn't help but smile. "That's a deft sidestep, too."

"I'm not a fan of politics," he said. "It's ugly and cutthroat. I like my ranch—my cattle, my horses, my neighbors…"

"Do they know who you are?" she asked.

"Yeah. And it doesn't make a heap of difference when someone's cattle break down a fence or someone needs help with haying, does it? Neighbors help each other—there's no other way to make it out there."

"You don't worry that they'll take little stories about you to the press?" she asked.

He shook his head. "Nope. They aren't like that. They've got personal ethics, and selling out a neighbor who gave them a hand in a hard time goes against what they believe in." He eyed her for a moment. "Getting ideas, are you?"

"No. I have a few ethics of my own."

"Yeah, me too." He met her gaze, and she wondered what he was thinking about as he scrutinized her like that. Outside, the wind moaned softly, but inside the house, all was warm and snug.

It was late, and George's words were still spinning around in her head. She should just focus on her vlog and let that be the end of it…shouldn't she?

"I'd better get to bed," she said, then she added after a moment, "Brett, I like you more than I thought I would."

"Thanks." He shot her a small smile. "I'll take that as a compliment."

"That's how it was intended." She rose to her feet and reached for her computer.

Brett was softer and deeper than she'd anticipated. Maybe even a little more vulnerable.

"Good night," he said.

Outside, the wind howled, long and low, and she looked out the window at the swirling snow, just visible through the glass. It was cold out there, and she truly hoped that Eeyore the donkey had found a safe little shelter somewhere.

They all needed a Christmas miracle this year…she could feel it.

CHAPTER FOUR

EMALINE CRAWLED INTO bed that night and plugged her phone into the battery pack on the bedside table next to the bed. She took a short video of the kerosene lamp glowing on her bedside table—zooming in on the wick and the flame. She also got a shot of the quilt in the lamplight—the stitching and the blocks of vibrant color. Her posts about Amish Country always got a lot of traction, and it brought out the best in most of the commenters. They'd talk about memories of their grandparents or a desire to live more simply and more gratefully than they currently did. Trolls who commented negatively got shut down pretty quickly by the others who enjoyed her positive, uplifting posts. She felt like she was contributing to people's happiness with her work. There was so much bad news out there that some good news went a long way to reminding people that life was still happy, and altruism and kindness were still plentiful.

With flannel sheets and three quilts, the covers were both heavy and warm. She flicked through some earlier video footage of Eeyore in the stable, and Eli's rubber boots as he forked fresh hay into a feeder. She liked that clip—it really accentuated the rugged charm of the place, and she was willing to bet that it would increase interest in the Butternut Amish B&B by quite a bit. She put her phone aside and sank into the pillow and listened to the soft pings and rattles of the cooling stove downstairs.

Her mind moved back to that text from George. He'd said that she was sitting on gold here, and she had to wonder how true that was. Emaline had a sensitive spot when it came to men who abused power. Her own father hadn't been a powerful man, but he'd abused the power he'd had over his family— and had broken their hearts. He'd lied and hidden his shameful secrets, and he would have continued doing so if his other common-law wife hadn't figured out that she wasn't the only woman in his life. There were two families that Emaline's father had kept going, unaware of each other. That betrayal had stabbed deep... It had torn out her mother's heart and left her and her brothers stunned. Maybe Emaline more than her brothers, because she'd always thought that she should find a man like her father to marry. But not after that! How was a girl supposed to navigate relationships when all she knew was that she needed to find a man who wasn't like her dad? That was when she'd started seeing a therapist. Best decision she'd ever made.

Now, every time she saw a news story about a man with sordid secrets, she wanted to see him pay. Men shouldn't get away with lies and betrayal. They should have to face what they'd done.

Not that her father really had…he'd gotten away with it, for the most part. He still had a family—he'd chosen the other one.

Senator Rockwell struck her as a man with secrets. Call it a gut instinct, but she wouldn't be surprised to find out he'd taken advantage of an aide and taken her baby, too.

What was it Brett had said about his brother when he was running for senator? She remembered the news story vividly, because it had caused such a stir.

Just because a family has money doesn't mean they deserve to run a state or the country. I mean, vote for my brother if you want to, but I'm not going to.

That had topped three full news cycles here in Pennsylvania and had made it all the way to Fox and CNN. Brett knew more about his brother than anyone else.

Just because the Rockwell family was wealthy didn't mean they had any right to wield the kind of power that they did. Dean Rockwell was out of touch with regular Pennsylvanians but still managed to say all the right things to keep them voting for him. She wouldn't be voting for Dean Rockwell this time around. Their state deserved better.

She picked up her phone and shot off a text to George: Is there any evidence that Senator Rockwell fathered Damian?

A couple of minutes passed, and then George answered: Just look at him. He looks exactly like his father.

She'd had the same thought. Damian's big, soulful eyes and the little dimple in his chin really were just like the senator's... But that wasn't enough to prove anything.

Anything more than that? she texted.

George replied: We can't get any nurses to talk, but an unnamed woman gave birth in a Pittsburgh hospital around the same time Celia gave birth. The Rockwells went home with the baby. No confirmation of who the woman was because of privacy rights, but we've followed Celia around for weeks, and there is no evidence of a child. If she's raising that child, she's hiding him or her very well!

Wow...still, a lack of evidence wasn't proper evidence. She could see why this was a tricky story.

Anything else? she asked.

Not really. The only hope of busting this story open is finding someone willing to talk. Maybe Brett?

Right. The chances of her getting Brett to open up and throw his senator brother under the bus seemed pretty slim.

Thanks, she texted back. Let me chew it over.

I'll send you a couple of contacts at the hospital. You might have better luck.

Snoring sawed its way through the wall, and she smiled faintly. Brett hadn't been joking about Eli. She heard the bedroom door close—Brett going to bed, it seemed—and there was a sputter along with creaking springs and the slow, loud breathing started up again.

Outside the window, Emaline could just make out the swirl of snow through a crack in the curtains. The wind moaned and whistled, and she closed her eyes.

It was a week before Christmas, and she was in a snug little Amish B&B with Senator Rockwell's son and younger brother. Who knew what this week had in store? Maybe even her first real news article and her chance at finally breaking into journalism.

She loved vlogging, but she'd fallen into it as a hobby that turned out to be lucrative. She'd never meant it to be a career.

What if she got a chance at the career she'd longed for, after all?

With that thought in the forefront of her mind, Emaline closed her eyes and drifted off to sleep.

THE NEXT MORNING, Emaline woke up to the scent of coffee and frying potatoes. She lay under the warm blankets for a moment, enjoying the coziness before she tossed back the covers and shivered in the chilly morning air. Downstairs there would be warmth and a hot stove, and the faster she dressed, the faster she could get down to it.

She pulled on a pair of jeans and a thick cable-knit sweater. She combed her hair and looked in the mirror, wondering if makeup was necessary today. Somehow the rustic bedroom made her feel like it would be over-kill. There was something about this Amish house that brought out the simple side of her.

After stopping in the bathroom to wash up, she headed down the stairs in the direction of those delicious cooking smells.

"Good morning, Emaline," Belinda said, casting her a smile from where she stood at the big black cooking stove. She had an iron skillet on the range and stood over it holding a spatula.

Eli and Brett were both seated at the table, mugs of steaming coffee in front of them. Damian sat across from his uncle, his head-phones on. He turned when he saw Brett look in her direction.

"Good morning," Emaline said. She glanced at her watch. It was half past eight. "It looks like I slept in."

"I don't wake sleeping babies or sleeping guests," Belinda said with a wink. "They both need their rest."

Emaline chuckled.

"Breakfast is almost ready," Belinda added. "Can I get you some coffee?"

"That would be great," Emaline said.

"I'll grab it." Brett stood up and headed by the counter for a mug, then over to the stove where a percolator sat. He poured a cup and handed it to her with a half smile.

Her gaze slid toward the window, where the snow was still spinning past the glass, veiling her view into the yard. He was right—they weren't going anywhere.

The cream and sugar were on the table, and she doctored her coffee up to her liking—sweet and pale. This was how her dad used to drink his coffee, too, and it had taken her a decade of dedicated coffee drinking to accept the fact that she liked her coffee this way. It didn't need to be about her father. Sometimes a cup of coffee was just a cup of coffee. She took a sip. It was perfect.

"Hi, Damian," she said. The boy was quiet this morning. "How did you sleep?"

"No comment." His little chin rose, and he met her gaze with a blaze of defiance.

"What?" She stopped stirring her coffee. "Are you okay, kiddo?"

"No comment," he repeated.

"Uh, Damian, you could probably answer those questions…" Brett said. "That's just polite conversation."

"Oh…" Damian sank a little lower in his chair.

"Is this a stranger danger thing?" she asked, casting Brett a curious look.

"Kind of."

Suddenly she got it. He'd talked to his parents last night, and they'd probably warned him about saying too much. But why worry about a travel vlogger?

"Today I thought we'd work on those Christmas decorations you wanted to film," Belinda said.

Belinda opened the oven door and pulled out two casserole dishes, using pot holders to protect her hands. She carried them to the table, and Emaline saw one dish filled with cooked sausages and the other with a French toast–looking casserole: egg and bread and what smelled like cinnamon all baked together.

"I appreciate it," Emaline said. "We talked about not including any Amish people in the videos, and I'll be true to that."

"Thank you, dear." Belinda deposited the dishes onto cork hot pads on the table and then turned back to the stove and began dishing fried potatoes into a ceramic bowl. "That is a rule that we take very seriously here. We Amish people don't pose for pictures or videos. But you could all participate in the decorating if you're interested."

Brett looked over at Emaline, and his dark gaze locked onto hers for a moment. It was like the rest of the kitchen melted away, and they were back in the firelight from last night. A smile touched his lips, and then he turned toward his nephew, leaving her with goose bumps on her arms.

She rubbed a hand over her sleeve, then took a sip of hot coffee. She could see why he had a reputation with the ladies. He had a dark, intense quality about him when he focused his attention on her like that, and her heart was still stuttering in her chest.

"What do you think, Damian?" Brett asked. "Do you want to help decorate for Christmas?"

Damian looked over at Emaline mutely. He obviously wasn't sure if he was allowed to say anything, so she figured she'd cast him a lifeline.

"I'm going to," Emaline said with a sneaky little smile.

"Okay, I will, too," Damian replied.

She shot the kid a grin. Maybe they were teaching him to be careful out there—and she didn't blame the Rockwells in the least—but she wasn't a danger. Not to Damian. It did make her wonder what his father was hiding, though.

"But first, we eat," Eli declared. "The Good

Book says not to muzzle the ox while it is treading out the grain."

"People don't like being referred to as oxen," Belinda said, returning to the table.

"But they do like to eat," Eli retorted, and then he looked toward the window.

They all looked then, and another swirl of snow blasted against the glass.

"I hope old Eeyore has found a warm sheltered spot somewhere," Eli said softly. "Is that too much to hope?"

"There is never too much hope," Belinda replied. "Eeyore is smart. If he can break out of a stable, he can get into a shelter. I know my donkey, and he's smarter than any others I've met."

The guests started passing food around the table, and Belinda and Eli bowed their heads for a moment, then joined in on the dishing up.

"Sometimes Eeyore goes up the mountain, and other times he heads down the road," Eli said. "There might be some natural shelter from the wind on the mountain. I know a few craggy spots. And down the road, there's always another farm."

"All our neighbors know him," Belinda added. "If anyone sees him, they'll put him in-

doors until the storm is past. I just hope someone sees him."

Emaline looked toward that blowing snow.
The poor donkey. She hoped someone saw
him, too.

The meal was delicious. That French toast
casserole was already sweetened, but Belinda
provided maple syrup to drizzle on top. The
potatoes were fried with onions and bacon
bits—the savory dish pairing perfectly with
the sweet casserole. There was applesauce on
the side, too, and it was that smooth, almost
pink color that could be found nowhere but
in the Ball canning jars of women who made
their own.

When Emaline had finished eating, her
phone dinged, and she looked down to see
a new email. It wasn't an address she recognized, and her first thought was that perhaps
this was an email from George with those
contacts at the hospital. All she could see was
the subject line: Just reaching out.

"I'm sorry, I should check this," Emaline
said.

"No problem, dear," Belinda said. "I completely understand."

Belinda broke into a story about her niece
who worked in advertising, and Emaline
walked over to the window to read the email.

Emaline,
I just wanted to reach out this Christmas and say hello. I know you're probably busy with your family and friends, but I've been thinking about you a lot over the years, and I wish we could sit down together and talk. I know our childhoods were complicated, but you're my sister, and I'd like to know you.

This wasn't a contact. Her heart thundered in her ears as she kept reading.

We're adults now. I want to put our father's mistakes behind us. Is there any possibility of us sitting down to talk?
You're always welcome at my place, and Mom and Dad assure me that you're welcome at their house, too. Dad says he's invited you before, but you didn't feel comfortable. We could meet at a coffee shop or a restaurant if that's better for you. But we're family. Please think about it.
Maggie

Emaline flicked off her phone's screen and tucked it into her back pocket. Maggie had written to her before in a similar vein a few years ago, reminding her that they were sisters. Biologically, they were. But they'd never been raised together. She'd been the only child of the other family her father kept hidden. And if Emaline couldn't sit down with her father and have a mature conversation about how he'd torn her life apart, she didn't think she could manage it with Maggie, either. Maggie had won. Dad had chosen her, had been there in her life from the start. Maggie had never grown up without one of her parents.

"Is everything okay, dear?" Belinda asked.

Emaline roused herself. "Yes, it's fine."

Eli's gaze was cast uncomfortably at the floor, but Brett was looking at her thoughtfully…like he could read her discomfort and frustratingly petty feelings all over her face.

"Just family drama," she said, forcing a smile. "'Tis the season, right?"

Brett smiled faintly, and she thought she sensed some understanding there. After all, he came from a dramatic family of his own.

"Let me help with cleaning up," Emaline said. "Then we can get decorating."

She needed to stay busy. She'd get some great footage of Amish Christmas decor in this old house, but Emaline had no intention of brooding over the problem of her hopeful half sister.

THERE WAS SOMETHING in Emaline's expression that gave Brett pause. She looked…sad. She looked at her phone once more, pressed her lips together, then pocketed it. Christmas seemed to be the season when all the big family triggers showed up, and the Rockwells were no different. One Christmas, his family had given him an intervention—a much needed one—and he'd headed off to rehab before the New Year. Another Christmas, Bobbie told Dean that he'd either have to spend more time with her and the kids, or she was taking the kids to California to be with her parents for the next school year. Dean had canceled his plans for the entire month and given Bobbie what she needed. And then there was the most memorable Christmas of all, when Brett sat down with his brother and sister-in-law and asked them for the biggest favor—no, a gift—they could possibly give him. It had been too much to ask, but he'd asked all the same…

So Brett knew a thing or two about family dynamics over the holidays, and he was curious to see what happened in a Piper family Christmas that could cause that kind of reaction. It couldn't be half as bad as the Rockwells', could it?

Emaline came to the table and picked up

her plate. Before she could reach for his, Brett gathered up his plate and piled it on top of Damian's.

"Oh, never you worry about that," Belinda said. "You're both guests here."

"I've also got to set an example for Damian," Brett said. "Boys have to learn to pitch in."

"Don't worry about it, Belinda. We're happy to do it," Emaline said. "It was a delicious breakfast."

"Thank you, dear." Belinda smiled. "It's one of my specialties. A good many of my guests mention my breakfast casserole in their online reviews."

"Do you check those?" Brett asked.

"Of course!" Belinda accepted the plates and carried them to the sink. "Well, mostly it's my niece Jill who does the checking." To Brett, she added, "She's the one I was telling you about, the one in marketing. She peeks over my reviews and tells me what I need to know. And she says my breakfasts are always mentioned." The old woman's cheeks pinked. "I'm always pleased when my guests enjoy my cooking."

"I'll make sure to post a review, then," Brett said.

"It's very kind of you," Belinda said. "Reviews help this business a great deal."

Brett glanced over his shoulder. Damian sat at the table, his headphones around his neck and his attention on the falling snow outside. He looked pensive.

"Damian?" Brett called.

The boy looked over at him.

"Bring those mugs to the sink, okay?"

"I hope the donkey is okay," Damian said.

"Yeah, me too, buddy," Brett said.

"Do you think he'll come back?" Damian asked.

"That stubborn old donkey?" Eli said. "If he doesn't, he's just chosen a new farm he likes better. He wanders all over the place, and everyone knows him. I, for one, wouldn't mind if a new farm kept him!"

"I would mind!" Belinda said. "Eeyore is special."

Damian's gaze moved toward the window again, and Brett sighed. The kid had been asking about Eeyore all morning. He was city-raised, so he hadn't learned the lesson farm kids learned about life, death and accidents.

Damian wordlessly got up and grabbed a mug, doing as he was told. Dean and Bobbie were sticklers for kids pitching in and helping around the house. Housekeepers were for the big jobs, not the little ones, Bobbie always said. Brett approved of that. Kids should learn how to pick up after themselves. Damian might have a nanny, but he also had a chore list. And for the next few minutes they cleared the table and cleaned up the kitchen.

When the work was done and Belinda had scrubbed the table down with a wet cloth, then put the same amount of energy into drying it with a dish towel, she turned to them with a smile.

"Would you like to help put out the Christmas decorations now? You don't have to, of course. Eli and I can manage—"

"We'd love to," Emaline said, and she gave Brett a meaningful look. "Wouldn't we?"

"*We* would." He shot her a teasing grin. He kind of liked that "we."

"Oh, I'm glad," Belinda said. "Now, every year I put candles on the window sills, and I make a little nest for each candle with some evergreen springs. They smell wonderful. Sometimes I tie a red ribbon around the candle, too. Just for a little color." She turned around. "Eli, do you know where I put the tree trimmings?"

"In the basement?" Eli guessed.

"In the basement. *Yah.* That's it," she said.

"I'll go get them," Eli said.

"Let me help," Brett offered. This seemed

like a man's job around here. He followed the old man down one creaking step at a time. The basement was as clean and neatly organized as the upstairs. The concrete floor was painted gray, and there were wooden shelves down there holding canned preserves with neat labels on the front of each jar. He noticed the dill pickles right away, being a fan of them.

The basement was colder, though, and seemed to act as a cellar as well. He saw some burlap sacks filled with potatoes and onions leaning up against one wall. There were two other sacks that were bulging full, but Brett couldn't make out what root vegetables were in those.

The pile of evergreen boughs lay on top of a chest freezer. It wasn't plugged in. It would be packed with ice to keep things cold, but chest freezers were well insulated, and so the Amish used them as their ice boxes.

"Eli, could I ask you a favor?" Brett paused next to the freezer.

"You can ask," Eli said, but his playful reply didn't match his solemn expression.

"Okay, well…" Brett eyed him for a second. "The thing is, Damian is a pretty sensitive kid."

"*Yah*, I noticed. I suggested you get that boy a horse."

"Right." Brett smile wanly. "He lives in the city, though, and there isn't a lot of room for horses. Anyway, he's pretty upset about Eeyore going missing. He's been asking me about it a lot."

"Hmm." Eli nodded.

"And while you and I both know that donkey probably isn't coming back, I don't want Damian to know that. This is already a tough Christmas for him. His parents are on the road, and he's stuck with me for almost the whole holiday. Maybe we could just tell him that story you made up about Eeyore finding a new farm."

"We could do that," Eli replied. "Or you could use it as an opportunity to talk about what happens if you wander off in a blizzard."

Brett waited for the old guy to crack a smile or show he was joking in some way, but all he got was that solemn, frank expression.

"He's five," Brett said.

Eli shrugged. "We teach our *kinner* young about consequences."

"No judgment there. I'm sure it's good when you raise a kid on a farm," Brett said. "And I probably would if I was raising him on the ranch. But I don't think my brother would appreciate me teaching him about freezing to death in blizzards this young. I'm going to play it safe there."

"Okay, if that's what you want." Eli shrugged.

"It is."

"It's too bad about old Eeyore, though," Eli said, rubbing the heel of one hand over the knuckles of the other. "That donkey hated me. He thwarted me every step of the way. But I think I understand him. I mean, sometimes a guy needs someone to butt heads with in order to really feel alive."

Brett chuckled. "Yeah, I get that."

The constant battle he'd once had with the press had been frustrating, but it did keep life interesting. He glanced toward the stairs. His verbal sparring matches with Emaline reminded him of those battles. Was that why he was so drawn to her?

"I didn't think the Amish were allowed to have frenemies," Brett said.

"Frene-what?"

"It's a made-up word that combines *friend* and *enemy*. People you keep around just to argue with."

"Ah. Clever." Eli chuckled. "And, no, we aren't supposed to, but people are people, wherever you find them. Belinda and I were like that for a long time. I drove her crazy purposefully, and she told me off on a regular basis. We enjoyed it."

"Did *she*?" Brett asked, squinting. Because from what he knew about women, they didn't actually enjoy that a whole lot.

"I kept her life interesting." Eli winked. "But I've decided that I'm done with that. It might have kept her talking to me, but it won't help me in the long run."

"No?"

"No. I intend to marry that woman," Eli replied.

Brett stared at the old man in surprise. "You do?"

"I've intended it for as long as I've known her, but *yah*, that's the plan. And seeing how driving her crazy isn't going to endear me to her, I've decided not to irritate her anymore."

"Just like that?"

"Yah." Eli picked up a handful of greenery. "Here." He handed it over to Brett, and he stood there as the old man loaded him up with evergreen fronds. Eli said it so matter-of-factly that Brett had to wonder about the history between those two. Did Eli have a chance with Belinda? Or was he destined to stay her frenemy?

"How will you get her to fall in love with you?" Brett asked.

Eli picked up his own two handfuls of greenery. "I'm working on that. It's a long game."

Eli headed up the stairs first, and Brett followed him. He hoped the old man was successful. Every guy might need someone to butt heads with to feel alive, but he also needed someone to come home to. That was probably more important.

They emerged into the kitchen, and Brett deposited his armload of evergreen boughs onto the table. Belinda had brought out pillar candles, some spools of red ribbon and a ball of twine. She smiled up at Brett.

"Thank you, that was very nice of you," she said.

"It was very nice of me, too," Eli quipped.

"Oh, Eli, you know I appreciate your help. But you aren't paying to be here, are you?"

Eli muttered something in Pennsylvania Dutch, and Brett chuckled. Maybe winning Belinda over was keeping Eli's life interesting, too. What would happen if those two stopped bickering and actually settled down together?

Emaline looked quizzically at Brett, and he just shook his head. He couldn't explain this in front of Belinda. Although he had to wonder what Belinda would think if she knew that Eli was telling her guests he intended to marry her. Would this be good news or not?

Damian stood over by the window again, and he shaded his eyes, looking through the falling snow. He had his headphones up over his ears again. He seemed pretty fixated on this donkey, and Brett wished he wasn't. This couldn't end well.

"Why don't you come help us at the table?" Brett said.

Damian didn't move.

"Damian?" He raised his voice.

The boy turned back and pulled off his headphones. "I'm watching for Eeyore."

"You know how they say a watched pot never boils?" Eli asked.

"No," Damian replied.

"It means if you just wait for something, it takes forever. But if you distract yourself, the thing you were waiting for happens," Brett said.

"Oh." Damian sighed and moved away from the window. "I hope he comes back. I wanted to meet him."

Emaline sat down at the table and patted the spot next to her.

"Damian, why don't you come sit with me?" she said. "This will be fun."

Damian moved over to the spot next to Emaline. She seemed to soften even more when Damian was close by her. And Damian responded to her. Maybe he sensed that Emaline sincerely liked him. He'd been struggling with making friends. The kid with the headphones didn't get asked to many birthday parties.

Suddenly Emaline's eyes widened and she pointed. Brett looked over his shoulder in the direction she was gesturing, and his heart hammered to a stop.

A large snowy donkey's nose pressed up against the window. What Brett could see of the donkey was covered in snow, and he blinked a snowflake off his long lashes.

"Eeyore!" Damian shouted, and Brett shook his head in wonder.

That donkey had survived the night and made his way home.

CHAPTER FIVE

EMALINE STOOD UP at the same time that Belinda did, and suddenly the house burst into excited confusion. Eli headed for the mudroom to put on his boots, and Belinda started dashing around the kitchen muttering about finding that halter, although why a halter would be in the kitchen, Emaline had no idea. Damian ran to the window, and by some miracle didn't startle the donkey away. Eeyore must be happy to have found his home again, because he was waiting patiently by the window. Belinda came up with an actual rope halter from a kitchen drawer—there *had* been a halter in the kitchen!—and dashed over to the mudroom after Eli. Brett followed her, and the door opened, letting in a swirl of frigid air, boots thunked against the steps, and then the door slammed shut.

It all happened so fast that Emaline wasn't even sure she knew what was going on. She stood there for a moment, then hurried across the kitchen to the window next to Damian.

She pulled out her phone and started to record, doing her best to keep from filming Eli's or Belinda's faces, but maybe she could blur them out later.

Outside, Eli had the halter over the donkey's head, and Belinda was brushing snow off his back. The snow was deep, and Brett was lifting his knees high to get through it as he walked into the veil of blurring snow toward the stable. Emaline stopped filming.

"I think that counts as a Christmas miracle, Damian," Emaline said.

"Santa did this," Damian said soberly.

"I think he did." Emaline smiled. It was sweet to see that Christmas faith in little kids.

"I gave up my Christmas wish," Damian said.

"What?" Emaline looked down at him.

"I gave it up. I wished on a star last night—even though I couldn't see any stars, but they're still up there, you know."

"Yes, they are."

"So I wished on a star that I could undo my Christmas wish and have Eeyore come back instead," Damian said.

"Oh, sweetie, that was very selfless of you." Emotion tightened her throat. "What was your Christmas wish before?"

"I wanted a hoverboard. My dad said he'd

help me learn how to ride it. He said it's probably harder than a bike, but I can ride a bike already."

"Good for you!"

"So I won't get the hoverboard now," Damian concluded. "And I don't mind. Maybe Santa will give it to me next year. I'm glad Eeyore is home again."

He honestly thought he'd given up any hope of getting the toy he'd been yearning for, and he'd done it so willingly. His sacrifice was so sweet.

"You are a very good kid, you know that?" Emaline said.

Damian smiled bashfully, and just then the door opened again, and Belinda came inside, stamping her boots on the mat.

"No, no, no!" Belinda said. "There has to be another way."

"There isn't another way," Eli said from behind her.

There was more stamping, and then Belinda appeared in the kitchen, her cheeks wind-reddened.

"I have guests!" Belinda waved a gloved hand toward Emaline and Damian. "There are hygienic issues and food preparation laws, and…and…and *online reviews*!"

"What's going on?" Emaline asked.

"There's a snow bank in front of the stable door," Belinda said. "And the rolling door at the back is frozen shut. There was a leak of some sort that made an icy chunk right in front of the wheel—" She gestured a couple of times futilely. "Anyway, it won't open, and we can't dig through a snow bank that big in the storm."

"And the only solution I can see is bringing the donkey inside the house," Eli said.

"Bringing him in here?" Damian's whole face lit up.

"We cannot bring a donkey into the house!" Belinda retorted. "It's not done!"

"It's only getting colder out there…" Eli murmured.

"It's not done!" she repeated. "I have food in here and guests, and we cannot have a donkey wandering around my clean floor!"

"Belinda, I'm not wanting to argue with you or make you miserable," Eli said. "I told myself I wouldn't do that anymore. You are absolutely right that this isn't done. It's like living in a barn—you've told me that a hundred times. I know it's uncivilized and wrong and goes against the better instinct of any good woman, but there's a storm blowing out there, and Eeyore, by some miracle, is back. And alive! But he won't stay that way if we don't warm him up. While I think he's a cantankerous old beast and he loves nothing more than pitting himself against me, I would very much like to see that donkey live to fight another day."

Belinda's eyes misted and she seemed to deflate a little. "Oh, Eli..."

"I wouldn't breathe a word of it to anyone," he said. "It'll be our secret."

"I do have a reputation to protect." A smile touched her lips, and she looked over at Emaline. "I fear that Eli is right. Eeyore will die if we don't take him inside. Would you be okay with that?"

"I don't see a way around it, either," Emaline said. "And getting that donkey home cost a great deal." For Damian, it had cost a full Christmas wish. She looked down at the boy who was holding his breath. "I'm fine with it. Let's get that donkey warmed up."

"Then it's settled?" Eli eyed Belinda.

"It's settled." She sighed. "Bring him in."

Eli had a little hop in his step as he headed back outside, and Belinda shook her head.

"You don't understand," Belinda said, stepping out of her boots and carrying them back into the mudroom, her voice echoing back until she reemerged again. "Eli and I have disagreed for decades over his tendency to bring farm animals into his house. Decades! He's had everything from chickens to calves to goats to..." she shook her head "...I'm sure there are more than I'm forgetting. But never in all those years of that man living like he was raised by wolves has he ever brought a donkey into his house. And what do I do? I bring in a donkey!"

Emaline burst out laughing. "You're losing a lot of high ground today, aren't you?"

"Like you wouldn't believe." Belinda started to laugh. "If you'd be so kind as to not mention this in any online reviews, I will personally promise you that I will never again allow a farm animal into this home, and I'll give you a free stay at a later date."

"This would actually make a really good vlog post," she said. "What if I made it clear that this was a life-or-death situation and expressed awe for your deep cleaning afterward? This is a Christmas miracle with a donkey who has to come inside to warm up or die in the elements. That's ideal for me."

"Is it?" Belinda frowned.

"It's gold."

Not quite the gold that George insisted she was sitting on, but gold nonetheless.

The door opened again, and this time the sound of Brett's voice mingled with Eli's as they encouraged the donkey to climb the stairs. The sound of scrambling hooves and one loud bray echoed through the house, and then Eeyore was inside, hooves clopping against the wooden floorboards. He stepped into the kitchen looking as surprised to be there as everyone else was to see him.

"Eeyore!" Damian rushed forward and put a hand up toward the donkey's nose. Brett moved to stop him, but Eeyore lowered his head to greet the boy as gently as a lamb. Belinda had a mop in hand and she was looking forlornly at the mud and snow on her floor.

"Would you help me get his feed? There's some under the buggy shelter," Eli said to Brett.

"You bet."

The men clomped back outside, and Belinda began to mop behind the donkey. Eeyore plodded farther into the kitchen, putting his nose up to Emaline's mug of hot coffee on the table and snuffling at it.

"Not for you, Eeyore," Emaline said, picking up the mug. "But we're glad to see you, all the same."

Eeyore moved on to the evergreen branches, snuffled at them, and took one small nibble at the needles, and then carried on forward toward the kitchen sink. Damian followed behind, his face glowing.

"He might be thirsty." Emaline looked over to where Belinda stood with an entirely defeated look on her face. "Can I put some water in the sink for him?"

"Might as well," Belinda said. "He's been in snow all night—I doubt he got anything liquid into him."

Emaline put the stopper in the sink and turned on the water. Once she got a couple of inches in the bottom of the sink, she turned it off and Eeyore moved forward and started to drink thirstily.

"Belinda, would you mind if I recorded some of this?"

"You'll express deep and abiding awe in my ability to deep clean afterward?" Belinda asked.

She chuckled. "That's a promise."

"You can't have me or Eli in it," Belinda said.

"I know. I'll be careful. I'll show you all the footage when I'm done so you can be sure of it. But this would be perfect. It's about heart. It's about visiting somewhere different from the city life that people are used to—different priorities, different challenges."

"I wonder what my niece would say about

having my Amish Butternut Bed and Breakfast mentioned in it…" Belinda murmured.

"Ask her!" Emaline said. "But what would you say if I took a little bit of video of Eeyore with my phone, and I wrote up a script that included all the things I promised? You could take a look, and I wouldn't post it unless you specifically gave me permission to do so."

"Eeyore does make a good story, I'll give you that," Belinda said thoughtfully. "All right."

"That's a deal." Emaline pulled out her phone and framed a shot of Eeyore drinking water out of the kitchen sink. She moved around the donkey, getting a view of him from all sides as he drank. Then she backed up to get more of the kitchen in the shot.

The side door opened, and the men came back in with a bale that they put on the floor next to the mudroom door. There was a rustle of coats and boots being removed, and then Brett came into the kitchen first. Emaline whipped the phone out of sight before he caught her eye.

"I had no problem with having Eeyore inside," he said. "Did you?"

"None." She grinned back. "This is great for me."

"These are not the sorts of memories I want

to leave my guests with," Belinda said. "But since there's no avoiding it, Brett, would you be so kind as to use the broom and get the snow off Eeyore's back? I might as well mop it all up now."

Belinda grabbed a straw broom from the corner and passed it over.

"Can I get some video of you sweeping off the donkey?" she asked with a grin.

Brett paused. "Can you keep my face out of it?"

Was he really agreeing to this? She nodded. "Of course."

"And I think we can put down some newspaper once we figure out where Eeyore wants to stand," Eli said, cocking his head to the side thoughtfully. "Trying to force him into one corner isn't going to work. Eeyore is too opinionated. Let's figure out where he wants to be, and put newspaper down behind him for...the inevitable."

Belinda shuddered and Emaline laughed. "That sounds smart."

"As much as Belinda loathes this," Eli said, "I have a fair amount of experience in keeping things clean with large animals around the house. We will manage."

Eeyore finished his long drink of water and

clopped across the kitchen toward the bale of feed.

"Are you hungry, old fellow?" Eli asked, cutting the length of twine that bound the bale and pulling up the hay so that Eeyore could get at it. Eeyore immediately pulled up a big bite and started to chew. Eli stood back, watching the donkey with a satisfied smile. "Now, I'll have you know I fought for you, so you'd better be nicer to me going forward."

Brett started brushing snow off Eeyore's back, and Emaline took some video. True to her word, she avoided capturing any human faces in the video. Then she turned it off and grabbed the dustpan to scoop the clumps of snow up off the ground before they melted. Keeping up with an indoor donkey was going to be a group effort—no way around it.

"You need to thank Damian for Eeyore coming back," she said softly.

"Oh?" Brett looked down at her.

"He used his Christmas wish." She glanced toward the boy who was standing proudly next to the bale of hay watching Eeyore eat. "He reversed his first wish and asked for Eeyore's safe return instead."

"Are you serious?" Brett kept his voice low, and she saw his expression soften. "Wow."

"Yeah."

He met her gaze again and his smile was tender now. He needed to know. Damian might get that hoverboard all the same—parents had a way of making sure they got their kids the gifts they wanted most if they had the financial ability to do it, and the senator could afford it. But that little boy's tender heart needed to be protected.

Suddenly, Emaline realized that Damian's headphones were on the kitchen table, and Damian didn't seem to miss them, even with a donkey in the middle of the kitchen. That felt like a good step.

BRETT BRUSHED THE last of the snow off Eeyore's back, and then he stood back as Belinda took a towel to the donkey and continued to wipe him down. She worked slowly and gently, Eeyore looked over his shoulder at the old woman, and Brett could see the love shining in the donkey's eyes.

Yeah, Eeyore had been rescued this morning, and heaven knew what he'd endured overnight on his own in that storm.

Brett headed over to the table, and Emaline followed him. She was closer than he'd thought, and his hand brushed across hers as he turned to pull a chair out. His heart thundered in his ears, and she looked up at him, eyes widened in surprise. He smiled sheepishly.

"Small kitchen," he said by way of excuse, but truth be told, he liked having her this close. She was the kind of pretty that tugged at him in a deeper way. He wanted to know what she was thinking. He wanted to hear her talk.

"Hmm." A smile tickled her lips.

Eli and Belinda worked together to clean up the floor around the donkey, and Damian seemed just thrilled to watch Eeyore eat. Brett pulled out a chair and sat down, then nudged out the chair next to him. Emaline accepted the silent invitation and took a seat.

"Is this a good start to a vlog?" Brett asked.

"You bet." She showed him a video on her phone of Eeyore drinking out of the sink.

It was good stuff, he had to admit. He liked that she was a travel vlogger, not some cutthroat journalist. It meant he could relax around her and not worry quite so much about what he said or what impression he made. Although, he wanted her to like him—he had to admit that.

"You might not know me very well, but I do have a sensitive touch with these things," Emaline said.

"I've seen your work," he countered.

"I mean…I could do more than this."

He paused, wondering what that meant. Dean had mentioned not wanting to put her on the map with a news story… He wasn't right about her, was he? Her phone pinged and he saw an email notification pop up. Just the first line: Here is my contact info if you want to talk… She took her phone back and looked down at it grimly.

"Is that the family drama you were talking about?" he asked.

"Yep." She pulled up the email, then flicked her finger to dismiss the notification.

Once again, he found himself wondering what family drama looked like for Emaline Piper. Most people didn't have the Rockwells' level of practice in keeping dirty laundry hidden behind bright smiles and family unity.

And the Rockwells had plenty to hide in that respect. Brett, personally, had plenty to hide from the press.

Emaline reached for a candle. Her eyes had lost their luster. Whatever that email was, it had upset her.

"Belinda, how do you want us to put together the candles and the evergreen twigs?" she asked, raising her voice a little.

"Well—" Belinda turned from the donkey and came over to the table. "I use that twine to secure it together in whatever way seems to work. But I like to have a little nest of greenery to hold the candle."

She demonstrated, deftly twisting a sprig of pine needles around the base of a candle, then adding another and another. Then she nodded to the twine, and Emaline cut a piece off for herself. It looked simple enough. Belinda smiled and left the table again. Emaline placed the candle in front of the pile of greenery and pulled out her phone. She held up a finger, then pressed Record. He watched the screen as she got a shot of the finished product, then stopped recording.

"What do you normally do for Christmas?" Emaline asked, glancing over at him.

"Normally, I'm at Dean and Bobbie's place," he said. "Bobbie puts together an amazing holiday. Everything is organized to perfection. She used to put on dinner parties to get supporters for Dean's campaigns, and she single-handedly brought in more donations and pledges than anyone else on the fundraising team."

Emaline looked over at him, her expression veiled.

"Don't tell me," he said with a rueful smile. "You don't like my brother's wife, either."

"I don't know her," Emaline replied. "But

from what I understand, she came from a lot of money, so moving in those circles would be a lot easier for her."

That was a cautious answer. And she was right.

"She came with connections," Brett replied. "That's true. But it doesn't make throwing together a dinner for sixty any easier. Sure, they had the money to hire a catering company and a cleaner for the house. But it was her touch that gave it that feeling of being intimate yet important."

"So…Christmas was the same as those dinner parties?" she asked.

"No, Christmas was private. It was one holiday where we all let our hair down, so to speak."

Emaline nodded. "At least you got that."

"How about you?" he asked.

"We always go to my mom's place—me and my three brothers. Andy got married recently, so his wife will be there, too. This year we all went in together and bought my mom a new stove. Hers was on its last leg, so we splurged on a really beautiful one with double ovens and the works."

He shot her a smile. "Is it a surprise?"

"Yep. Paul is going to bring it in the back of his truck, and he's going to arrive Christmas Eve. So, we have this plan that we'll get Mom to come outside to look at something, and this big box will be in the back of the truck with a huge red bow on it. Honestly, we almost didn't spring for the bow. They're pricier than you'd think. But I think the bow is important."

"I agree. It's all about the presentation," Brett replied. "I kind of envy you."

"Me?" She broke a sprig off the branch. "Why?"

"You can get your mother something she needs, and she'll be deeply grateful," he said. "She'll probably cry."

"You could buy something like that more easily than I ever could," she said with a chuckle.

"Actually, I can't." He broke off his own bits of greenery. "You're right that we have the cash at our disposal, but my mother doesn't need anything that she can't easily buy for herself. So she wouldn't be deeply grateful. It's…it's a weird blessing to be able to meet someone's need."

"Oh…" Her voice softened.

He was talking too much. He glanced up to see Damian still looking adoringly at that donkey. They might be a political family, but they *were* a family.

"I try to get Mom sentimental gifts," he said after a moment, "but there's only so many thoughtful gifts you can even think of. One year I framed a picture of my brother and me for her. Another year, I bought her a new dinner ring. But again—nothing she couldn't have done for herself easily enough."

He glanced over at Emaline, and her gaze was locked on him. He swallowed. Somehow, he couldn't look away. And some too-trusting part of him wanted to keep talking. He hadn't had anyone listen quite like she did before. Was this how regular people got to know each other?

"You see these videos online of guys having made it big, and they go back to their parents' house, and they have some lavish gift for them," he said. "A car, maybe. And their parents tear up and are so grateful. The problem is, I didn't make it big. I came from privilege and simply maintained it."

"I'm sure your mother is proud of you," Emaline countered.

"She is…" Mostly. Brett's mother was relieved that he'd turned his life around. "The only thing I've done that's brought tears of gratitude to my mother's eyes was checking myself into rehab."

Had he just said that out loud? He hadn't meant to open up quite this much!

"When was that?" she asked.

Too late now, anyway. At least he could keep the focus off Damian.

"About five years ago," he said after a beat.

"When you dropped off the party circuit." Emaline nodded. "That adds up. What made you decide to do it?"

"Is this just between us?" he asked.

"Of course. I'm asking as a fr—a fellow human being."

Had she been about to say "friend"? He realized ruefully that he wished she had. But she'd asked, and the words just kept flowing, even if this wasn't entirely wise.

"My family had an intervention for me one Christmas." He remembered the tension, the embarrassment of it all. "They sat me down and told me that my partying had gotten out of control. They were right. What they didn't know was that the week before that intervention, I'd looked at myself in the mirror and decided I needed to change something. I had nothing I was proud of. I was going to ask my mother if I could run the family ranch—get away from the friends and the booze and the constant parties. Just go cold turkey."

"And when they did the intervention?"

"I figured rehab was a good idea. It would dry me out before I started fresh. So I went."

"And that's why you disappeared and made a life for yourself out here," she said.

"It is."

"I knew there had to be a reason for it," she said thoughtfully. "You seem like the kind of man who has good reasons for what he does."

Did he? It was rather sweet seeing himself through her eyes. She might think better of him than she should.

"People don't normally say that. Have you read the news stories about me?"

"Not in about five years." She shot him a teasing smile. "You've done well staying out of the public eye."

"Thanks, I tried." He chuckled and she dropped her gaze.

Emaline set down a completed candle decoration on the table in front of her. "People tend to be jealous of your family."

"Are you?" He shouldn't ask that, but he was curious.

"Absolutely!" she replied, then her face pinked. "I shouldn't admit that to you. But us regular people don't have the opportunities that you've got. I mean, most people can't go run a family ranch because they want to, you know? I do envy the life your family leads, even though I know it isn't quite as easy as it looks on the outside."

"What would you do if you had the privilege?" he asked. What he really wanted to know was what would she do if she were his girlfriend? What if she had access to the comfort he did?

"I'd get my mother the matching fridge," she said.

He started to smile, and it took him a beat to realize that she wasn't joking. He was half inclined to offer to buy her mother the fridge, but he had a feeling that would land wrong. People didn't want the handout. She reached for the ribbon and cut off a piece, then tied it around the candle.

"And what would you do if you *didn't* have all that privilege?" she asked, breaking the silence.

That was a fair question. "I wouldn't have had the opportunity to go to rehab, for one," he said. "And I probably would have picked up a few friends in low places. I think I'd be a guy in the city, working a job, paying my bills, and dreaming of a rural life that would never be mine."

"Just as well you aren't a regular guy, then." She smiled again, and he felt better in the warmth of it.

She was probably right. The family money had rescued him more than once, but he had to wonder, if he hadn't had it to fall back on, would he have gotten serious about his life a little bit sooner? It might have changed everything…although he couldn't blame anyone else for his own mistakes. Family money behind him or not, he'd been the one to mess things up.

Belinda came back to the table then and starting breaking off some twigs to work with, too.

"You know, we Amish believe that a simple life is the shortest path to happiness," Belinda said, and when Brett and Emaline both looked up at her in mild surprise, she added, "I'm sorry to have overheard your discussion."

"That's okay." Brett leaned back in his chair. "I suppose we come visit your Amish farms and shops for a reason, don't we?"

"I think so," Belinda agreed. "We do have something that others long for—that everyone else lost along the way somehow."

"It's contentment," Emaline said.

"I disagree," Belinda replied. "Yes, we are content, but it's more than that. It's relationships. When relationships go wrong, it doesn't matter how much money you have. You aren't happy if you're lonely or heartbroken. So we

Amish focus on those personal connections—we focus on our friends and our families and the ones we care about. We order our lives to spend more time at home together as a family. And when we have those relationships in line, we have that contentment, too. No Amish person is ever alone."

Brett exchanged a look with Emaline. Never alone. Oddly, he was the least lonely he'd been in his life right here in an Amish kitchen with a pretty blonde vlogger making candle wreaths beside him.

"Do you ever worry about your privacy, Belinda?" he asked. "With all those people in your life, I mean."

"Oh, all the time!" Belinda said. "But that's our pride getting in the way. If we just own up to our mistakes and face them, then there isn't anything to hide, is there?"

A simple life, to be sure. And maybe your average Amish guy had fewer mistakes in his past than Brett did.

"Take the two of you," Belinda said. "I imagine you've felt lonely a lot over the last few years. But since you arrived here and were snowed in with a perfect stranger, two old people, a little boy and now a donkey, are you lonely at all?"

"Not a bit," Emaline said softly.

Brett looked over at her, and her cheeks were flushed with color. She wouldn't look at him.

"See?" Belinda smiled brightly. "We need each other. We need people in our business and asking us questions and challenging our ideas. We need people who know our histories and our shortcomings and who love us anyway. We need people to stop minding their own business and start paying attention to the people around them. That's the secret to happiness." Belinda winked. "And now I'm going to start a fresh batch of muffins. Snacks also help."

Emaline had a wistful look on her face. Funny, but out here in Amish Country, it was easy to believe in a different way of living and a different set of rules, where opening up was a good thing, and people kept you company instead of tilling you under.

But that was the one thing Rockwells avoided—people in their business. If they were regular folks, it might be different. But the senator's family didn't have the luxury of opening up too much. People weren't interested in supporting the Rockwells' hopes and dreams. They'd vote for them if they could get the job done, but no one wanted the best for them on a personal level. The average person wanted to tear them down. Wealth didn't make the friends that people thought.

The rules might be different out here for the likes of Belinda and Eli, but not for the Rockwells.

CHAPTER SIX

"Uh oh!" Damian said at the same time that Emaline heard a plopping sound. The inevitable had happened. With a farm animal in the house, they'd have to deal with droppings.

"That's why we have newspaper back there." Eli grunted as he bent over and picked up the newspaper and its contents. "Put more down, Damian. If we pick it up right away and get it outside, it won't smell like a barn in here."

"Or at least not as much…" Belinda murmured.

Hund plodded along after the old man and even tried to sniff the contents of the newspaper. When Eli tapped Hund's nose away, he fell in behind him and followed the old man to the door.

Funny though the scene was, Emaline's mind was on her half sister's email. Maggie wanted to talk. If Emaline was back home in the city, she'd have a hundred pre-Christmas errands she'd be running, a vlog or two to prepare and parties with friends to attend.

She'd be busy, and pushing her half sister out of her mind until that lull between Christmas and New Year's Eve would be easy enough.

But snowed in at the Butternut Amish Bed and Breakfast, ignoring her own feelings surrounding her half sister wasn't so easy. Sure, she wasn't lonely, but it didn't stop her from thinking, either. Especially with honest Amish wisdom about family and connections.

But those honest Amish families wouldn't have a mess like hers did, either, would they?

That was her silent argument as she worked on another candle display.

She'd been seeing a therapist for a few years now. And it had helped her a lot in sorting out her issues surrounding her father's lies and betrayal. Where were the warning signs that her father had been lying all those years? She'd had to sift through all the things about her parents' relationship that she'd figured were normal to find out if they actually were! She'd picked through her memories with the help of Dr. Bernice, and she'd come to the point where she could confidently date nice men and not feel like she was going to step into the same travesty her mother had. In fact, at this point, she might even be better equipped than most to spot deceit. She'd done a lot of emotional work, but she hadn't gotten to the point of sorting things out with her father's other family. That was still a tender spot.

She pulled out her phone and looked at her sister's most recent email.

Here is my contact info if you want to talk. It would be really nice to talk to you—just the two of us.

Maggie had left a litany of different ways to contact her: cell phone, email, social media accounts. One of these times that Maggie attempted to contact Emaline and Emaline pushed her away, Maggie would take the hint and stop. She'd attempted two times before this over the years. One of these times, Maggie might develop a grudge of her own... Was that what Emaline really wanted?

Emaline's finger hovered over the call button on her phone, and for a moment, she hesitated. But maybe now was as good a time as any. She pressed it, then stood up and slipped away from the table. The sitting room was empty, and she eased in there. It was also much cooler, the potbellied stove and the regular oven being in the kitchen.

The sound of hooves clopped behind her, and Emaline turned to see Eeyore standing in the entrance to the sitting room. He stretched his muzzle toward her and started into the room.

"No, no, you silly donkey!" Eli hollered from behind. "Pick a room and stick to it, old man!" Then a pause. "Hund, sit!"

Emaline chuckled as Eli squeezed past the donkey and proceeded to herd him back out again. Eli stood in the doorway with his arms spread to discourage Eeyore from trying again.

"Hund, I said to sit." Then he said something in Pennsylvania Dutch. The dog sat.

"Hello?" A woman answered the phone.

"Maggie?" Emaline turned away, toward the window. It was the most privacy she'd get in this house.

"Yes."

"This is Emaline."

"Oh!" There was a pause. "Just a minute. I'm at work. I'm going to go to the break room."

"Sure."

Emaline watched as Eli herded the donkey back into the kitchen, and she sucked in a deep breath, willing her nerves to calm. When she was alone again, Maggie came back on the line.

"Thanks for calling me," Maggie said. "I wasn't sure if you would."

"I wasn't sure if I would, either," Emaline replied. "Where do you work?"

"At an insurance company. I do data processing."

"Oh…neat."

"It's really nice to hear your voice. Dad says we sound a lot alike. I'm not sure I hear it, though."

Dad… Emaline rubbed a hand over her eyes. Her father hadn't talked to her in years. Or more accurately, she hadn't spoken to him. "Can I ask you something?"

"Sure."

"Aren't you mad at him?" Emaline asked.

"Our father?"

"Yes, our father. The man who kept two families for ten years. Hasn't he messed you up at all?" This was coming out more aggressively than Emaline intended.

"Well…I forgave him."

"Just like that."

"Not really. It was hard. I mean, we had no idea about you guys, either. I was about eight, I guess, when it all hit the fan. How old were you?"

"Sixteen."

"Okay, so you were old enough to really understand what was happening," Maggie said. "I wasn't. I suppose that made it easier at the time. And Mom and Dad got through it, so…"

Got through it… That sounded so innocent, as if they'd simply had a disagreement. *Sorry about having a whole other family, sweetheart. Let me bring you some flowers to make it up to you.*

"Do you know what really happened?" Emaline asked.

"I think I do," she said. "Maybe you should tell me what you know, though."

"Your mother figured out Dad was lying. She somehow got my mother's phone number, called her and told her that Dad had you two in another city. Our mothers were both enraged. They both said they deserved better. They promised they'd help each other get through this. So my mother kicked Dad out, and instead of staying true to her word, your mother took him in. That's what happened."

There was silence for a moment. "I didn't hear that version."

"What did you hear?"

"That…Dad chose us."

Those words were like a kick in the gut. That sentiment was the very one she'd been working through the last ten years in therapy.

"Our father was emotionally lazy. My mother kicked him out. Your mother didn't. It was easy for him. Path of least resistance."

"So, you blame my mom…"

Emaline sighed. Sixteen hadn't really been old enough to understand all of this. Thirty-one wasn't old enough, either. It had been a mess.

"I don't blame your mother," Emaline said after a beat of silence. "I blame our father. But what I'm saying is it wasn't a matter of a little marital spat that they worked out. Dad had two complete families in two different cities. And he simply chose the easier path. My mother wouldn't put up with it, and so he went to yours. He left me and my three brothers behind. You grew up with a father. We lost ours."

"I'm sorry he did that, but the lying had to stop."

Such a high horse to land on. Yes, the lying had to stop, but the lying had crushed a lot of lives. Just not Maggie's, apparently.

"Do you think he's faithful to your mother now?" Emaline asked.

"I think so. Yes. Of course. He loves her."

"He's a phenomenal liar, you know. He can hug you and tell you how much he loves you, and go to a new city and do the same thing with someone else."

"Why are you saying all this?" Maggie asked, tears in her voice. "I contacted you because you're my sister, and I wanted to know you!"

"Maggie, you say we're sisters like we grew up together or something. We're related to each other. Yes. We share DNA. But we didn't know each other. We didn't bond. We didn't have anything to link us in our childhoods."

"Spoken like someone with three siblings," Maggie said bitterly. "I was an only child. I kept begging my parents for a little brother or sister. So when I found out I had four siblings in Pittsburgh, I was secretly thrilled. I knew it broke my mother's heart. I knew it made my father a terrible guy, but I had siblings. More specifically, I had a sister. I was just a kid, and I couldn't reach out or anything, but I told myself that when I was older, I'd find you. You were good news to me!"

"You were the family that decimated mine," Emaline replied quietly.

"Right." Maggie's tone sounded tired. "But that was our parents messing up everything. I had just as much choice in being born as you had. So I get that you're angry, and I can even understand that you might hate our father, but I didn't cause this mess. I was born into it. And like it or not, you're my sister. So forgive me for wanting to find some sort of human connection with you."

Emaline sighed. Maggie was reaching out, and she was right that neither sister had had a choice in any of this. That was the infuriating part. Their father had lied and destroyed his children's ability to trust, and they'd had no choice in any of that.

"Are you going to therapy?" Emaline asked quietly. Maybe they had that in common.

"No." The answer was curt.

"I was just checking," Emaline said. "I am. I've been in therapy for years now. What we both grew up with wasn't normal. My parents' relationship, your parents' relationship—all very messed up. And if you want to avoid that in your own romantic life as much as I do, then do yourself a favor and start therapy now. There's a lot to work through."

"Well, between the two of us, you're angry and bitter, and I'm reaching out," Maggie said. "Which one of us do you think is handling things better?"

Emaline was tempted to snap, but she took a calming breath instead. "Getting angry is actually a step forward. When you really face this, you're going to be furious, too. And that rage can't be avoided. It can't be skipped over. It can't be sidestepped."

"I'm not angry," she said, her tone tight. "Okay, maybe I'm a little bit angry at you right now. But I'm fine. I'm trying to fix this. I'm trying to unite us."

"Maggie, you can't fix what Dad broke!" Emaline said.

There was a tense silence, broken by the distant sound of a phone ringing on the other end.

"Message received," Maggie said after a moment. "But you say that one day I'll face this and I'll be furious. Well, one day, you're going to face having had a sister that you pushed away, and you're going to wish you hadn't. Because I'm the only sister you've got. We both may have a few regrets."

But this was all surface stuff—two sisters getting to know each other. And Maggie was awfully young. Twenty-two wasn't the mature adult Maggie thought. Were they supposed to pretend the rest of their family drama hadn't happened? Maggie had won—her mother had won the competition. Dad went to them, and Emaline had gone the rest of her adolescence without a father and with a burden of emotional baggage she'd have to sort through for years to come. She couldn't pretend to be some cheery sister who was thrilled for the contact. She wasn't.

"I'm sorry I wasn't what you were hoping for," Emaline said.

"That's okay. Apparently, that feeling is mutual."

Emaline had offended Maggie, and she hadn't called her to do that. She wasn't sure what she'd hoped to get from this phone call. Maybe she should have followed her original intention and simply ignored the email.

"This is probably pushing it," Maggie said, "but Mom and Dad say you're welcome at their home anytime. I told my mother I'd pass along the message."

Maggie's mother could probably use a good, healthy rage fest, too. She'd won her man, but in Emaline's humble opinion, her father wasn't much of a prize to hold on to. He might be fun and tender and thoughtful when he wanted to be, but he was also capable of some huge secrets. Trusting him was a bad idea.

"I'm not going to visit your parents," Emaline said quietly. "But thank you for reaching out to me this Christmas. I know it came from a good place."

"No problem," Maggie snapped. "Take care."

"You too."

Emaline hung up the call and looked down at the phone. She didn't feel any better. If anything, she felt worse. Maggie wanted a sister, and while Emaline had three brothers, she had to admit that she'd longed for a sister more than once, too. But not like this—not with *them*.

"Eeyore!" Damian hollered from the other room, and the donkey came clopping into the sitting room again, not to be dissuaded. He plodded up to her and put his velvety nose into her hand.

"Hey, you," Emaline said softly, and suddenly all the hopes she didn't know she had and all of her sister's dashed expectations seemed to crumble inside of her. Her eyes misted, and she stroked the donkey's nose.

"Eeyore, you have to come back!" Damian said, sliding on sock feet into the sitting room. "He has to come back, right, Emaline?"

"He does." Emaline forced a smile and wiped at a tear on her cheek.

"Oh." Damian sobered and looked up at her.

Emaline wiped her face again. She didn't mean for the boy to see this.

"Are you sad?" Damian asked.

"I'm okay, Damian. Don't worry about me," Emaline said.

"But you're crying," Damian said. "That means you're sad."

"I am a little bit, but I'll be okay." She

didn't need to upset this little kid. The ugliness in her family didn't need to touch him.

"Let's get Eeyore back into the kitchen," Brett said from the doorway, and then his eyes locked with hers. His expression softened into a face exactly like his nephew's—stunned and helpless. "Everything okay?"

"Yep." She licked her lips and pocketed her phone. There really was no privacy in a place like this, was there?

"Come on, Eeyore," Belinda called, joining them in the sitting room to shoo the donkey into the right direction. Hund came into the room next and loped around the back of Eeyore, and the donkey picked up his pace to head in the right direction. Hund seemed to know his job.

One good thing had come out of her adolescent trauma, and that was that she had a keen nose for deceit. But somehow, she hadn't been prepared for Maggie's perspective. Their father wasn't the bad guy for Maggie. He was just…her dad. And Emaline didn't know why that made her so angry, but it did.

But her father wasn't the only man who seemed to live his life with zero consequences. How many powerful men did the same thing—had families, mistresses, extra kids—and there was never any consequence?

Even senators. Where had Damian come from? And why would his wife just go along with this? Was the life of privilege really worth her own self-respect?

Men got away with an awful lot that they shouldn't. They should be held accountable, and the women who should be putting their feet to the fire weren't. And that fact left Emaline angry.

She just wished that she could stay mad, instead of having it all erupt in tears.

BRETT STOOD BACK as Eeyore was hustled into the kitchen again, ears high and a playful look in his eye. The donkey seemed to be in good shape, considering his long stay out in the freezing cold. Damian followed the old folks back into the kitchen, eager to go wherever the donkey and dog went, and Brett looked over at Emaline.

She stood with her arms crossed, and tears shone in her eyes. His heart gave a squeeze. What he wanted to do was hug her—just wrap his arms around her in a big bear hug, and make it better. But he couldn't… That would be overstepping big-time.

"Are you really okay?" he asked.

"Yeah. Yeah." She sucked in a breath. "I'm fine."

She didn't look fine. She looked a bit shaken. He'd overheard some of that conversation—the house wasn't exactly soundproof—but should he say anything? Belinda had said they needed people in each other's business, but that was the sort of advice that sounded nice when applied to others. He wasn't so sure that Emaline would appreciate it from him.

"Family drama?" he asked cautiously.

She nodded. "I'm sure you aren't immune to that, either."

"We Rockwells just hide it really well."

She smiled faintly. "I'll bet you do."

Her tone sounded like she was talking about something specific, but she didn't elaborate. A wisp of hair lay across her cheek, and he reached up and brushed it away. She raised her gaze at the same time, and he froze, his fingers lingering on her soft cheek.

She was so beautiful… What he wanted to do was dip his head down and catch her lips, but he wouldn't. That would be all kinds of inappropriate!

"Do you know what we need?" Eli's voice echoed from the other room. "We need to get that wheelbarrow at the side of the stable and bring it over here to put our soiled newspapers into."

Brett swallowed and stepped back, dropping his hand. "Why don't we do that? I don't know about you, but I could use some fresh air."

Emaline's cheeks pinked and she licked her lips. "So could I."

Sometimes a distraction was good for the soul…and for avoiding making a big mistake like kissing a pretty vlogger he had no business kissing. He knew enough about that.

This Christmas with Damian was another distraction—a chance to spend some time with the kid and pretend that everything was fine. But over the last couple of years, things had been less and less fine. This arrangement was supposed to be the best for everyone, but it was getting tougher for Brett to make his peace with lately.

"Eli, Emaline and I will go get that wheelbarrow," Brett said, heading into the kitchen. Emaline followed him, and they headed into the mudroom.

"Can I come, too, Uncle Brett?" Damian asked.

"No, bud, you stay in here. It's cold out," Brett said. "Besides, I think Eeyore needs you, don't you?"

"Oh yeah…"

That was all it took to distract Damian. He went back over to Eeyore and put a small hand on the donkey's shoulder. The donkey looked down at him with big liquid eyes. Eli had suggested a horse for the kid…maybe he had a point. Damian had definitely opened up since Eeyore came inside, and maybe Dean would agree to having Damian spend more time at his ranch if the kid had a horse of his own.

Emaline shrugged on her outerwear in silence. Brett did the same. They headed into the blowing snow, and he pulled the door firmly shut behind them.

The wind stung Brett's face with icy little pellets, and he ducked his head against the gale. The snow swirled across his field of vision so that he could hardly see. His red Ford truck was covered in snow, and he could make out one crimson splash on the side of the vehicle, but even that blurred out of sight when the wind picked up.

"Stay close!" The wind whipped his words away from him, and he reached out and caught Emaline's hand. He pulled her firmly against him. She felt good there at his side, her gloved hand in his. Getting out of the house was one thing, but getting lost in a blizzard was another issue all together.

They tramped through the snow toward the stable, and it flickered in and out of his view as the wind swept the snow sideways in front of his eyes. But having Emaline's hand in his, he felt better. At least when they got to the stable, they'd be together.

His boot slipped, and Emaline put her hand through his arm.

"Don't fall…" she breathed. She wasn't going to hold him up—not when he was about seventy pounds heavier than she was—but he appreciated the gesture all the same. She felt soft and close, and some elemental part of him was responding to that more than he should.

"Thanks," he said, and they drove forward toward the stable.

The snow had only made a bigger bank against the front door, and he guided Emaline past it toward the buggy shelter, where a black buggy used up most of the space. But there was a gap next to the building that was mercifully snow-free. That was where the wheelbarrow waited. Brett pushed into the shelter, and he tugged Emaline in after him.

"Now this is a storm." Emaline was breathing hard.

"Maybe I should have done this alone," he said. "Sorry about that."

"No, this is good for me." She leaned against the side of the buggy and looked back out into

the falling snow. There was a light visible from
the house—a lantern from inside—that flickered in and out of visibility with the blowing
snow.

"You looked pretty upset," Brett said. She
looked over at him a little sheepishly. "Yeah,
you don't hide it very well."

"It doesn't matter. I'm fine."

Except she didn't look fine to him. She
looked deeply upset, and that had pricked at
him in a strange way.

"You can talk about it, you know," he said
quietly. "I know I'm a virtual stranger, but
I'm actually a pretty good listener."

For a moment she didn't say anything, and
he thought she might brush him off, but then
she looked back up at him and smiled faintly.
"I decided to give Maggie a call—my half
sister."

"The other family," he murmured.

"That's the one." Emaline brushed snow
off her gloves. "I'm not as petty as I sound,
though. It isn't like my father left us and
then met someone else. I'm in my thirties.
I could handle that—forgive it, even. But it
was more complicated. He had two families
for ten years, and none of us knew about each
other. The other woman figured it out first
and called my mom to fill her in. My mother

was irate, my dad didn't deny anything, and she kicked him out. The other woman didn't kick him out. And that's how he decided which family to stick with."

"Ten years!" he said. The reality of her childhood was startling. That was a long time to keep that kind of secret. "Who could do that? How did he manage to keep all of you in the dark?"

"He was a truck driver," she said. "We thought he was on the road. And sometimes he was, but obviously not all the time. He and mom had separate finances. I can only guess he had mountains of debt she didn't know about. That's all I can figure out as an adult looking back on it."

"I'm sorry."

"Thanks, but he's got this whole other family that I'm supposed to embrace because we're related, and I can't do it."

It made sense now. "I don't blame you."

She shot him a wary look, and he met her gaze. He could see her relax then. What had she expected, judgment? From him? He wasn't exactly pure as the driven snow.

"That means more than you know," she said.

"So, your father is still with them?" he asked.

"Yep."

"Have you seen much of him since all this went down?"

"I've only seen him a handful of times. That's on me. He wanted to see me, and I was furious. The longer we went, the easier it was to say no. We met up at a coffee shop a couple of times, just the two of us, but he couldn't give me any explanation for why he did that. I even asked him how he'd feel if I was with some guy who did the same thing to me, and all he could say was that he did his best. I dare say he *didn't* do his best. He was a liar, and it took me another ten years of therapy to figure out how to avoid men just like him."

"And your sister wants…"

"My half sister," she corrected him. "She wants to connect, be all warm and fuzzy."

Her expression told him that wasn't going to happen. "Wow. And people think my family is complicated."

Her laugh was bitter. "See? I can't judge you, either."

Her gaze moved out to the falling snow. Wind swirled it around, but where they stood, they were sheltered from that biting cold.

"Are you going to talk to your dad about it?" Brett asked.

"I've been avoiding this for a long time,"

she replied. "My dad made a few feeble efforts to stay connected with me, and then he put all his attention over to the other family. Maggie had her father in her life from birth. She has him now. She forgave him… and maybe that was easier to do when he chose them."

"Do you miss him?"

"I miss the family I thought I had. I resent him, mostly. I'm angry. I haven't forgiven him for what he did to us—to *me*! I had to comb through my childhood, looking for all the red flags in my dad's behavior so that I'd know what was weird and what wasn't. You tend to assume that the things you grow up with are normal and safe. So if you see them in someone else, you think it's fine. But nothing in my childhood was normal, and I want to avoid that for all I'm worth. I have to go through everything, every memory. Do you know how much emotional labor that is?"

"Sounds like a lot."

She pressed her lips together and looked back out into the falling snow. "I'm sorry. I don't mean to unload any of this onto you. It's not your problem."

"I can still listen," he said.

"This is where most men run," she said with a wry smile.

"It's snowing pretty hard. I don't think I'd get far." He gave her a deadpan look and was rewarded with a low laugh. That felt good—he'd amused her, at least.

But not all secrets were nefarious, like Emaline's father's had been. Some started out as good ideas that got more complicated as time went on. He had too much experience with the latter.

"If I were to guess why he did what he did," Brett said, "I'd say he was probably just too much of a coward to make a choice. Sometimes a man's excellent reason is pure spinelessness."

"I'd agree with that." She shook her head. "You're insightful."

He wasn't sure if that was a compliment or not, considering his insight was into some pretty base behavior. But he had some experience with that, too.

"I've seen a lot," Brett said. "I've also made a lot of my own mistakes. Sometimes, you think you're just taking your time and thinking something through, but that turns into doing absolutely nothing. It's just as bad. I have regrets of my own."

"Can I ask you something?"

"Sure."

"*Did* you vote for your brother?"

Brett looked down at her in surprise. "That sounds like an interview question."

"Nope." She shook her head. "I'm curious about your relationship with him. You defend him. You believe in him, even. But I'm curious if you vote for him."

Brett eyed her for a moment. He could put her off. He could change the subject, but she'd opened up.

"No," he said. "I didn't. And it wasn't because I don't think he's doing a great job. It's because my life has been a lot harder with his political career. It was petty of me, but I voted for his competition. It was purely selfish. I'd love nothing more than to get back to a more normal existence where I could see a pretty travel vlogger and not worry about how it would look in the papers if I took her out on a date."

Shoot. Had he just said that out loud?

Color rose in her cheeks. "You're a flirt."

"I'm actually not." Maybe he wasn't thinking this all the way through before he opened his trap, but he wasn't a flirt.

"I beg to differ." She smiled, though.

"Fine, I'm flirting with you right now, but I'm not a flirt by nature." He shot her a smile, hoping for the best. She froze for a moment, then laughed softly.

"I don't know...you always had a different woman on your arm when you were in the papers."

"That was before. This is now. I'm a different guy." And she wasn't his usual type, either, not that he'd say that out loud.

"I don't know what to make of you," she said.

Coming from the family he did, he was used to that. Really decent women were wary of him, and the less decent women's eyes sparkled with dollar signs.

"If we put my brother aside, and you didn't know me from tabloids and newspapers..." He met her gaze. "What would you make of me then?"

He really wanted to know.

Emaline arched an eyebrow. "I don't know. I'm still trying to figure you out."

Yeah, maybe he was trying to figure her out, too.

"Out here in Amish Country with a snowstorm and a donkey inside the house—" Brett let his smile drop "—it feels like the real world rules don't apply somehow. If we were in Pittsburgh, I don't think our paths would cross. But out here? I don't know. You almost feel like a friend."

"Weird how that works." She looked up at

him, and they were so close together that he could feel the warmth of her breath. Her eyes shone in the shadowed light. "I feel the same way. An actual friend—even a friend for a few days—is a rare thing."

That was probably the most complimentary thing he'd heard in years. But a friend was not exactly the way he was seeing her right now. He didn't want a buddy or a pal...

He touched her cheek, his finger lingering on that soft skin, and her lips parted.

"You're really something," he murmured.

The color in her cheeks deepened, and he went against every better instinct he had and lowered his lips over hers. She leaned into him, the cold air blocking out the closeness of their winter coats, and he kissed her carefully, tenderly then pulled back.

She blinked up at him.

"Is that okay?" he asked softly.

She nodded. "Yeah, I think so."

"Good. Because I've been wanting to do that..."

Emaline stepped back, a bashful smile on her lips, and she nodded toward the wheelbarrow. "I'm also freezing out here."

And if he were still the confident playboy, Brett would be tempted to tug her back against him to warm her up...enjoy a few more stolen minutes alone with her. But he should be careful. He was here to connect with Damian, not start an ill-fated romance with an influencer. Even if he'd just kissed her...

"Yeah. We should get back," he said. "Stay close to me, okay?"

Brett hoisted up the wheelbarrow from where it leaned against the wall and carried it out so he could put it on the ground properly. He was looking forward to some of that cozy warmth in the kitchen, too.

What was it about this B&B that made everything seem possible? Somehow with Amish hosts and the simple life out here influencing him, it made him wish for something more.

CHAPTER SEVEN

BRETT POSITIONED THE wheelbarrow beside the side steps, the wind and snow swirling around him. Emaline opened the side door. A rush of warm cooking-scented air met her as she stepped inside first. She held the door for Brett, then they slammed it solidly shut against the prying cold.

She'd kissed Brett Rockwell… He'd kissed her! And somehow that kiss had been the sweetest, purest kiss she'd ever experienced. If he'd been a playboy back in the day, he certainly hadn't kissed her like she was a conquest. He'd kissed her like she was a piece of china, afraid to break her…and goose bumps ran up her spine at the memory.

"You're back!" Belinda called from the kitchen. "Thank you for doing that. I normally don't put guests to work like this!"

"You normally don't get massive snow storms like this, either," Brett called back. Then he glanced over at Emaline and cast her a private smile.

Eeyore hee-hawed in reply, and Emaline laughed softly.

"We've got another one," Eli said, coming into the mudroom with a newspaper-wrapped package in his hands.

"Here—" Emaline took it, ignoring the weight of the thing, and Brett opened the door for her to step outside and drop it into the waiting wheelbarrow.

"*Danke*, my dear," Eli said. "It's some cold out there. I wonder how my chickens are doing…"

"They are in their coop, huddled up together and sharing warmth, Eli!" Belinda called. "Just like we are. When the snow stops, we'll check on them. But you know as well as I do that if you open that coop door in this cold, you're just letting out their warmth."

Eli sighed. "That woman has ears like a cat."

"I just have ears for your shenanigans, Eli!" But Belinda laughed.

Eli rolled his eyes, and a smile tickled his lips. "She's right, of course."

"She is," Brett agreed. "It can't snow forever."

Eli pottered out of the mudroom, and Emaline peeled off her coat and stepped out of her boots. Brett took her coat as she slid it off her shoulders and hung it up for her next to his own. His fingers lingered over hers...and the sight of their coats side by side warmed her a little. She cast him a smile.

"Thanks."

"Yep." The corners of his eyes crinkled just a little bit. He looked more serious now, but there was still a glitter of something softer in his gaze, and it made her stomach flutter.

She shouldn't enjoy this attention so much. Brett Rockwell was trouble, and whatever was sparking between them here couldn't last.

Emaline headed into the kitchen first, Brett behind her. Damian was feeding Eeyore handfuls of hay, and Belinda was at the stove with the black dog next to her, enjoying the heat.

"What smells so good?" Emaline asked.

"Chicken cutlets," Belinda said with a smile. "I'm going to make an Amish staple to go with them, brown buttered noodles."

She reached into the sizzling iron skillet with a fork, plucked up a piece of breaded chicken, checked the bottom, then put it back into the pan. Then she gave another pan a stir with a spoon.

"Can I record some of this?" Emaline asked.

"If you like." Belinda waved the spoon in the direction of the cupboards. "There's an extra apron hanging up over there if you want to grab it."

Emaline went over to the peg. The apron was wide and wrapped around her all the way to the back. Maybe it was made for a larger woman, or Belinda just believed in being well covered, because Belinda's apron was only a couple of inches away from meeting in the back, as well. Emaline pulled out her phone and started to record.

"Brown buttered noodles are an Amish favorite," Belinda went on. "My mother made them, and my grandmother made them. I've got a recipe for brown buttered noodles going back as far as my great-great-grandmother. If you've got flour to make noodles and butter from your cow's milk, you can make them."

"I've had them in an Amish restaurant before," Emaline said. She zoomed in on the sizzling chicken cutlets in the pan.

"And?" Belinda raised her brows expectantly.

"They're amazing," Emaline said.

Belinda nodded, satisfied. "They certainly are."

Emaline's phone pinged, and a text message from George popped up on the top of her screen. She stopped recording.

I talked to my boss about you and how you're snowed in with Brett Rockwell. He wants to see what you can put together for an article.

Her heartbeat sped up. This was a golden opportunity. This could very well turn into a job. Instead of Emaline Piper, travel vlogger, she could be Emaline Piper, honest-to-goodness journalist. At last!

"I just have to answer this," she said, stepping farther from the stove and from any prying eyes.

I don't have any research done, she texted back.

I'll send you what I've got, he replied. I've been nosing after that family for years. Plus, you need to contact those nurses—they're the linchpin in the whole thing. Just write up what you've got. He won't publish it without confirmation. It'll show him you know how to write news, at the very least.

Why would you give me your own research? This was maybe too nice of George. Why would he put himself out like this?

Because it adds up to nothing without confirmation. And you're the one who might actually get it! If it gets published, we'll both get the byline. It's a win for me, too. Besides, I told you before I'd like to have a friend in the bullpen over here.

George obviously knew what she was afraid of.

"Everything okay, dear?" Belinda asked.

"I need to take care of something," she said.

"Sure." Belinda smiled. "Take your time."

Brett gave her a curious look as she headed up the stairs to her room. She still had the apron on, hampering her movements just a little. She'd already discovered how much could be overheard in the sitting room, and this conversation needed to be private. She went into the small bedroom and shut the door behind her. Then she punched George's number, glancing down at her reduced battery life on her phone.

"Hi, Emaline," George said, picking up.

"I'm not sure that chasing down this story is a good idea," she said.

"How come?"

Because she'd just kissed Brett in the buggy shelter, that was why! But there was more to it, too...

"Because the kid you're questioning the paternity of? He's just a sweet little boy," she said. "Finding out that he's adopted—if he doesn't know—could be massive for him. He matters, too."

"And his dad is a very powerful man. What if there's a biological mother who was pushed out of his life?" George countered. "Sure, Dean and Bobbie Rockwell are raising him, but what if his mother didn't have a lot of choice in that? A stolen baby. Doesn't she deserve contact with her child?"

George was right. What about the mother? What about the abuse of power?

"I know...it's murky. I'm just—"

"Look, Emaline." George's tone softened. "This is the big leagues. You either have the spine to dig up those big stories, or you don't. There's no shame in admitting that you're better suited to social media and travel pieces. We need all kinds of media. Plus, you're very good at what you do. I'm not knocking it. But journalism—as you know—takes a certain type of person."

That stung, and she had to push back a wave of annoyance.

"Hey, I've told you from the start that I have what it takes to go after a big story," she snapped. "But I'm not being pushed into anything."

"I know," George said. "Look, my editor has to see what your writing looks like. You've got the journalism degree, so use it! Write up the story, and leave the confirmation blank. If you get the confirmation, it's a go. If you don't...it's dead."

"And I have your word that we're equal partners on this? You do nothing without my okay on this?"

"Yes, yes, send it. It's a writing sample."

And it was her chance to do the one thing she'd dreamed of—make a powerful man face the consequences of his abuses of power. It was why she'd gone to journalism school to begin with.

"All right. I'll write it up and send it to you in an hour or so."

"You've just entered the big leagues, Emaline. Welcome."

Emaline hung up the call and exhaled a shaky breath. Journalism was an odd mix of lone-wolf mentality and teamwork. No journalist stood alone, but there was fierce competition, too. And this was a once-in-a-lifetime opportunity based on an old journalism school friendship. She should be grateful. The memory of Brett's kiss left her feeling guilty, but Brett and Dean were two different men, she told herself. Dean could be a louse and Brett could be a nice guy.

And this was just a writing sample, right?

She opened up her computer and pulled up a blank page.

But what would this article mean to Brett if they got strong enough sources to confirm their suspicions? Did Brett know what his brother had done? Did he know his brother was a cheater who'd fathered a child and then managed to get the mother to sign the baby over to him and Bobbie?

Would Brett be shocked and betrayed that his senator brother could be so cold, or was Brett helping to hide the secret?

She wished she knew. Brett seemed decent, and after that kiss, she wanted so badly for him to be a good man. She was getting attached. Maybe it was this Amish B&B. Maybe it was just being locked in with a handsome guy…or his soft lips out in a storm…

But this wasn't about Brett. This was about the Pennsylvania senator and making sure he was accountable for his actions. The state deserved that…and so did Damian's biological mom.

Emaline started to type.

BRETT SAT AT the table as Belinda had instructed him. A large dish of brown buttered noodles sat in the center, and it all smelled amazing. There was something about swirling snow outside a window that made the food smell even better. That was one thing he liked about running the ranch—good old-fashioned fresh air and hard work made everything more pleasurable, from putting his feet up after a long day to eating a hearty meal. Damian sat up on his knees, elbows on the table. Brett was tempted to tell him to move his arms back, but Damian had left his headphones across the room on the kitchen counter, and that seemed too much like a win for him to ruin it.

Emaline appeared on the staircase. Something had changed—her earlier cheerfulness had waned, and she looked a little pale.

"Emaline, not a moment too soon," Belinda said. "Come sit down. The food is ready."

"It looks wonderful," Emaline said. "Sorry that took so long."

"Oh, that's no trouble at all," Belinda said. "You're my guest, dear."

Eeyore came clopping over to the table too.

"Hey, there," Emaline said. "This isn't for you, Eeyore."

The donkey poked his nose toward Emaline's plate and snuffled his nostrils over it.

"Eeyore!" Eli said. "How rude. Belinda, she'll need a new plate now."

Damian started to giggle and Belinda threw up her hands.

There was something about a busy kitchen that made Brett comfortable. Food, chatter, laughter—it was the combination that couldn't help but infect others with happiness. Except Emaline still looked distant, and he couldn't help but wonder if she'd been dealing with her family again. He caught her eye and she smiled then, and it was like sunlight coming out from behind clouds—warm, bright and enveloping. But then her attention moved, and she passed her plate to Belinda. Somehow, all he could think about was getting her to smile at him like that again.

"Eeyore!" Belinda said, bustling over. "Honestly, I don't know how we're going to have a meal around him."

"Come on, Eeyore..." Eli stood up, and together the old couple blocked the donkey's path. Eeyore's nose appeared over Eli's shoulder, snuffling toward the table.

"He wants to eat with us!" Damian laughed. "We should let him."

"He cannot eat with us," Belinda replied, grunting as she pushed the animal away from the table. "Eeyore, your hay is over there."

Eeyore hee-hawed plaintively, and even Brett had trouble not feeling sorry for him.

"We can't just put him in the sitting room, though," Eli said. "He'd never stay there.

And if we blocked him off, he might damage things. Your home isn't as…animal ready… as mine is."

"Animal ready…" Belinda muttered. "No home should be that animal ready, Eli."

"And yet, these situations do arise," Eli replied. "All the same, I think it's best to keep him in the kitchen."

"What do we do then?"

Belinda and Eli were looking at each other; they weren't interested in outside input. Eeyore nosed around Eli and came toward the table again. The old man caught his halter and pulled his head around.

"Eeyore, old boy…" Eli met the donkey's gaze meaningfully. "We are in unprecedented times. Do not push it if you want any chance of staying inside again."

"There will not be any other times!" Belinda exclaimed. "Eli—"

Then the old man shot her a teasing grin. "I was joking."

"Oh, you!" Belinda's eyes snapped in rage and she marched off toward the sink.

"Mostly," Eli finished under his breath, and Brett smothered a grin.

"Can Eeyore eat with us?" Damian asked again.

"I think the boy has the only solution," Eli

said. "Eeyore only wants to be included, and seeing how he's inside and we can't put him out yet, we can either fight him this entire mealtime, or we can make room for him."

"How?" Belinda almost wailed.

"Scootch," Eli said, gesturing toward Brett. "You all just move on down the table, get a little closer together, and we'll put Eeyore here at the head of the table. This will work... I think."

Belinda just stood back and watched as they all scooted their seats over, the sound of scraping chair legs filling the air. A full third of the table opened up, and Emaline leaned forward and slid the food over, too. Eli picked up a handful of hay and put it on the table in front of Eeyore, who took a bite and placidly began to chew.

"I'll sit closest to Eeyore," Eli said, pulling his chair up and looking at the donkey thoughtfully. "And don't you ever say I haven't done anything for you, old boy. I think you're going to owe me a truce at the end of this." He looked down at the dog. "Hund, come sit. Good boy."

Belinda settled in her place on the other side of Brett, and she gave Eli a tired look.

"Dare we bow our heads?" she asked.

"For just a moment." Eli bowed his head,

but his eyes stayed open and locked, side-eyed, on the donkey. Then he lifted his head.

"Eat up!" Belinda said cheerily.

Brett scooped a spoonful of noodles onto Emaline's plate, then Damian's.

"Ladies first, you see," Brett said quietly.

"Oh…" Damian murmured.

Brett passed the noodles to Belinda, who also handed him the plate of chicken cutlets. For a couple of minutes all was rustling silence with the clink of cutlery against plates as everyone got served. Eeyore, from his place at the head of the table, chewed his hay happily enough, and when a piece of hay drifted into Damian's noodles, Brett reached over and plucked it out.

"Is it dirty?" Damian whispered.

Right. This kid had a thing about germs, too. He took Damian's plate, emptied his noodles onto his own, and then dished him up a new serving. Would this be enough? Or would Damian need a new plate, too?

To Brett's relief, Damian picked up his fork and started to eat.

"Uncle Brett…" Damian whispered softly.

"Yeah?" Brett leaned closer.

"I think Emaline is mad at me."

"Why do you think that?" he whispered back.

"Because she's not talking to me."

Damian had trouble with figuring out what other people were feeling. That was part of the diagnosis he'd received earlier that year. Sometimes he couldn't tell the difference between mean laughter and happy laughter. Or between a quiet mood and anger. He tended to assume the worst.

"No, she's not mad at you," Brett whispered back. "She's quiet. Sometimes people just don't want to talk."

"Is she the sad quiet?" Damian's whisper was getting louder. "Because Dr. Sam says sometimes people feel sad and they get quiet, and the right thing to do when they're sad quiet is to go sit next to them."

"No, she's—" Brett looked up and he saw it. Emaline did look a little sad. Was this because of that phone call with her sister or something else?

"Good call, buddy," Brett murmured.

"I got it right?"

"Seems that way. But it's okay. Maybe we can help to cheer her up, okay?"

"I can make her a present!" Damian was talking at full volume now, and Emaline looked over in curiosity. "I'm going to make you a Christmas present, Emaline!"

"You are?" She smiled. "That's very sweet."

Damian seemed pleased enough now, and he tucked into his meal—his solution decided upon.

If only it was that easy for adults. But then… looking across the table at Emaline, Brett wondered why it shouldn't be. Maybe he *could* cheer her up a bit. He couldn't just leave her like this. She was starting to feel like his responsibility, and he wasn't sure why.

Brett felt the dog's head on his thigh and looked down to see a twitching black nose.

"Hey, Hund," he said, and he scratched the dog behind the ears. Then he cut off a piece of chicken cutlet and handed it down. Hund took the gift gently between his front teeth and backed slowly away underneath the table as stealthily as a spy.

"Is he begging?" Eli asked.

"He just asked nicely," Brett said with a chuckle.

"Hund, come here, I have your food for you," Eli called. The scratch of dog toenails against the floor headed in Eli's direction.

Eli was the neighbor—Brett knew that much—but he very much seemed like the man of this home, too. He glanced over at Belinda, who was eating her meal calmly enough. Who knew? The Amish were private people, and from what Brett knew, even engagements stayed secret until a couple of weeks before the wedding.

Emaline looked up from her meal, and she caught Brett's eye. She did look sad, but he was gratified to see that she wasn't hiding it from him, either. When they'd arrived, Belinda had said something about everyone leaving here friends, and he wondered if that would happen between him and Emaline. Friendship for him—the real, deep, honest kind—didn't come easily. People either wanted something from him or from his family. So he didn't use the word lightly... Would he end up considering this influencer his personal friend?

He hoped he would. Emaline wasn't like the others; there was something special about her.

There was much more drama in this Amish B&B than anyone ever guessed.

CHAPTER EIGHT

THE REST OF the day slid by. Emaline helped Belinda put pillar candles with their greenery in the upstairs bedroom windows and in the windows for the front room. But then Eeyore came ambling in and tried to eat them, so they had to be put up above the cupboards in the kitchen.

Damian was her little shadow. Apparently, he forgot about the "no comment" rule, and he followed her around, his headphones on his ears, until Eli called him over and offered to show him how to do something with long pieces of straw. That caught the boy's attention, and he pored over that. Eeyore stood by the big kitchen window, looking out at the snow, and Hund lay down by the potbellied stove and went to sleep.

Emaline and Brett didn't get any more time alone, but he was good company, all the same. She'd sent off that writing sample to George, and she was relatively certain it would remain just that—a writing sample. All the same, she was proud of it. Maybe it was the script-writing that had kept her sharp, but writing a news piece still came like second nature. George had sent her the phone numbers and email addresses for some contacts: Senator Rockwell's aide and three different hospital nurses. That nagged at her. If there was a mother out there who'd had her child taken away from her so that the senator could keep up appearances and have his son in his life at the same time, then she deserved justice, didn't she? She doubted that Brett was going to tell her any unvarnished truths about his nephew's parentage, and she couldn't exactly dig for it. Not like this…not with their blossoming friendship.

So she went outside to the front porch and made a few phone calls. Celia, the aide, answered her call but wouldn't say anything at all.

"What paper are you with?" she asked warily.

"I'm pitching this story to the *Chronicle*."

"No comment."

"Look, men like the senator get away with travesties all the time. They're powerful and wealthy, but that doesn't mean that no one else has rights. If you had a child with him, you have rights. I want to see you get those."

"Are you a lawyer?"

"No."

"Then I have nothing to say to you."

It was close to a confirmation, but not quite.

"Are you saying there was a child?"

"Yes, I had a child. A boy. I gave him up for adoption. But I had no relationship with the senator. It was strictly professional. He was a good boss, and he was good to his family. He was never anything but professional with me. That is not my son."

A lie? The truth? How could Emaline even know? So she'd thanked her for her time and moved on to the nurses.

Two of the nurses didn't pick up, but the third one did, and she refused to answer any questions at all based on patient privacy. Of course, that was the right thing to do, but not terribly helpful for Emaline.

"If a woman was strong-armed into giving up her child, wouldn't you want to help make that right?" Emaline asked.

"If the mother wants to find her child, she can petition the family courts. I could lose my job if I reveal anything."

"So there was a baby and a mother who might not have wanted that adoption?"

"I'm not saying anything else."

"Are we on the right track, at least?"

"Goodbye, Miss Piper."

There was something here, she could feel it. The women were all a little slippery for there to be nothing to the story. She could see what George meant. *Something* had happened. But what? And without sources who were willing to talk, they'd never find out. A snowed-in few days with the senator's brother wasn't going to change that.

Besides, there was a little boy in the middle of this, and while she wanted his mother to have access to him, she could also see how traumatic this would be for Damian. Small, sensitive and misunderstood as he was...

But could she abandon the mother's justice in order to keep peace for the child? Was that the right thing to do?

It might not matter at the end of the day. If the mother wouldn't talk, they couldn't help her. Maybe she'd just given up, and another powerful man had gotten his way at the expense of the less powerful people beneath him.

When Emaline came back inside the warm little house, she hung up her coat, her mind still chewing over those phone calls. Everyone sat around the kitchen table, and Belinda was telling stories.

"The most recent wedding in our community was one I helped set up between a young woman named Miriam and Obadiah—the least likely suitor you could imagine..." Belinda said.

Eli cleared his throat, and Belinda's cheeks pinked.

"To be entirely honest, I didn't think they'd make a good match at all, and I tried to convince Obadiah to go in another direction. Quite frankly, Miriam was too high above him."

"So what happened?" Emaline asked, pulling up a chair.

She cast Brett a smile, and he put an arm up over the back of her chair. His arm didn't touch her, but she could feel him there, all the same. Brett couldn't know...could he?

"Well, a guest who was staying here struck up a little friendship with Miriam and pointed out Obadiah's virtues," Belinda said. "Simple as that. She came to me once the *Englisher* woman left and asked me to tell her honestly what kind of man Obadiah was."

"And she told her, all right," Eli chuckled.

"I was honest!" Belinda protested. "He'd never be able to afford to keep her in the comfort she was accustomed to, but he was honest and decent and kind. Anyway, despite everything I said, she said she'd have one formal date with Obadiah. He took her on a buggy ride, and when they returned from that buggy ride, Obadiah was holding her hand."

"And that was that," Eli said triumphantly. "Obadiah got his girl."

"They got engaged, planned a wedding, and then, Obadiah's *Englisher* second or third cousin passed away, leaving twin toddlers behind," Belinda went on. "That was just before the wedding. And with all the stepping down Miriam was doing to marry Obadiah, I wasn't sure he should even bring it up to her. But he did. He asked what she thought, and she agreed to adopt them. Today, they have three little ones—the adopted twins who are about three now, and a baby of their own."

"That's really something," Emaline said.

"Our way of life is all about family," Belinda said. "You see, life doesn't always unfurl the way we think it should, and when things go wrong, it's important to remember our top priorities. And family always tops that list."

Emaline nodded. "That's beautiful."

"Even…sisters." Belinda's gaze flickered toward her uneasily.

Eli murmured something in Pennsylvania Dutch.

"I am not, Eli!" Belinda retorted, then she turned toward Emaline apologetically. "I'm so sorry, but I overheard a little of your conversation with your sister. Eli just said I'm being pushy."

"And I sound like the bad guy, don't I?" Emaline said. As if her own guilt over the matter weren't enough. Maybe it was better to focus on her own problems right now, anyway. The Rockwell secrets would very likely stay buried.

"You sound hurt," Belinda replied.

"I guess I am. You're lucky. In your community, people get married, have kids, get old…all in the usual order. But my family was seriously messed up."

"And that isn't your fault," Belinda said, putting a warm hand on Emaline's arm. "Not one bit of it. But from what I gathered, neither was it your sister's, though."

"I know! Of course it wasn't," Emaline replied. "In fact, I've been thinking it over, and I should probably try to connect with my sister more. She's a lot younger than me, and I could probably help her. I suppose for me, she's my father's preferred daughter, so that hurts. But I'm also the only sister she's got, so…"

Belinda nodded. "Parents can let you down, dear. Even the best of parents. My father had a terrible argument with my brother, and he ran away from home. My father never forgave himself for it. And truth be told, I didn't forgive him, either, for a long time. It took ten years for my brother to return and make things right with Daet. The thing you have to decide is who you will be as an adult. That's the important decision, and you let the mistakes of your parents remain the mistakes of your parents."

"That's wise," Emaline replied.

"Trust me, in the best of families this is a lesson we have to learn," Belinda said. "I eventually had to forgive my father and simply decide that I wouldn't let nitpicking about rules get between me and my children. I was going to learn from his mistakes and do better, myself."

Emaline shook her head. "I'm going to therapy, so if that isn't learning from my father's mistakes, I don't know what is."

Belinda nodded. "Here, you'd go visit a wise friend. But I understand the idea. You talk it out. You dig down and figure out why you feel what you do, *yah*?"

"Pretty much. There's a bit more to it, but… yeah."

"We Amish believe that *Gott* doesn't make mistakes," Belinda said. "And there is good to be mined from every situation. Maybe this insight you have gained will be needed to help others. You never know!"

Eli cleared his throat warningly. Belinda was getting dangerously close to preaching. But Emaline understood the point. If it weren't for her father's betrayal, would she be keen to make the powerful men of the world pay for the pain they caused? Probably not.

Belinda put her hands up. "That's all I wanted to say. Please forgive a nosy old lady. I get overly attached to my guests, I've been told."

"She does," Eli murmured.

"And I have been known to put my nose where it doesn't belong," Belinda added. "My conscience insists that I admit to that."

"Her conscience isn't wrong on that point," the old man said quietly from his seat at the table, and Belinda cast him a baleful look.

Emaline had to stifle a laugh. "It's okay. No harm done. You're right—maybe some good will come out of it. It's probably time I made peace with Maggie. She wants a relationship with me, and that's a miracle in itself."

"Well, I hate to intrude," Belinda said, and before Eli could say anything she waggled a finger in his direction. "Enough, Eli!"

"What?" Eli looked around innocently.

Emaline did think more about her sister

that day. It was wrong of her to take her anger at their father out on Maggie. She was just as stuck in the middle of their dysfunctional family dynamic as Emaline was. What she needed to do was sit down and talk to her father. Maybe he needed to hear what Emaline thought of him now. He was the one who'd decimated their lives, after all.

That night, Emaline went to bed early. There was something about kerosene light and snow falling in the darkness outside that made 9:00 p.m. feel like midnight. Plus, all that physical work in the kitchen and in decorating for Belinda's family Christmas left her feeling exhausted…right up until she crawled under those three thick quilts. And then she lay awake. She couldn't even blame the sound of snoring from the other room, because there was none—just silence. So much silence that Emaline was left with only her thoughts, and tonight that wasn't calming.

Emaline fiddled with her phone. Should she text Maggie? But what would she say?

She started typing: Hi, Maggie, this is Emaline. Just wanted to…

She deleted the words. Wanted to do what—reach out? Say hi?

She tried again: Hi, Maggie. I'm sorry if I upset you. I…

She deleted it.

She started again: Hi, Maggie. I was wrong. I'd like to get to know you, too. I'm sorry I took my anger out on you. Let's plan to get a coffee, just the two of us. I'm sure we'll find a lot we have in common.

That was better. She pressed Send.

Emaline wasn't tired yet, after all. She tossed back the covers and grabbed her thick terry cloth bathrobe. She shivered as her toes hit the chilly wooden floor, then slid into her slippers. She opened her bedroom door, and downstairs, she heard the murmur of voices.

Were the old people still up? That was a good sign. Maybe she could go down and get something hot to drink.

Brett's bedroom door was shut, the soft golden glow of kerosene light shining from underneath. So he wasn't asleep yet, either. She tiptoed across the hallway to the staircase, and about halfway down, she saw Eli and Belinda at the kitchen table. There was a plate of cookies between them and two mugs, but their eyes weren't on the treats. Something about the scene made her pause instead of joining them.

Eli said something in Pennsylvania Dutch, and Belinda replied in kind. They seemed to be having an intense conversation, and Eli suddenly burst out in English, "Have I been a good friend to you?"

"*Yah*, Eli."

"Have I ever lied to you?"

"Sometimes I wished you would," Belinda chuckled, and she reached for a cookie.

Eli said something else in Pennsylvania Dutch, and Belinda turned back on him.

"Where is all of this coming from, Eli? You sound like you're dying or something." She sobered. "You aren't sick, are you?"

"No, I'm not sick! I'm as healthy as that donkey over there!"

All Emaline could see of Eeyore was his tail swishing. She shouldn't be here. Obviously, this wasn't a good time for her to interrupt, but somehow she couldn't pull away.

Eli said something else that Emaline didn't understand, but Belinda suddenly stilled.

"I've been trying to say it for years," Eli went on quietly in English. "I tried over and over again."

"I know I can be pushy sometimes," Belinda said, "but I don't think I've ever stopped you from speaking your mind. If I have, I do apologize, but—"

"Belinda, let me speak, woman!"

Belinda looked miffed and spun to face the table again. If Emaline had her guess, Belinda probably didn't like being called "woman" by her neighbor.

"It started when we were teenagers," Eli said quietly, and Emaline held her breath. "I wanted to ask you home from singing, but..." He melted into Pennsylvania Dutch again for a little bit and finally switched back to English with, "Anyway, my glorious plan was that I'd be your friend, and then through friendship, I'd show you that I'd be the perfect husband for you."

"What?" Belinda whipped around, and Emaline put a hand over her mouth. Was Eli declaring his feelings?

"*Yah*. But that didn't work as well as I'd hoped," the old man went on. "So I went to your home to ask you to let me take you home from singing that weekend, and when I got there, you were asking me about Ernie and what kind of man he was."

"Oh..." Belinda breathed. "You said he was a good man..." The rest was in Pennsylvania Dutch.

"He was," Eli said. "I couldn't lie to you. And you chose him. So I let it go."

"But you could have married anyone else!" Belinda said earnestly. "Anyone!"

"I could have..." Eli turned his cup on the table. "I didn't, though. The problem was that

Ernie knew how I felt about you, and living next door, it irritated him something fierce."

"It didn't!" she countered.

They went back and forth for a minute in Pennsylvania Dutch, obviously disagreeing over this point.

"He never said a word to me!" Belinda finally said in English.

"Well, he said a word to me," Eli countered. "He told me to keep my eyes on my side of the fence. So I did that. For all these years. When Ernie passed away, I thought I'd be your friend while you grieved, and maybe later..."

"Later?" she whispered.

Emaline leaned forward to catch the words that were so quiet now she almost couldn't hear them.

"Later you'd love me," he whispered.

And then there was silence. No Pennsylvania Dutch, no English, nothing.

"Oh, Eli..." Belinda breathed.

"The thing is, I have waited all these years for my turn," Eli said, his voice trembling with emotion. "And that was probably very silly of me."

Tears shone in Belinda's eyes, and she dropped her gaze to her hands. Emaline breathed as softly as she could, and she wondered if she should escape now, get back up the stairs before she was seen. But somehow, she couldn't force herself.

"Why now?" Belinda asked.

"Because I won't have another chance. Or I might have the chance, but not have the courage. Chances and courage don't always occur at the same time, you know. It's not easy being the man. We have to be the ones who go out there and set the machine in motion. We have to say our piece. You have it much easier. You just wait."

"We do not have it easier!"

"We shouldn't get sidetracked with an argument. We do that too often." Eli's voice stayed low. "And, to be clear, how I feel is... I love you still, Belinda. I loved you then, and I love you now. It's just a fact." He took her hand and lifted her fingers up to his lips. He pressed a gentle kiss against them.

Belinda didn't answer at all. She was just silent, and Eli's hands trembled ever so slightly. She pulled her hand back.

Eli said something in Pennsylvania Dutch, his gaze locked on Belinda tenderly. What had he said? Emaline wished she knew, but it didn't really matter. The question shone in Eli's watery eyes. The old woman didn't answer, and for a moment, Emaline thought

Belinda might lean into Eli's arms. But she didn't.

"I would just hate to ruin a seventy-year friendship, Eli…"

Emaline squeezed her eyes shut and suppressed a sigh. Belinda wasn't interested. After all that courage it had taken for old Eli to declare his feelings. After all those years of loving her and waiting, and…apparently driving her crazy. Emaline could almost cry on his behalf.

She couldn't stay to watch anymore. Whatever else happened between the two of them, Emaline's heart wouldn't endure watching it. She eased to her feet, her knees aching with the sudden effort, and tiptoed back up the stairs.

Poor, poor Eli.

BRETT STOOD IN the doorway of his bedroom watching as Emaline crept back down the hall. He hadn't gotten into his pajamas yet—figured he'd read for a bit. He couldn't help but smile wryly as Emaline looked up and saw him. She looked even more petite in that white bathrobe that threatened to swallow her whole.

"Hi," he whispered.

She put a hand against her chest. "You scared me." She kept her voice to a whisper, too.

"Sorry." He grinned.

"Is Damian sleeping?" she asked.

"Like a log." He cocked his head to one side. "Why? What happened?"

"Eli just told Belinda he's been in love with her for years," she whispered. "And Belinda turned him down."

"What?" Brett scrubbed a hand through his hair, and he looked toward the staircase— the faint glow from the kitchen shining up at them. "Are you serious?"

"I wish I weren't. I just saw it all go down."

He nodded toward his light-splashed room. "You want to come in?" Emaline peeked in the door. Damian was in a single bed, completely flaked out, his mouth open and breathing deeply. He had a braided bit of straw in one hand—the gift he'd made for Emaline with Eli's help. "I think the kid counts as a chaperone, if that worries you."

"He probably does." She came inside, eased the door shut, leaning back against it. "I don't want them to know I saw anything. They'd be so embarrassed."

There were two chairs by the window, and he led the way over there.

"The poor guy. He spent a lifetime loving

her," Emaline went on. "If you'd seen him—the way he kissed her hand and told the story of how he'd loved her and waited…"

"And she wasn't swayed by that?"

"Nope." She winced. "Poor guy."

"Wow." He leaned back in the chair. "Is that going to make it into your vlog? That would get you all sorts of clicks."

"No. Not a chance. What do you think I am?" Emaline shook her head. "That was a private moment I should never have seen. Entertaining readers isn't worth embarrassing an elderly couple."

She was decent—truly decent. He didn't come across a lot of people like that in his circles. A couple of years ago, a story had hit the tabloids quoting Dean's oldest two kids talking about a teacher they'd disliked. Their insult about the man was calling him poor. Sure, it had been rude of the kids to say it, and definitely out of touch with how most of the country lived, but they'd said it in the privacy of their own home. They were young and thoughtless, and had a lot to learn still. Dean had had to take a closer look at the people he employed. But someone had written that story in exchange for a payout.

"You really do have your boundaries," he said. "I respect that. You're honest."

"I try to be." She was silent for a moment, and she chewed the inside of her bottom lip. "Brett, I feel like I need to come clean with you."

"Okay..."

"I have a friend from journalism school who I've kept up with over the years," she said. "His name is George. He's a good guy, and he works for the *Chronicle*."

"All right."

"We were chatting—catching up like we do—and I mentioned that I was snowed in with you," she said.

His stomach sank. Right when he was thinking she was decent, she told a journalist where he was...

"The thing is, he's offering to help me get a job with the *Chronicle*, and they're hoping that I can give them a scoop."

"On me."

"On...your brother."

"And you said?"

"I was tempted. I even did a little research," she said. "I won't lie about that. You don't know how crushed I was when I graduated with a journalism degree and couldn't land a job. I thought that would be the easy part. Far from it. I had to reinvent myself, find a way to use my education and make it lucrative. I started a blog first and added an Etsy shop, making travel-themed journals, then closed the Etsy shop because it was just too expensive—anyway, long story short, I found my niche in travel vlogging."

"But you always wanted to be a journalist," he concluded.

"I really did. I wanted to dig up those stories, and bring dirty secrets into the light of day."

"Okay…" He nodded. "And you're asking me for…"

"Oh, I'm not asking you for anything." She shook her head. "I know you wouldn't roll over on your brother, and it's almost cruel to ask you to. You're family. I don't think I appreciated that before, but I can see it now. So I've given the newspaper a writing sample. If they're honestly interested in hiring me, seeing how I write should be enough for them. I'm not digging any further. If I hadn't gotten to know you, I would have, no question. I can own up to that. But now?"

"Now?" he murmured.

"I think we might be…friends."

"And you couldn't do that to a friend?"

"Oh, I could definitely dig into your brother's campaign," she said with a roguish gleam in her eye, "but I can't use a friend to do it. Maybe I'll get into some serious journalism, but if I dug up some dirt on a politician, I'd do it the right way. I have my own integrity."

Brett looked over at his sleeping nephew, one arm flung over his head and his hair rumpled across his forehead. So small and vulnerable. Everything was hard for him—kindergarten class, being away from his parents, just the regular noise level that everyone else dealt with so easily. Brett worried about protecting this boy from the news cycles, but this particular vlogger wasn't the threat his brother feared she'd be.

"How ticked off will that editor be when you come back with no story on the Rockwells?" he asked.

She smiled faintly. "Not impressed with my journalistic teeth, I suppose."

"Will you lose your chance?"

She raised her eyebrows in thought. "I hope not. But I've got a gig already that's working for me, so..."

She looked over in the direction of Damian's bed, and her expression softened. "I have what it takes to be a hard-hitting journalist. But I'm more than a job."

"At least you told me," he said. "I appreciate that."

It was something, at least. The sound of shoes on the staircase silenced them, and then the bedroom door opened with a soft squeak. Eli stood there looking sad and tired, and Emaline stood up.

"I'll get out of the way," Emaline said.

"We don't normally have women in a man's room," Eli said, his tone quiet but disapproving.

"I'm on my way out," she said. "I assure you, Eli, there was no impropriety."

"None," Brett confirmed. He hadn't even gone so far as to touch her hand.

Emaline paused in the doorway. She looked back at Brett once and then disappeared into the hallway. He felt like their conversation wasn't over, yet at the very least, he'd wanted to wish her a proper goodnight, but Eli was here now, and the old man sank onto the side of the cot.

"Are you okay, Eli?" Brett asked.

"*Yah*. I'll be fine." He pulled off his shoes and socks one by one with slow, laborious effort. Eli looked older tonight, the lines in his face deeper.

"Thanks for helping Damian make that straw bracelet for Emaline. It meant the world to him."

"He's a good boy." Eli glanced toward the

slumbering child. "And who am I to stand between a boy and the woman he wants to impress?"

Brett smiled sadly. The irony was deep. "Story of our lives, huh?"

Eli nodded, his watery brown eyes lifting for just a moment to meet Brett's. "Story of mine, at least."

"Do you want—" Brett began.

"I just want to sleep," Eli said. "I'm tired out."

Right. This wasn't a new heartbreak for the old man. He'd been shouldering it for a lifetime, from what Brett understood. Maybe he was more used to this burden than Brett gave him credit for.

Brett went to the bedroom door and looked out. Emaline was gone, and her bedroom door was shut. A faint glow still came from the kitchen downstairs. Belinda must still be up. Brett shut the bedroom door softly, and Eli lay down in his cot. Brett turned down the oil lamp until the flame extinguished, leaving a faint red glow at the top of the wick.

So, Emaline's journalist pal was trying to use her to dig up some dirt on his family. Wherever he went, the press wanted something, even here in Amish Country. That in itself wasn't surprising. But Emaline was principled enough to tell him what was going on. Was Brett naive enough to believe her? Was this just a ploy to win his trust?

She didn't have to say anything. She could have just carried on and tried to dig up some details. She *could* have, but she didn't. Emaline Piper was a woman with integrity, and he'd never met anyone else like her.

CHAPTER NINE

EMALINE WOKE UP early and refreshed. Outside the bedroom window, she saw rays of sunlight stretching across the fresh snow. The storm had ended.

She quickly got dressed and ready for the day. She reached for her phone and realized she hadn't plugged it into the battery pack last night. That was so unlike her. She decided to go with it, leaving the phone on low battery for now instead of reaching to check her feeds.

Brett's room door was still shut when Emaline made her way down into the kitchen. She felt better having made a decision about that news story. Let them see how she wrote, but she wouldn't use Brett for her own career gains. That was wrong.

Belinda stood at the stove in front of a large pot, slowly stirring with a wooden spoon. The scent of bubbling oatmeal filled the kitchen. Eeyore stood by his bale of feed, contentedly grinding a mouthful of hay. Emaline stopped at Eeyore's side and gave him a pet. His side rippled in pleasure. This donkey seemed to be getting used to being indoors.

"Good morning, dear," Belinda said. She looked more tired than usual, her face pale. "The snow has stopped."

"I see that," Emaline said. "What will we do now?"

"We'll have to dig ourselves out," she replied. "In fact, Eli took Hund out to his own farm to check on his animals. They'll need new feed and water before we do anything else."

So Eli headed back to his own space as quickly as he could. Emaline could understand that. But she couldn't help wondering how Belinda felt this morning about Eli's declaration. The older woman seemed pale and quiet.

"Can I help with anything?" Emaline asked.

"No, thank you, dear."

"You look like you could use a rest," Emaline said delicately. She looked like she could use a good cry, quite honestly.

"I'm fine." She turned back toward the stove again. "Do you know how long I've had this old stove?"

"How long?"

"Since Ernie and I got married. This house used to be *Englisher*, and Ernie chose the stove himself and had it delivered, and I stood right where you're standing now and watched the men install it."

"How long were you married?"

"Forty-three years."

"Do you miss him still?"

"Every day." Belinda sighed. "But it's easier now. It's not fresh grief. I was sixty when he passed."

"Do you ever think of getting married again?" Emaline asked.

Belinda chuckled softly. "At my age? Women my age don't get married again."

"Why not?" Emaline asked. "I know of a woman who got married at eighty-two."

"Amish women don't get married at my age," Belinda clarified.

Belinda was throwing up barriers. Some things—like men and loving them—were universal, and Emaline would not be convinced otherwise.

"What makes us so different?" Emaline asked. "Amish, English... We're more alike than you might think. We both say we're fine when we aren't."

Belinda's cheeks pinked. Her stirring got faster, and for a moment, she just stood there mixing almost fast enough to whip cream, and then she stopped. "You heard, then?"

"I did. I'm sorry."

Belinda sighed. "I can't just marry him, you know. He's a good man. He's worked hard to get more civilized—all for me, might I add. And if we could just carry on like we do now, I'd be so very happy, but I can't just marry him."

"Why not?"

"Because marriage involves whole families! I have children and grandchildren. I have brothers and sisters, and in-laws and nieces and nephews from my late husband's side, and…and…" Belinda wiped her cheek. "And there would be opinions—all of my children and friends and relatives would have opinions on the matter."

"Yours is the opinion that matters most."

Belinda sighed. "I suppose I'm scared. It would change everything. It would be a massive risk. I don't know that I've got the strength to civilize a whole new husband."

"Are they so much work?" Emaline asked.

Belinda glanced over her shoulder and smiled wanly. "You have no idea."

At the sound of footsteps on the stairs, Belinda turned away, wiping at her face once more. Emaline looked back to see Damian bounding down the stairs. His uncle came behind him, his steps slower.

"Hi, Eeyore!" Damian sang out, and he

beelined for the donkey. Eeyore looked over at the boy with a tender expression on his donkey face. Those two had bonded.

"Good morning." Brett's hair was a little disheveled, and she smothered a smile at his bed head.

"Good morning, dear," Belinda called. "You can all sit down and I'll get breakfast on the table. The snow has stopped."

"Time to dig out," Brett said, and he nudged Emaline's arm with his as he walked past her. "How are you with a snow shovel?"

"I can hold my own," she said.

"Good, because we'll need to dig out the stable and clear a path to it," Brett said.

"He's right," Belinda said, coming to the table with a stack of bowls. "We have to get Eeyore back out where he belongs and check on the horse."

It sounded like a lot of work, not that Emaline minded. It had to be done, and it would give her a bit more time alone with Brett. She was almost embarrassed that that was her first thought. It might be her last chance to spend any time with him alone. Once they dug out and the road was plowed, they both would be headed in opposite directions. This time together would be over. Her stomach twisted. Whatever this was here in Amish

Country, it wouldn't survive when she returned to Pittsburgh. At least not in the same form. This connection would be a memory.

"Eeyore is going back outside?" Damian asked.

"Yes, dear, of course," Belinda replied. "Donkeys don't belong in the house."

"But he likes it inside," Damian said plaintively.

"Donkeys belong in barns," Belinda replied. "He'll have his horse friend, and no one will bother him when he makes messes. It will also smell much better in here when he's back in the stable." Belinda set the table with bowls and utensils, then placed a hot pad in the center of the table. "Come sit, everyone."

Emaline took her seat next to Brett, and Belinda filled bowls with steaming oatmeal. Damian was looking at Emaline, his eyes wide, and then he'd look at Brett, then back at Emaline.

"Go ahead," Brett said, his voice low.

Damian came around the table and stood next to Emaline, his head down. Then he slid something prickly into her hand, and Emaline looked down to see a braided strip made out of straw.

"That's for you," Damian said. "A Christmas present."

"For me?" Maybe she was emotional from the previous night's events, but Emaline felt tears rise up inside of her. "Really?"

The boy nodded. "I made it. It's a bracelet. Like the one that Bethany made for Michael S. Because friends wear them. But no one ever gave me one before because I don't have a friend at school."

Emaline's heart skipped a beat, and she blinked against the blur in her vision.

"Sweetie, thank you so much," Emaline said. "I'm going to treasure it always. I'm really honored to have your friendship bracelet. And if Belinda will lend me some yarn, I'm going to make you a friendship bracelet that you can wear at school when you go back after the holidays. Every time you look at it, you can remember that you do have a friend and that she cares about you very much."

"You'd make me one back?" Damian whispered, leaning a little bit closer.

"I absolutely will," she said. "Can I tell you a secret?"

Damian nodded solemnly.

"I never had one of these growing up, either. I used to watch the other kids exchange them, too. So this is very special for me."

Damian smiled. "Don't worry, Emaline,"

he said, leaning his head against her shoulder. "I'll be your friend."

"Okay, come sit down and eat," Brett said, but there was a catch in his voice, and when Damian went back to his chair and dug into his bowl of oatmeal, Emaline looked over at the boy's uncle. His Adam's apple bobbed up and down.

This poor little boy...so sweet and so misunderstood by the other kids.

"He needs a horse," Brett said gruffly, pitching his voice low enough for Damian not to hear. "And this Christmas, Santa's going to do just that."

Emaline shot him a surprised smile. "Really?"

"Yep." Brett's gaze was locked protectively on the little boy across from them. "Santa's on it. In fact, he already has one in mind."

"You can tell me about it while we clear snow," she said.

Brett's smile suddenly relaxed. "Deal." He raised his voice a little louder. "Damian, don't give toast to the donkey."

It was too late. Eeyore had poked his nose over Damian's shoulder and had grabbed a whole thick slice of toast.

"Oh, Eeyore!" Belinda said. "Stop being so naughty!"

"He just wanted breakfast," Damian said.

"I have no idea how well donkeys digest toast," Belinda said with a grimace.

Emaline couldn't help but chuckle at that.

"It's his last breakfast inside," Brett replied. "Where's Eli, anyway?"

"Checking on his own animals," Belinda said.

"He'll be back?" Brett asked.

"I hope so…" Belinda turned back to her own meal, but Emaline saw her gaze flicker toward the side door. Belinda was hoping to see him return, wasn't she?

"Do you know what we should do now that the snow has stopped?" Brett said. "We should introduce this kid to a snowball fight." Then he raised his voice. "Hey, Damian. Do you want to have a snowball fight with me?"

Damian lowered one side of his headphones and looked over at Brett warily. "But I don't like snow on my face."

"No headshots," Brett said.

"What does that mean?"

"It means we don't throw snowballs at someone's head."

"But I don't like getting hit with snowballs," the boy replied.

Brett deflated a little bit. "Okay… So what if we made a snow fort instead? Then if there

are any snowballs thrown, you can get behind the wall."

"A fort?" Damian squinted.

"What do you think?"

"Maybe..."

Emaline looked out the window. How long
had it been since she'd actually played in
snow?

"Emaline, do you want to make a fort?"
Brett asked, casting a hopeful smile at her.

What she actually wanted to do was
film that snowball fight between uncle and
nephew, but that might be pushing it.

"Sure." How could she say no to that plead-
ing face?

When they'd finished eating, Damian
thumped over to the mudroom and Brett followed him. It was a chance for Brett and Damian to do something together, and she didn't
want to take away from that.

Brett poked his head out of the mudroom.
"Damian doesn't like snowball fights, but I
could challenge you to one."

"You think you can take me?" she laughed.

"We'll discuss it when you get out here."
Brett grinned, and then he disappeared again.
He and Damian headed outside, and she
watched them through the window, tramping out into a section of unbroken snow.

The snow had stopped falling, and Eeyore was going to get back to the stable, and life was going to return to normal. She'd miss Brett a lot when they all went their separate ways. She'd gotten attached, hadn't she?

BRETT PACKED ANOTHER snowball and started rolling it through the snow, collecting a thick layer of padding with each rotation. How long had it been since he'd done this…twenty-five years? Damian stood back watching him warily.

"I used to be good at making forts," Brett said. "Your dad used to rely on artillery in our snowball fights. He'd have big piles of snowballs, but I always had a fort with thick walls and good defenses. I didn't need a hundred snowballs. I needed twenty."

Damian's eyes widened.

"What's so shocking?" Brett asked with a laugh. "Your dad had snowball fights with your siblings, too."

"He doesn't do snowball fights with me," Damian said. "I don't like it."

"That's fair enough," Brett said. "They can be fun, though. Maybe you and I could challenge your dad to a snowball fight together. We'll make a big fort, and I'll be your muscle."

"What does that mean?"

"That means I'll be the one who gets hit in the head with snowballs for you."

Damian grinned. "Okay!"

"Really? You'd like me to do that?" Brett chuckled. "You'd sacrifice me up that easily?"

"It was your idea!"

Brett beckoned Damian over. "Okay, come on, this one is almost done. You take over now. Put your back into it."

Damian squatted down and took over rolling the ball, but even with all of his strength and weight, it was too heavy to move very far on his own. Brett bent over him and helped put it next to the other snowball they'd already made.

"We need another one!" Damian said.

"We do." Brett packed another snowball between his gloved hands and stood up. The side door opened and Emaline stepped outside.

He lobbed his snowball toward her. It landed at her feet.

"That was a warning shot!" Brett joked. He cast her a smile. "Come on. The snow has stopped. I hear snowplows out there—" He paused, listening to the distant sounds of growling and scraping. "We don't have too much time left where we're snowed in, do we?" He crossed the yard and stopped a couple of feet away from her. "And...I'll miss you when this is over."

He shouldn't have said it, but he was thinking it.

She stilled. "Will you really?"

Emaline had already sunk past his defenses. There was something special about her, and impossible or not, she was going to be hard to forget. He pulled off his gloves and touched her chin with the pad of his thumb.

"Yeah," he said. "I really will."

Out there in the real world, he and Emaline probably didn't make much sense together. But here at the Butternut Amish Bed and Breakfast, they were just a man and a woman who were starting to really care for each other. Maybe he liked that simplicity. What would it be like to live his life this way—where a snowstorm could stop every wheel from turning?

Color touched Emaline's cheeks, and she brushed a stray strand of hair out of her eyes.

"I'll miss you, too, Brett," she said. "But with the roads opening up, the real world is waiting for us. I should probably plug my phone in, check the news—"

"No!" he said with a short laugh. He didn't want to see the stresses of the country, the updates on the election, the insults slung between Dean and his competition. Not yet. "We don't actually have to keep up such a fast pace in our lives, you know. Everyone can reach us every second of the day. Everyone needs something. But we can slow down. Let's just leave the news outlets and the election and all of that stuff to fend for itself for a while."

"All right. Deal."

He bent down, packed a snowball and handed it to her. "This is me being gentlemanly."

"How so?" But she was smiling now.

He packed a second snowball, took two big steps back and tossed it at her. She squealed and ducked, then whipped her snowball at him, catching him in the center of his chest.

"You've got a good arm!" he laughed.

"I grew up with three brothers!" she retorted. "I don't need special treatment in a snowball fight!"

She stooped to grab another handful of snow, her eyes glittering with amusement.

"Here I thought I was being magnanimous," he laughed. "Damian, build up our fort! She's going to be tougher to beat than I thought!"

"I wanna be on *her* team!" Damian hollered back.

"Are you abandoning me now?" Brett laughed. "Fine, go be on her team, but you remember who's buying you McDonald's on our way home!"

"Come on, Emaline!" Damian called. "You gotta get behind our fortress so you don't get any snow on your face!"

The snowball fight was on. Emaline, it turned out, had excellent aim, and she threw a hard snowball that packed a punch. Damian squealed a lot and dived behind the fort, and Brett lobbed the snowballs toward Damian high or wide to give him lots of opportunity to find cover. He did manage to get one good shot in at Emaline that took her by surprise, but he paid for it when she pelted him with four more snowballs that exploded against his shoulders and chest, spraying his face with snow.

"Okay, okay!" he laughed, putting up his hands. "You win!"

Emaline dropped the snowball in her hands, her glittering gaze meeting his. "It's been years since I threw a snowball."

"I hate to see what I'd be up against if you had practice." He grinned.

"Did we win?" Damian asked. "Did we win, Emaline?"

She raised an eyebrow at Brett.

"Yes, yes, you two beat me fair and square," Brett laughed.

The side door opened again, and this time, it was Belinda coming outside with a snow shovel in one hand.

"Belinda, I'll do that," Brett called.

He wasn't having an elderly lady shoveling snow while he played games. He shot Emaline a grin.

"You want to help me shovel?"

Her eyes sparkled. "Sure."

Hanging out, playing in the snow, doing some chores side by side…this could transfer over to his ranch pretty easily, he realized. *Dang.* He could get used to this…

Her phone rang, and she fished it out of her pocket and looked down at it. Her smile slipped.

"Everything okay?" he asked.

"It's my father…" He could see the hesitation in her expression, and then she picked up the call and turned away. "Hi, Dad…"

He'd get started on the shoveling. He took the shovel from Belinda with a nod and glanced back at Emaline. Her back was to him, her shoulders hunched up, and he suddenly felt a surge of protectiveness.

Emaline had been through a lot the last few days, and he knew that her relationship with her father was damaged and traumatic at best. What did the man want from her? That's what Brett wanted to know. Because Emaline deserved some healing, some apologies, and Brett had a feeling that she wasn't going to get that from her father that easily.

What Brett wanted was to pull her into his arms and shield her from everything that would hurt her, including her old man.

But it was futile. She wasn't his to protect, was she?

CHAPTER TEN

EMALINE HAD PICKED up the call before she could think better of it, but the sound of her father's voice in her ear suddenly brought tears to her eyes.

"Hi, Emmie…"

When was the last time he'd called her that…when she was ten, maybe? Back when her father had been her hero, and she'd never even guessed at the secret he was holding.

"How did you get my number?" Emaline asked.

"I asked Maggie, your sister, for it," he said. "The thing is, she said you weren't comfortable coming to my house to see us…and that's my fault. I should have tried harder with you. So this is me…trying."

Emaline let out a shaky breath. "I don't know what to say to that."

"You don't need to say anything," he said. "Look, I know you got caught in the middle of our divorce, and—"

"No. No." Emaline shook her head. "I got

caught in the middle? Dad, how could I not be in the middle of that? You and mom didn't decide to get divorced, you started a whole other family! She caught you! That's not the same thing!"

"It was...complicated," he said.

"It was flat-out wrong."

"Okay. Yes, I agree with that. I have regrets," he said. "The timing wasn't good..."

"The timing was ten years *overlapped*!" This was why she'd stopped talking to him. This right here! He made excuse after excuse for himself, pretending that what he'd done hadn't crushed her on a soul level.

"Can we not talk about that right now?" he asked.

Emaline's gaze moved out over a snowy field lined with trees on its far side. Out here, everything seemed so wholesome and fresh.

"Fine," she said. "What do you need?"

"I need my daughter," he said. "I miss you. Don't you ever miss your old man?"

"Yeah, but I miss the dad I thought I had. You crushed more than Mom. You crushed me, too."

"Look, with adults things can get messy," he said. "Adult relationships aren't easy. You should know that by now."

"Have I ever told you what your lies did to me?" she asked quietly.

Her father was silent.

"I don't think I have…" She licked her lips. "When you're a girl, you think you'll marry a man just like your dad. I thought that. And then I realized that my father was capable of hiding some very big secrets. He was capable of hugging us and bringing us presents and, at the same time, hiding a whole other family he was loving, too. So I figured out that I couldn't marry a man like my father. My father wasn't a good man."

"Hey…"

"No, listen." Emaline's voice firmed. "Do you want that for me? Do you want me to be with a guy who's a phenomenal liar, who cheats on me and does to me what you did to us? Well, I don't want that. So that meant that I had to look back on every single memory, every single aspect of your relationship with Mom that I could remember, and figure out where the warning signs were. Because otherwise, I'd end up with a man just like you, and I don't want that." She swallowed against the lump in her throat.

"There are worse men than me," he said testily.

"On a scale? Probably. But you know what?

That doesn't matter. I'm not the same young woman with her ability to trust crushed out of her. I've been working on that. I've been going to therapy and thinking stuff through and coming to a few of my own conclusions. It hurt, and your betrayal was formative in my adolescence, but it doesn't define me anymore. Your mistakes are your own, and I'm stronger and smarter because I saw what you were capable of up close."

"Emaline, are you telling me that you've never come close to a gray area? Not once?" he demanded. "Because I very much doubt that. Yeah, I messed up. I fell in love with Carmen, and I couldn't let her go."

"You couldn't let Mom go, either, apparently."

"I loved them both!"

"Enough to lie to them both. To betray them both. That's not love. That's selfishness."

"You might find yourself in a similar situation one day—"

"Like you? No. I will never become that, Dad. Or if you're saying that I'll end up like Mom—well, I've got a decade of therapy under my belt to help me avoid it." She paused. She should be angry. She should be simmering mad, but somehow, she was in a bubble of calm. "Can I ask you something?"

"Fine."

"Did you ever once think about what you were doing to your own daughter?"

"I have more than one daughter," he said tersely. "Magdelena manages to love me. My relationship with your mother is not your business. It shouldn't be. I'm your father."

"I have news for you, Maggie is going to have to do the same thing I did," Emaline said. "And she will. She'll start sorting through her memories, her experiences, and start looking at where the lies were, where she naively believed you. She's strong, that one. She just hasn't gotten there yet, but give it time."

"Are you ever going to stop being angry with me?" He suddenly sounded tired.

"I'm not angry," she said. "I used to be furious, but I'm not angry anymore. I'm just… wiser. If you want a relationship with me, you'll need to own up to what you did, not keep making excuses for yourself."

"You don't want to hear my side?"

"Not if your side is you saying how tough it is to be honest," she said. "I don't want to hear that. And maybe you aren't honest yet. Maybe you're still the same guy, and you're doing the same thing to Carmen. I have no idea."

"I am not!"

"Great."

"You think you're better than me." He was whining now.

"Actually, I've got a really low tolerance level for men taking advantage of women now."

It wasn't like this behavior was limited to her family. What about the Rockwells? What about a senator who could pick up a child right under everyone's noses and have no questions asked because he was too powerful to cross?

"Emaline, I want you to leave Magdalena alone," her father said curtly. "That's why I called. I hoped that you and I could find some common ground, but that doesn't seem possible right now. You're upsetting her, and if you want to be bitter, then do it by yourself. If you want to be part of this family, then come by the house and visit us civilly. I'm married to Carmen, and you're going to have to accept that. She's your stepmother."

"It isn't about Carmen," Emaline replied, and suddenly she had a rush of clarity, the whole messy situation laid out in front of her like a map. "It never was. It isn't about Mom, either. Or about us kids. It's about you. You lied for years. It became a part of who you were. You lost my trust—that's just a fact. Blaming me, calling me a troublemaker, or whatever else you were going to, is only a diversion. So, no, I'm not coming by to make nice with you and Carmen. I don't want to. But I will keep up with my sister if she still wants that. She and I are blood."

Her father was silent for a beat, and Emaline didn't have the patience to argue further.

"Bye, Dad," she said, and she hung up the call.

And suddenly, all that calm evaporated, and her heart hammered hard in her chest. It felt good! Her father had said his piece. Somehow, hearing him say all the things she knew he would say didn't hurt as much as she thought it would.

Because he was wrong. He'd never admit it. But he was wrong.

Emaline wrapped her scarf a little bit higher on her chin. Brett was already shoveling a path toward the stable, and she picked up a shovel leaning against the house and followed his lead. When he saw her, he stopped working and came over to her.

"You okay?" he asked.

"I actually am."

"That was your father?"

"Yeah…" She shook her head. "And he

hasn't changed a bit. But one thing scares him, and that's me and Maggie getting close. I'm going to keep up with my sister."

"Out of spite?" he asked with a low laugh.

"No, because I think she and I both want a better future than our mothers got. And together, we can help each other do it. She's not quite as far down the path as I am, but she'll get there."

"Good for you." Brett shot her a grin. "Why don't you keep shoveling here, and I'll start on the snow bank in front of the stable door. And then when we meet in the middle—" his dark, sparkling gaze locked onto hers, and her breath seeped out of her "—we work on the stable together."

Alone. That was the word between the lines.

"Okay."

"Uncle Brett! Emaline!" Damian hollered from the snow fort. "I'm going to make the walls higher!"

Emaline turned and forced a smile in the boy's direction. He was so innocent. These were the real victims in powerful men's games. A clearer image formed in her mind of a senator who was willing to crush anyone in his path, so long as he got his way.

Men like that might not often get their due, but this time, it needed to happen.

BRETT CLEARED THE front of the stable. The snow was wet and heavy, and when he looked over at Emaline shoveling the path toward him, he felt a bit bad about how hard she had to work. But she wasn't flagging—she tossed her scarf aside into the snow and undid the zipper on the front of her coat a few more inches.

Brett had to wonder how she'd fare on his ranch. Granted, he had a ranch manager who kept things running, but Brett did a lot of work himself, too. That was the only way to keep it profitable.

Besides, when he got tempted to go back to his pre-rehab habits…well, some good sweat and hard work helped to get his mind back to where it needed to be. He was working toward his six-year sobriety token, and it mattered a lot to him. Without it, he wouldn't be half the man he was now.

He finished shoveling out the snow bank and pulled the door open, scraping the last of the snow out of the way with the bottom of the door. The stable was warm inside, and he heard the nicker of a horse.

"Hey, there," he called in a low voice. "Have you been lonely?"

Daylight spilled into the stable from the open door, and a horse blinked back at him from a stall. Hay had spilled across the ground. He looked over his shoulder and Emaline was almost done. She stepped through the last of the snow and joined him at his side.

"Is he okay for food in there?" she asked.

"I'll go check," he replied. There'd be some mucking out to do, and the horse would need fresh water and more feed. The work never stopped with large animals. He tried to open the rolling back door that led into the corral, but it wouldn't budge. So he filled a feeder in a spare stall and led the horse over there for some new hay and a few handfuls of oats. He could hear the scrape of the snow shovel outside getting closer, and then the door opened again, and Emaline came inside.

Her cheeks were pink from exertion, and she leaned the shovel against the wall and closed the door behind her. She looked good in this setting—a stable, the animals. It took a special kind of woman to settle into a barn.

"This is the dirty work," Brett said.

"Looks like," she said, but there was a smile in her voice.

She pulled off her gloves and hung them

over a stall rail. He looked away again, trying to focus on the work in front of him. What was it about her that tugged him in like this?

"I guess we'll be leaving soon," he said.

She stilled, and he stole a look up at her. She was watching him, her eyes filled with unnameable emotions. Would she miss him? That was the question circling his mind. He wasn't sure he had any right to it, but he'd miss her. That was the thing that had lodged in his chest—the certainty that he wanted to see her again. He'd want to talk to her, make plans to spend time with her. Was it crazy?

He nodded to a wheelbarrow leaning up against the far wall. "Could you bring me that wheelbarrow? I'm going to muck out this stall."

Emaline pushed it over to him, and he started to shovel out the soiled hay. He worked in silence for a moment, then looked up at Emaline to find her watching him still.

"What?" he said.

"I've been wondering something," she said.

"What's that?" He smiled at her, hoping to crack that serious look on her face.

"Do you know who Damian's mother is?"

His heart skipped a beat, then hammered hard to catch up. He straightened. "What do you mean? Bobbie is his mother."

"His biological mom." Her gaze didn't leave his face. "It's important. I just wonder how much you know."

This seemed to be coming from a different place. She was serious; her blue gaze seemed to read every passing emotion he was trying to hide. He dropped his eyes, wondering how much he should even say. It was better than talking too fast, saying something he might regret.

Emaline sucked in a wavering breath. "I'm going to take the first step, and I'm going to trust you with something."

"Okay…"

"Damian's real parents—that's the story the journalists are trying to crack. Bobbie was never pregnant, was she?"

Brett's mouth went dry. He was surprised no one had starting digging earlier, but with the election coming up, it was probably understandable.

"He's adopted," Brett said. And that was one hundred percent true.

"At the same time that Damian was born, a woman working for your brother's campaign had a baby, then that baby vanished."

He squeezed his eyes shut. It had been a difficult delivery, and for a little while they'd thought she might change her mind. She could have. They wouldn't have tried to stop her if she'd wanted to raise Damian herself. They would have helped her out financially. The Rockwells were many things, but they were not deadbeat parents.

"People have babies," he said, trying to evade her. This was getting too personal.

"The question is, did your brother impregnate one of his aides and then strong-arm her into giving up her son? That's the running theory right now."

Brett swallowed. *Strong-arm?* "That's what you really think?"

"I'm telling you what they've got. If my friend knew I was saying anything about it to you, he'd cut me off for the rest of our lives. No exaggeration."

"So why risk it?" he asked gruffly.

"Because you aren't just a story to me. And I don't believe Damian should be anyone's story, either. I think you're a good guy, but I don't know that your brother is." She looked at him pleadingly. "If my friend is right—if there's a woman out there who had her child taken away from her—"

Yeah, he could see why that thought hurt. It stung him, too.

"I can assure you that my brother did not

cheat on his wife or strong-arm anyone to give up her baby."

She frowned and shook her head. "Damian looks like Dean. He's got the same dark hair, the same little dimple in his chin, the same face shape…"

Brett rubbed a hand over his own dimpled chin. It was a family trait.

"Have you ever considered it, at least?" Emaline softened her tone. "I talked to Celia Jenkins."

"You what?" He was shocked.

She held up a hand. "Before I decided to let this go. She wouldn't say a thing. If she had kept her baby, why not just say so? That would end that line of investigation right away. But she doesn't have a child. The *Chronicle*'s been tailing her for weeks—no sign of a child."

Brett was silent. It was an excellent question, and one that he'd been afraid would come up more and more as time passed. Damian definitely looked like a Rockwell. If only fate had made him look a little more like his mother. He stepped a little closer to Emaline and looked down at her.

"You're on the wrong track," he said quietly. "Please drop this."

"How can you be so sure, Brett?" she said.

"I just am. My brother isn't the bad man you think he is. Dean is not Damian's biological father." He said the words slowly and distinctly.

"But his mother is Celia Jenkins, isn't she?"

He didn't answer that. She was too close to the truth—and yet miles away from it. "Trust me, you're getting it wrong."

"Real life doesn't have this many coincidences! Look, I know what it's like to love someone and not want to believe the worst about them. I know what it's like to suspend your disbelief because the truth is incredibly painful. I remember how hard I tried not to believe that my dad had a whole other family. I wanted it to be lies, people jealous of my parents' marriage—stuff like that. So I get it. But if you don't know who his parents are—"

He didn't answer.

"Unless you're covering for your brother?" Her brow furrowed, and he hated that he could watch the possibility of him lying cross over her face.

"I'm not covering for him," he said gently.

Brett had removed himself from the public so he'd never have to lie. Maybe it was time to just own it and let the chips fall where they may. Dare he tell her?

"Then who are you covering for? Who are his real parents?" she pressed.

"Dean is not Damian's biological father," Brett burst out. "I am!"

CHAPTER ELEVEN

EMALINE'S BRAIN WAS still running at full speed, and it took her a moment to mentally skid to a stop. Brett's eyes filled with regret, and he pulled off his glove and rubbed the faint stubble on his chin.

"What?" she breathed.

Brett dropped his hand. "I shouldn't be telling you this, but you need to stop hounding Dean and Celia. They've done nothing wrong."

Emaline slowly shook her head. "You're his dad?"

"Biologically, yes," he said.

"And Celia Jenkins is his mother?"

"Yes. She gave birth to him, and she was going to give him up for adoption. I was in no position to take Damian in and raise him myself, being an addict in need of rehab. She wasn't ready to be a mother, and she wanted to focus on her political career. There was no strong-arming there. But I couldn't face the thought of never seeing my son again. Do you know what that does to a guy? So I asked my brother to do me a favor."

"What about your relationship with Celia?" she asked softly.

"I'm not proud of it, but we made a mistake at a Christmas party. That was it. I'm embarrassed about that now. But back when I was partying hard, I didn't make great choices. That's another reason I won't touch a drop of alcohol again. When I found out Celia was pregnant and everything started to unravel, I knew I needed to make some big changes in my life. It took me a few more months to acknowledge that I needed rehab. Long story short, my brother and his wife agreed to adopt my son, and we didn't say anything to the public because it wasn't anyone's business. The press would have had a field day with it."

"Have you seen Celia since?" she asked.

"A couple of times. I wanted to make sure she was comfortable with her decision. She was. She left Dean's office because she said it would be too difficult being adjacent to Damian, and I respect that." He paused. "And now, I guess I'm trusting you with this."

Emaline's heart hammered. He had just told her the big Rockwell secret, and all the pieces fell into place. It explained Damian's arrival. It explained the family silence on the matter and why Damian looked so much like Dean. So did Brett, for that matter. All the Rockwell men had the same tall, dark, chin-dimpled look. But Dean wasn't the liar she'd thought he was...

Brett said, "Dean and Bobbie *are* his parents. I gave up my rights. Dean is very much Damian's dad. I'm..."

He didn't finish the statement.

"You're on the outside," she said.

"Yeah." His eyes misted and he swallowed hard. "It was supposed to be better this way—easier on Damian and maybe even easier on me."

"Supposed to be?" she whispered.

"It's harder than I thought."

Emaline reached for his hand and he squeezed her fingers hard.

"To Damian, I'm Uncle Brett. That's all he knows. I have to stand back and let someone else call the shots," he went on. "Before rehab, I couldn't be the dad Damian needed. True. But then I went into recovery. I stopped drinking. I never touched another party drug. I turned myself around, and when I did that, I grew up, I guess. It took time and focus, but I grew into a man who was capable of fatherhood—just a couple of years too late.

Damian was a toddler when I knew I wanted him back."

"Did you tell your brother?" she asked softly.

"Sort of. I brought it up a couple of times. He shot it down. I don't blame him, really. They'd raised Damian since birth. He's theirs in every way that mattered. Bobbie is deeply attached to him."

"It's complicated," she said.

"Yeah. Incredibly. But Dean hasn't done anything wrong. He selflessly took in my son when I couldn't be there for him. He raised him as his own and gave him every advantage his own kids had. My brother is very much the family values guy he puts out there."

"And what about you?"

Brett's Adam's apple bobbed as he swallowed. "I'm the guy who volunteered to take Damian the week before Christmas because I wanted a chance to act like his father even if he'd never know that's who I was."

"Oh, Brett…" Tears blurred her vision. She couldn't tell him everything would be okay, because she had no idea how far his family would go to protect their secrets. And she couldn't comment on his choices—they were personal and understandable. Still, she could see the regret, and the deep sadness, the futile love for his son shining in his eyes, and it struck her that it was a testament to his strength of character that he was going through this sober. Another man would have found a way to dull the pain in the bottom of a glass or a pill bottle.

So instead of saying anything, she stepped forward, slipped her arms around his waist, and pressed her face into his coat. Without missing a beat, he wrapped his strong arms around her and tugged her in close against him. She could feel his breath against her hair.

"I'm sorry it was so hard," she whispered.

"I still think it was the right choice at the time," he said, his voice rumbling in his chest. "At least considering the options I had in front of me then."

She pulled back and looked up at him. "And what about now?"

"I already gave up the chance to raise him. That's over and done with."

But she could see the pain in his eyes.

The door rattled and then opened, and Emaline took a quick step back out of his arms, her face heating with the embarrassment of being caught.

"There you go, Eeyore…" Belinda led the donkey into the stable, and she looked at them mildly surprised. "You two don't need to muck out a stable! I've come to do that."

"It's no problem," Brett replied. "I'll get it done."

Brett cast Emaline an apologetic look. Whatever time alone they'd stolen was officially over. Her heart fluttered in her chest, and she swallowed, trying to get her balance back.

Then, something occurred to her. She'd promised something to Damian.

"Belinda, do you have some spare yarn I could use?" Emaline asked. "I promised Damian a friendship bracelet."

"Of course, I have plenty," Belinda replied.

And Emaline's mind went back to the writing sample she'd sent in to the *Chronicle* based upon George's research. Before, it had been about nailing a corrupt politician, exposing ugly lies and making a man pay for the damage he caused everyone around him. It was about making a man like her father pay. But now she knew better. Dean Rockwell hadn't taken advantage of anyone.

SHE LOOKED BACK at Brett as she headed for the door, and he met her gaze. Nothing had turned out the way it appeared, including Brett. He wasn't a selfish man with too much privilege, after all. He was a guy who'd had to give up his own child and now had to live with the heartache of his choice.

Back in the house, all was warm and cozy. Outside the window, she could hear Damian playing in the snow. It was quiet play, though. He wasn't a boisterous kid. He talked to himself and tramped through the smooth snow.

Emaline slipped upstairs to plug her phone into the battery pack in her room. The little lightning bolt appeared, showing that it was now charging, and she decided to check her notifications.

The first thing she saw was a text from George. It read, My boss loves your writing sample. He says you write a tight article. Thought you might want to know!

Emaline was glad he liked her writing, but the content was useless. She replied, I did what you asked and did a little more digging. I get why you thought there was more to the boy's adoption, but there isn't. You aren't going to find the proof. Might want to let your boss know.

She pressed Send, then dropped the phone onto the bedside table and hurried back downstairs.

Belinda appeared and held up a basket of yarn. "He's a sweet little boy," Belinda said. "He seems lonely, though."

"He's the youngest, and his siblings are teenagers," Emaline said.

"Hmm. Here, even if that were the case, he'd have a buggy-load of cousins to grow up with. And friends."

"I think it's tough raising your kids in the spotlight," Emaline said quietly. "They can't do anything, go anywhere, say anything without being scrutinized and judged. He can't just be a regular kid, because regular kids make mistakes. The press would use it against his dad."

"Would you?" Belinda asked.

"Me?" Emaline tore her gaze away from the window. "No, of course not. I'm not a journalist. I do something different. But even if I were working for a paper or something…I've met him. I've seen what a sweet, vulnerable little boy he is."

"Aren't all little boys vulnerable and sweet?" Belinda asked softly. "I have four grandsons about his age. They might be livelier and more rambunctious, but little boys are so very sensitive. Every last one of them."

"Uncle Brett!" she heard Damian's voice ring out.

Emaline looked out the window again, and Brett appeared across that expanse of snow in the doorway of the stable.

She heard the boy ask something about Eeyore, and Brett waved him over.

Damian started tramping in the direction of the stable, and Emaline smiled. Would Damian ever know who Brett really was to him, or would he just stay "the best uncle," never knowing why Brett had been so dedicated to him? Regardless of how much Damian would learn, he'd be a well-loved boy with an uncle who cared and wanted only the best for him. A lot of kids grew up with a whole lot less.

BRETT AND DAMIAN stood side by side as they watched Eeyore and the big quarter horse contentedly chewing their oats together. He'd said too much. He'd told Emaline everything, and while it had felt right on a heart level, he had no idea what the fallout would be.

Would he find his personal business on the next news cycle—Damian's paternity on front pages for all the see?

He didn't think Emaline would do that, though. She didn't have to tell him what the journalists were digging at. She didn't have to open up to him at all. But she had, and there was no denying that there was some powerful chemistry between them.

"Santa might not bring me presents this

year," Damian said quietly, pulling Brett out of his thoughts.

"What?"

Damian looked up at him mutely.

"I think you're on the good list this year, Damian."

"I sure hope so…"

"Why wouldn't you be?" he asked.

"I get in trouble at school." Damian looked up at him, his dark gaze filled with worry. "I don't like the noise."

Brett tried not to frown. "I thought you had a special teacher who helped you."

"Sometimes I run away from her because I want to be by myself."

"You shouldn't do that."

"None of the other kids have extra teachers." Damian picked at his mitten.

"Do you have kids to play with at recess?" he asked.

"There's kids I try to play with."

"What do you mean, try?" Brett's stomach sank.

"I go over to where they're playing tag, and sometimes they make me it, and then they all run away."

Brett's heart clenched. What was Damian going through every day? That was the best private school in Pittsburgh. His brother had spared no expense. All of the Rockwell kids had gone there.

"Do you tell your mom and dad about it?"

"No."

"Why not?"

"I dunno."

Maybe they were too preoccupied; the election was coming up. Brett didn't blame them, but it was tough on a little guy who just wasn't wired like other kids.

"Do you like that school?" Brett asked.

Damian shook his head. "No. They don't like me, either."

"Are you sure?" Brett asked.

"Yeah. The other kids make the mad face at me a lot."

Brett blew out a breath. "I'll talk to your dad about it. There are other schools, you know."

"Are there?" Damian's eyes widened.

"Lots."

"Could I go to a different one?" Damian's whole face brightened. But would it make a difference? There had to be a solution.

"Maybe. Look, I'll have to talk to your parents. Does the teacher tell your parents that you get into trouble?"

"Sometimes. Daddy says I should do what the teacher says."

"Right." It sounded like Damian was left

shouldering his emotional burden alone. "Don't worry. You did the right thing to tell me, okay? I've got your back, kid."

He gave Damian a playful nudge, and the boy smiled.

"Okay."

If Dean and Bobbie didn't have the time, Brett would be glad to go down to that school and discuss the situation with the principal. If Damian was struggling this much socially, he might need more than just a teaching assistant. Maybe there were some social options where kids could learn those skills, or they could pull him out of the school entirely and find a school or a classroom that was gentler for the kid. Potential solutions were already tumbling through his head. No son of his—

The second the words formed in his brain, his breath caught. No son of his would be treated like that... And yet, legally speaking, Damian wasn't his son, was he? That was a thought he didn't have the luxury of entertaining.

But Brett loved this boy in a way he didn't love his other nieces and nephews. He felt that tug toward him, and as the years went by, it only got stronger. He'd asked Dean and Bobbie to adopt his son so that he could still be close to him—still get to know him and see him grow up. He hadn't realized how hard it would be to keep an appropriate distance when he was now fully capable of being a dad. He was a different man than he'd been when Damian was born.

Brett had more than that on his mind right now. Everything seemed to be mixing together into a mess inside of him.

"Look, Damian, I'm going to go help Eli on his farm. I saw him a few minutes ago, and he could use a hand," Brett said.

"Okay."

"I need you to go in the house. I've heard stories of how this donkey escapes, and I don't want you to accidentally let him out."

"Okay." Damian looked up at him, and there was so much that Brett wanted to say, so much he wished he could do, like bring the kid to the ranch and maybe find a Montessori school for him, somewhere that would be able to accommodate him. He wanted to say he loved him and that he would make it all better, but it wasn't his place to do that. So Brett ruffled Damian's hair. The boy made a face and smoothed it back down.

"I don't like that."

Of course. Damian hated anything too disruptive touching him. Brett had heard that he wouldn't even take a shower because he didn't like the feeling of water falling on his head.

"Sorry." He should have known better. Brett squatted down, and Damian pushed his hair off his forehead. "I'm going to talk to your parents. I know they'll want to help fix all of this for you."

Damian nodded, his eyes wide. Would Damian let Brett hug him? He wasn't sure he dared to try—not after that hair ruffling.

"And Santa's coming...okay? You don't have to worry about that. You're a good kid. I know it."

"Okay." Damian smiled then.

"Now you go inside, okay?" Brett said gruffly.

Damian turned for the door, and Brett watched as the boy headed back out of the stable and trudged toward the house, one small child against a very big world. Brett had told himself that he'd made the right choice, and it had been the only one he'd been able to see. But today, a new realization hit him like a falling brick. If he'd been able to see to the other end of his own troubles, he might not have asked his brother to adopt Damian. He might have made the arrangement more flexible. But he hadn't been able to see what healing looked like.

Damian disappeared inside the house, and Brett turned toward the property next door. He'd seen Eli cross the farmyard a couple of times already, and he was pretty sure the old man was in the barn.

When he saw Eli appear at the barn door, he waved. Eli waved back and waited while Brett plunged through the deep snow toward him. By the time he got to him, Brett was breathing hard.

"I came to give you a hand," Brett said.

"*Danke*, young man," Eli replied. "It's getting harder and harder to keep this place running on my own."

"Did I hear you're going to retire?" Brett asked.

"*Yah*. After the holidays I'll put the farm up for sale. It'll be sold in a week or two."

"You think?" Brett raised his eyebrows.

"This is Amish Country." Eli gave him a funny look. "Farmland is hard to come by. Trust me, it'll sell, and quickly."

Eli headed back into the barn and Brett followed him. There were stalls at the far end of the barn, five of which were filled. Brett's practiced eye counted three steers and two heifers.

"This is my herd." Eli gestured toward them with a rueful smile.

"You got them in before the storm hit," Brett said. "I'm impressed."

"Don't be too impressed," Eli replied. "I tend to mollycoddle my animals. I bring them in every night in the winter. Five cows aren't enough to really keep warm if the temperature drops."

"I heard you mollycoddle your chickens, too?" Brett asked with a grin.

"They are my princesses, and *yah*, I do." Eli picked up a shovel and handed one to Brett. "I appreciate the help. My knees aren't what they used to be."

"Will you miss your animals?" Brett asked.

"Terribly. I love them, and handing them over to some other farmer—it feels like a betrayal to them. No one will care for them as tenderly as I do. But that's life. Sometimes it hurts."

Brett helped to move the cattle as they got ready to clean out the first stall. Eli paused with the steer and smoothed a hand down its head. The animal noticeably calmed under Eli's touch.

"My advice to you is don't get old," Eli said as he locked the gate on the animal and came hobbling into the empty stall.

"It's better than the alternative," Brett said.

"Barely." But Eli smiled faintly. "I hate leaving this farm. I hate it so much."

"Then stay," Brett said. "I know the Amish help each other—"

"It's more than that," Eli said. "It's the woman I live next to. I've loved her for decades, you know."

"All the more reason to stay?" Brett asked hopefully.

"I've told her how I felt," Eli said. "I thought she must have known. I'm not a man who hides his feelings very well. But she doesn't feel the same way."

"I'm sorry, man."

"Danke."

Eli bent to the work at hand, and Brett joined him, but he could feel the sadness coming off the old man like a wave. He was truly leaving everything behind—his farm, his animals and the woman he loved.

"People say I should have married," Eli said, breaking the silence.

"Yeah, they tell me the same thing. So, why didn't you?" Brett asked.

"Because I loved Belinda, and I couldn't pretend I didn't," Eli replied. "I'm nothing if not loyal, it turns out."

"Do you regret it?" Brett asked. "Not marrying someone else, I mean."

Eli straightened and pursed his lips. "Some have said I wasted my life."

"That's a little harsh," Brett said. "I'm not married, and I wouldn't say my life's a waste."

"Life is short, I discovered," Eli said. "I didn't know that at your age. When I was young like you, I saw old men and thought it took forever to get there. But it flies by. You blink, and you're suddenly this old man in the mirror. That's what they mean. I didn't use the time I had to find a woman, marry her and have some *kinner* of my own to take care of me in my old age. If I had a son or a daughter, I'd be moving in with one of them, not into an old folks home." Eli bent to shovel up more soiled hay, the blade scraping against cement. "But no, I didn't waste my life loving Belinda."

"Good for you." Brett picked up the handles of the wheelbarrow, waiting for Eli to finish with the last little bit of soiled hay.

"But not loving me back was a waste of half of her life, I'll tell you that."

That sounded bitter. Brett looked over at Eli quizzically.

"I mean it," Eli said. "When she was married to Ernie, she had a good life. After he died, I was here. I was the one helping her with chores and being the man within stone's throw if she needed any kind of defense or support. Once a man dies, an Amish woman normally remarries pretty quickly because she needs the help. I gave her the help without demands. I loved her and I protected her. I might have driven her a little batty, too, with my unique ways, but she missed out on years and years of being loved truly and purely. I would have done anything for her—anything! And I did. I changed myself so I'd be husband material for Belinda, and even that wasn't enough. So she grieved Ernie, and she ran her bed-and-breakfast, and she lived alone. She didn't have to do that. If she'd just let herself love me back, I'd have been so grateful…"

The old man's voice caught, and he stopped talking.

"Maybe give it some time?" Brett asked. Eli cast him an irritated look, and Brett smiled wanly. "Sorry, you've done that."

"Maybe I did waste my time," Eli said at last. "I didn't tell her sooner. I should have told her how I felt while we were younger. There's no worse feeling than looking back on your life and realizing that you didn't do the most important thing because you were afraid."

"You were afraid of her rejecting you?"

"Of course! Wouldn't you be?"

Brett nodded. How many things did a man hold back on out of that fear of being told to take a hike? Like his growing feelings for Emaline... Like his desire to be an actual father to his son.

A man held back for good reason. Brett couldn't get involved with just anyone! He'd been born into the wrong family for that. And he couldn't tell Damian who he really was, either. He'd made choices already, and he was honor bound to stand by them.

But how would he feel looking back at himself when he was Eli's age? Would he have regrets? Would he wish he'd done the hard thing and blown up the entire family plan for Damian to be raised by Dean and Bobbie, and never know the difference? Would he think back about the problematic blonde who made him feel things he'd never felt before and regret not having told her? Because there was a chance he'd never feel this way again, either. He thought he had lots of time, but apparently, it flew by.

On this end, telling Emaline what he felt was a scary thought.

"Did you know you'd have regrets?" Brett asked, wheeling the barrow out of the stall.

"I thought I was being pragmatic," Eli said.

"That's the irony. You don't know what will be a regret until later."

"That's not comforting," Brett murmured, then he heaved the wheelbarrow forward and glanced over his shoulder. "What direction is the manure pile?"

"Go left," Eli said, and when Brett was headed in the right direction, he called after him, "And as for the rest, it wasn't meant to be comforting!"

CHAPTER TWELVE

EMALINE SAT IN front of Damian, who held one end of the friendship bracelet she was braiding. He held on to the yarn tightly, the tips of his little fingers turning white. He was taking it so seriously. He'd chosen the colors—red and blue. She braided the yarn slowly and snugly, making sure it was the best she could do.

The memory of the anguished look in Brett's eyes was seared into her heart. It must hurt to have his son so close but so far away, to be a father but not to be your son's comfort or his solution. And yet she respected Brett for turning his life around and becoming the kind of man whose heart broke over this. A lot of men never matured enough to feel that pain.

Emaline crossed the last of the threads over, then used another thread to tie off the end. She smiled at Damian.

"Hold out your hand."

He let go of the yarn and thrust a hand out, and she tied the friendship bracelet onto his thin wrist.

"There," she said. "What do you think?"

Damian beamed. "I've finally got one!"

"I'm glad you like it. Now, whenever you look at your wrist, you can remember that you've got a friend." She paused. "And you know, your uncle Brett is a pretty special uncle, too."

"Yeah..."

But Damian wasn't really listening now. He pulled his headphones up over his ears and looked happily down at the braided bracelet. Then he headed over to the window and looked outside. That blocking out of sound seemed to give him a rest that nothing else could give him. The world could be a very overwhelming place for this kid.

"Uncle Brett is coming," Damian announced. "And Eli."

Belinda perked up, and she smoothed her hands down her apron, then patted her hair and *kapp* in a quick check. Had she been in waiting mode for Eli in spite of it all?

Emaline got up from her seat and headed over to the potbellied stove, mostly because she was full of nervous energy. She heard the door open, the sound of boots and male voices, and then the door slamming shut. She glanced over her shoulder as Brett came into the kitchen. Eli was still in the mudroom, but his voice filtered out to them.

"The chickens are doing fine," Eli called to them. "And so are the cows. It's a good thing I had them in the barn. If they'd been out in that storm, it would have been something else."

Eli appeared behind Brett, and he rubbed his hands together. The dog was at Eli's heels, as usual.

"I'm glad to hear it," Belinda said, and Emaline noticed that Belinda sounded just a little bit breathless, and there was pink in her cheeks that hadn't been there before.

Brett's gaze found Emaline's, and his smile held new warmth. He joined her beside the stove, his sleeve brushing hers. He smelled of hay and snow. Was this what he smelled like on the ranch after working outside? It would be awfully nice to be the woman he came home to, she realized.

"I think I said too much earlier," he murmured. "If I'd been thinking straight, I would have kept my mouth shut."

"You opened up," she countered. "That's what ordinary people do when they get close to each other."

"Are we…getting close?" His voice was low enough for her ears only, and his dark gaze caught hers and held it.

"I thought so." Her pulse sped up.

A smile touched his lips. "Just making sure that wasn't one-sided."

"Nope." She smiled back. "Not at all."

Across the kitchen, Belinda had brought Eli a mug of something hot to drink, but he hadn't taken off his coat, as if he didn't intend to stay. Damian stayed by the window, his earphones up, blocking out the rest of the world.

"For what it's worth," she whispered, "whether you tell him or not, Damian is better off with you in his life."

Brett looked over at Damian by the window, and for a moment, the only sound in the kitchen was of Belinda and Eli talking in low tones in Pennsylvania Dutch.

"Sometimes when you love someone," Brett said, "you step back and…let them go."

That sounded ominous, and she searched his face, looking for a clue of what he meant.

"What are you thinking of doing?" she asked.

"Either we tell him the truth," Brett said, "or I need to step back from my brother's family."

Sadness glimmered in his dark gaze.

"Brett, my family was messed up," she whispered. "The thing that turned us all upside down was the lie. It would have been better to face my parents' marriage ending than live in that fake in-between world made up of deception. If you do step back, keep in mind that the truth will probably come out sooner or later. As kids get older, they start asking better questions. I know I did."

"Everything inside of me is screaming to tell him who I am," Brett breathed, and his fingers brushed against hers. She spread her fingers, and his twined through hers. "But my instincts aren't necessarily right. My brother adopted him, and I can't tell my son anything without Dean and Bobbie's okay. We have to talk about it. He has a good home and loving adoptive parents. He has every privilege…"

"I'm not saying what the right thing is to do." She looked up at him. "I can see how complicated this is, and how well-meaning everyone is in this situation. You're a good guy, Brett."

"You think? Damian is worried Santa will skip him this year, but I'm the one who should be worrying about the naughty list."

"Nah. Your heart is in the right place. That counts."

The door opened and shut again, and Emaline tugged her hand free of Brett's warm grip. They were in front of people, and she'd forgotten herself. She turned to look behind her. Belinda stood at the door, the empty mug in one hand and her shoulders squared. For a moment, Emaline wondered if she was angry, standing so ramrod straight, but then she wiped at her face, and Emaline realized that she was trying not to cry.

"Where did Eli go?" Brett asked.

"Home." Belinda gave a wobbly smile.

"Are you okay?" Emaline asked.

"Of course." Belinda gave a curt nod, then headed out of the kitchen and disappeared into the sitting room.

"He loves her," Brett murmured. "He really loves her."

"Yeah…" But love was never simple, was it? Belinda was afraid of that step, and she might miss it all together. Time wasn't on their side.

"Can we do anything to help?" Brett asked.

Could they? This was a private matter between two people who had known each other for decades. What could two relative strangers do to help them fix things?

"I doubt it," she replied. "But we could get out of her hair for a bit. Let her have a cry in peace."

They exchanged a somber look.

"I need to make sure my car will start and

then check to see if my phone has charged," she said.

"That's a good idea," he replied. "The battery pack in my room is out of juice, and my phone's dead, too." He raised his voice a little. "Damian, I'm going to charge my phone in the truck. Do you want to come along and call your parents?"

Damian pulled off his headphones. "Yeah!"

Emaline dashed up the stairs to grab her phone, and then they bundled back up and headed out of the house together. Emaline went to her car, and Brett and Damian carried on to his vehicle a few yards away. She brushed off a thick layer of snow from the door handle in order to open it. Down the road she could hear the growl of snowplows, although she couldn't see them yet. The lock chirped, and her lights blinked. She eased into the cold seat and started the vehicle. It rumbled to life, and she leaned back, scrolling through her messages in the relative privacy that the snow-covered windshield afforded her.

It was a relief to have her phone charged again. She was definitely a person who was tied to the device, and she wouldn't even apologize for it.

She idly flicked through her personal social

media—just the regular happy Christmas-themed photos being shared by her brothers' girlfriends. All three of them had picked nice women. Then she went over to her professional profiles to check on the status of her latest posts. They were still doing well, but it never ceased to be a relief to see. She'd uploaded some video of Eeyore drinking out of the kitchen sink, and that post had gone viral. She had a lot of followers, but she had about ten times the normal activity on that one! She'd jumped in followers again. She scanned the comments—lots of positive responses and people saying how much they liked to see the Amish treating their animals well, which counteracted some loud anti-Amish sentiment out there on the internet. She was glad to be part of spreading good news and helping to show the Amish the way they really were, as good people doing their best. Then she moved on to the newsfeeds to see what was happening in the world.

She flipped through story after story until she got to the local news in Pennsylvania, and a prominent story caught her eye, and her heart thundered in her ears. *Senator Rockwell's Adopted Love Child*. It sounded more like a gossip rag's headline than a proper news outlet's. Her first thought was that someone else had gotten to the same story that George had given her. All of that spun through her head in a split second before her gaze dropped down to the byline, and her heart thudded to a stop.

By George McDonald and Emaline Piper

George's editor had released her article. Hadn't George seen her text? She checked her messages and found a reply from George.

We have confirmation from a solid source. You did good. Don't worry, you get to share the byline.

But the story wasn't true!

Or was it? If a source confirmed it, either that source was lying…or Brett was.

BRETT AND DAMIAN reclined in the warm comfort of the truck.

He'd have to have a heart-to-heart chat with his brother one day soon, but right now Damian needed to talk to his parents. It wasn't about what Brett wanted or about who deserved what. This was about Damian—starting with the security of knowing he could talk to his parents whenever he needed to. Brett dialed Dean's cell phone number. It rang twice, and Dean picked up.

"Brett? I've been trying to reach you for ages!" Dean's voice broke into the silence.

"It's me, Daddy!" Damian said. "I won a snowball fight!"

"Oh, did you?" Dean's voice softened. "That's great buddy. Seriously? You had a snowball fight?"

"Yeah, and we beat Uncle Brett fair and square!"

"Who's we?" Dean asked, and his tone turned wary.

"Me and Emaline. She gave me a friendship bracelet, and Uncle Brett likes her."

"Yeah?" Dean's voice cooled just a bit more. "Hey, buddy, can I talk to your uncle for a minute? Then you can tell me all about it, okay?"

Damian handed the phone over and Brett took it off speaker and put it against his ear.

"Hi, Dean. We've been snowed in. My phone died. Sorry for not checking in earlier."

"Is Emaline our little travel vlogger?"

Brett didn't like the tone his brother used or the diminutive. "She's not a problem, so leave her alone, okay?"

"Has he looked at the news?" Bobbie asked in the background.

He frowned. "No, I haven't looked at it in a couple of days. Why? What's going on?"

Brett's phone pinged and he looked down at the screen. It was a text from Bobbie, and when he touched it, he could see it was a link to a news article.

"Do I need to read this now?" Brett asked.

"Yes, I think you should," Dean replied.

Brett clicked the link, and the title made his heart gallop: *Senator Rockwell's Adopted Love Child.* But it was the journalist's name that made him shut his eyes for a moment.

"It looks like your fluffy little influencer has teeth, after all," Dean said dryly.

Brett looked up out the truck window to see Emaline standing there, her expression agonized.

"What does it say in a nutshell?" Brett asked gruffly.

"Can Damian hear this?"

"No."

"It says I impregnated my aide and then forced her to give up the child so that Bobbie and I could raise him," Dean said.

"Right." Brett gritted his teeth together. This was the story she'd told him about—the one her newspaper was planning on investigating. It seemed there was more to that story than she'd divulged.

"I hope you've been on eggshells the last couple of days," Dean said grimly, "because that vlogger has ambitions, and she's already proven that. Obviously, the story is false, but they're getting a little too close to something that is no one else's business. I'm calling my lawyers now."

"Can I talk to Daddy now?" Damian asked.

"Sure," Brett said and his knees felt weak. "Dean, I'm handing you back to Damian now."

He passed the phone over and Damian grabbed it and punched at the speaker button.

"Uncle Brett and me made a snow fort!" Damian said. "And the snow is just right for snowballs, too. Remember when the snow was like sugar, and it wouldn't make balls? It's not like that at all!"

Brett left Damian to talk to his parents, and he ran a hand through his hair, and his brain spun. The story had come out under her name. They couldn't possibly have confirmation of any of it unless someone was lying. Was it Celia? Was someone paying her to spread lies? He couldn't imagine so. She'd always been loyal to Dean.

He needed to sort this out. With a quick word to Damian to stay in the truck, he opened the door and swung out. He saw Emaline by her own car, her arms crossed in front of her coat and her agonized gaze locked on him. He slammed the truck door shut and headed over to her.

"I saw your article," he said. "The one with your name on it. When were you going to tell me that was coming out?"

"I didn't know!" she said. "I'm so sorry. I'm trying to reach George now. I used the information he had for my writing sample to show what my investigative voice sounds like. It wasn't supposed to be published."

But she *had* written it and sent it to a newspaper editor.

How naive had he been? He'd told her *everything*!

CHAPTER THIRTEEN

WIND WHIPPED EMALINE'S short hair around her face, and she brushed it out of her eyes. Brett's expression was grim, covering anything he might be feeling. She didn't blame him, and maybe she shouldn't want to see the depth of that betrayal.

Damian was visible in the truck, a smile on his face as he talked to his parents. He gestured with the hand that held the phone, then brought it back in front of his face.

"I didn't know they'd publish it," she said. "I knew they were investigating. George wanted me to get more evidence, but that's not why I asked you about it. I'd already told George to back off from you and that I wouldn't participate in the investigation. I haven't told George anything about what you shared with me in the barn. In fact, I told him that they wouldn't find any proof for the story."

"What did he say?" Brett asked.

"He said they got confirmation on the story from some credible sources."

"What confirmation could they possibly have gotten?" Brett demanded. "Someone here is lying!"

Did he mean her? The thought made her stomach knot. She pulled out her phone, found the text and marched over to him.

"Look. I'm not lying to you."

He put his hand over hers to stabilize the cell phone screen and read the texts. He was still for a moment, then sighed and released her hand.

"I wouldn't tell anyone your private business, Brett. Damian's birth has nothing to do with your brother's election. I know that now."

"But you did write the piece," he replied woodenly.

"George said he'd share the byline with me if I used his research and got additional confirmation from you or any of the other sources."

"And you got them to talk?" Brett asked.

"That's the thing! They wouldn't give me any information. Not the nurses or Celia."

"But you did pursue the story. You did *try* to write about Damian's parentage."

Her phone rang, and she looked down at George's phone number on her screen.

"Yes, but that was before… Look, let me talk to George, and I'll tell you what he says."

Without waiting for Brett to reply, she picked up the call and headed to her car for privacy.

"George," she said.

"Hi, Emaline," he said. "Our story went live. Did you see it? Your first byline, and my editor says he'll look at more from you."

"I told you there was no evidence for it!" she snapped.

"A little late," he said. "And you're new at being in the actual trenches. Those Rockwells are charming. Trust me, I know how likable they are when you get up close and personal with them. There's a reason why our senator keeps getting reelected. Politicians are made up of half shark and half kitten. We want a man who will shake our hand, look into our faces, talk about his grandpa's hard work in the mines and then go tear the throat out of his opponent. That's how America likes them. It's a sexy combination."

It was, but that wasn't Brett.

"And you think Brett Rockwell talked me into giving up the story," she said.

"Didn't he?"

No! Sure, she'd texted George after Brett had told her the truth about whose son Damian really was. After he'd opened up, he'd trusted her with his secret, and proved that the senator was innocent of their accusations.

But she'd already decided not to pursue the story further.

"Let me guess," George said when she hadn't answered. "He believes his brother is a Boy Scout. He can't imagine his beloved sibling would do anything so crass as disrespecting a woman in any way. He's certain that the senator is faithful to his wife and is just as clean-cut as he appears on TV screens. And he looked deeply into your eyes and asked you to trust him on that."

"No. That's not what happened."

"Is he suggesting you might have a romantic future if you just go along with him on this?" George asked.

"It's not like that, George." Although, it was a little like that. Was she being manipulated? Was he taking advantage of her softer feelings for him? She'd feel like a complete fool if that were the case!

"Then why are you so certain that Dean Rockwell is innocent here?"

"I can't tell you that," she said. "But suffice to say, as much as I would have liked to prove otherwise both for my own career and because I believe powerful men should pay for their sins, the senator is in the clear with this one. If we're going to catch him up, it won't be about his youngest son's parentage."

"Then how come we have confirmation for all of it?" George demanded. "Two nurses came forward who worked on opposite shifts who both said they saw that the baby born that night was legally a Rockwell according to the paperwork. The father was a Rockwell, if you need that spelled out for you."

"Did they see Dean's name?"

"That would have been on the birth certificate forms that would be sent to the state. One nurse was in the room when the birth certificate information was filled out. There were other forms being filled out at the same time for an immediate adoption."

"So maybe she was confused."

"She knew what she saw."

"And was she willing to give her name?"

"Of course not! She's a credible source that I'll protect to the death. She can't just relay a patient's private information without being fired and possibly sued."

"Exactly," she said.

"What is with you, Emaline?" George barked. "We also have a statement from the biological mother."

Emaline's heart hammered in her throat. "What did she say?"

"She said, and I quote…" There was the sound of a keyboard clattering. "'I'm not saying anything to you people. I told you to leave me alone. Haven't I been through enough? Yes, I had a baby. Yes, I gave him up for adoption. No, I was not coerced into doing so. That's a personal decision, and none of your'—a few colorful expletives here—'business.'"

"That doesn't prove anything," Emaline said. "That's pretty much what she said to me, minus the colorful part. And she's right about it being her personal choice."

"I'm not done." George sounded smug. "When we pushed her a little further, she said, 'My son will be just fine with his adoptive parents. I don't know why you're so determined to tear into this. The Rockwells take care of their own, and they did the right thing by Damian. I gave up my rights to him by my own choice. If you care so much about a woman not being pressured and manipulated, you'll leave me alone! You're the problem right now, not the senator.'"

"Oh…" Yes, she could see exactly how that sounded. Except that Celia meant he was a Rockwell not because of Dean but because of Brett.

"So what makes you so certain Damian Rockwell, who looks exactly like the senator, isn't his biological son?" George demanded.

Emaline sighed. "I just have…credible suspicion. You swore to me that what I sent you was only a writing sample! If you'd wanted to publish that story, you should have gotten my permission first. I would have told you to leave my name off it."

"I did you a favor," George said, lowering his voice. "This is your first big piece, and it's getting traction. It's already hit CNN, Fox News and MSNBC. Everyone is questioning Senator Rockwell's Boy Scout reputation right now. Granted, CNN is questioning the journalism, but we'd expect that since he's their boy, after all. But our story is solid. We've got the confirmation."

"And if it weren't solid?" she asked weakly. "If they did a DNA test and proved that Damian wasn't the senator's biological child?"

"Emaline, if it walks like a duck and quacks like a duck and looks like a duck, its father is a duck!"

And that father was a Rockwell, but there was more than one Rockwell.

"I want my name off that story," she said, trying to sound more confident than she felt.

"Too late," he replied. "This is yours. The nurses who called in said they were responding to voice mails left by you. You were able to do what I couldn't do alone. This story now belongs to the paper, and it's out there. Enjoy your success, Emaline. Don't wimp out now." There was a pause. "I've got to go. We've got other stories. Text me when you're back in the city, and drinks are on me."

He hung up without another word, and Emaline tried to curb the sheer rage coursing through her veins. She'd told him there was no evidence! She'd told him in time, too.

She put her hand on the door handle, and she realized she was trembling.

So what happened when the senator proved that he wasn't Damian's biological father? If the family came clean about Brett being his dad, and it was proven that she knew about it, she'd be in a whole different kind of trouble for having her name on that piece. There was no way for her to come out of this unscathed.

She got out of the car and slammed the door shut. A thick slab of snow slid off the front windshield with the force of it. Brett stood where she'd left him, his arms crossed over his chest, and his lips pressed together in a straight line.

"He's got what looks like good evidence," she said.

"What evidence?"

It was all in the article anyway, so she relayed exactly what George had told her. Brett rubbed his hands over his face.

"It looks bad," he said.

"I know. I'm sorry. If you told the truth about it all, it would clear your brother."

"And force us to talk to Damian about something we didn't want to tell him yet."

She could see the misery on his face, and she wished she could say anything that would make it better. But she had nothing.

"Brett, I'm really sorry."

He just nodded. The truck door banged, and she looked over to see Damian looking at them, eyes wide. He looked scared. He felt around his neck for his headphones, but she knew they were inside the house.

"Hi, Damian," she said, trying to sound cheerful.

The boy looked up at Brett, then stepped a little closer to his uncle.

"Daddy says I'm not allowed to talk to her anymore," Damian said, just loud enough for her to hear. He handed the phone to Brett, and Brett put it up to his ear.

"Yeah. Yeah…" Brett turned away a little bit. "Completely. Understood. Yeah."

There was a short conversation, most of which consisted of Brett agreeing, and then he tucked his phone into his coat pocket.

"You go on inside, Damian," Brett said. "I bet Belinda will give you some pie."

"Okay…" But he didn't move.

"Damian—"

Damian's feet started moving then, but when he passed by Emaline, he stopped, then lifted up his hand with the friendship bracelet on it. He looked down at his boots, his arm trembling.

"I don't know how to get it off," he whispered.

Emaline bent down, pulled off her gloves and untied the bracelet. When it was off, the boy looked up at her silently, his eyes filled with tears.

"It's okay, sweetie," she said softly. "You're being a good boy by obeying your dad. I understand."

He nodded. "Okay."

"Go get that pie. It'll be delicious." She tried to sound like nothing was wrong, but kids were smarter than that. He trudged toward the house.

Her heart squeezed, and she felt her chin tremble. So, he couldn't even have a happy memory about a friend he'd made. What had they told him about her? What would they say to make sure he gave her a wide berth? She looked up at Brett, and he gave her an apologetic look.

"You can't talk to Damian anymore. I'm sure you understand," he said.

"I do, yeah." She swallowed hard. "Are you, personally, worried about me? Or is this just from your brother?"

"My brother made it clear—" Brett swallowed "—and I understand why. I'm sorry."

Sure he was. So was she. But this had exploded, and there was going to be no putting it all back together again.

A SNOWPLOW GROWLED down the road, and Brett stopped to look as it deposited a dense pile of snow in front of the drive on its way by. Great. They weren't leaving in the next few hours, that much was clear. A quick escape wasn't going to be possible, and Dean would hate that.

"What did they tell him about me?" Emaline asked.

Brett sucked in a breath. "I don't really know. Dean didn't elaborate, but he probably said that you're a journalist trying to get a story on his dad, and he can't say anything to you. The kids know the drill pretty well."

"What a great way to grow up," she muttered.

"You can't say it's wrong," he said.

"Really?" Emaline's eyes snapped fire.

"Can't I? I know that story should never have come out, but that wasn't because I'm some career-obsessed witch! I tried to stop it! I even told you what I knew! And you can see what the evidence looked like. I'm not a monster, Brett, and now Damian is going to look back on this time at the Butternut B&B, and he's going to remember a lady he liked a whole lot who turned out to be just terrible. You think that won't be formative?"

"I'm not the one calling the shots here." His brother was, and his brother was Damian's legal father. That was what mattered—DNA gave Brett no rights here.

"Does your brother blame you for this?" she asked.

"He thinks I'm being phenomenally naive in trusting you at all," Brett said.

"Do you agree?" she asked.

Did he? How foolish was he going to feel later looking back on all of this? Except... he felt on a gut level that she was telling the truth. She'd believed him before, and he believed her. Not that it mattered right now.

"Em—" He crossed the snowy ground between them. "The truth is, I think you're a good person. I believe that you saw an opportunity at first and that you changed your mind when you got to know us. I believe you tried to stop this story, but the machine was bigger than you. It always will be. The political machine is bigger than me, too."

"Thank you," she said quietly. "It's the truth."

She looked down at the bracelet in her hand, then shoved it into her pocket. Brett swallowed. She'd been kind to Damian, and the kid had really responded to her. Telling Damian to give back the bracelet had been understandable, because Dean was freaking out over there, but from where Brett stood, it was also cruel. It was taking something precious away from both of them.

"What does your journalist pal think is happening here?" Brett asked.

"About the same as your brother," she replied. "He figures you're manipulating me and lying to me, and I'm buying it hook, line and sinker because you make my heart go pitter-patter."

He couldn't help but smile at the turn of phrase. "Do I make your heart go pitter-patter?"

"Shut up." She laughed softly and her cheeks colored. "A little bit."

"Good." She wasn't just some journalist. She was…a good woman. He was glad he made her feel something, because she had stirred up his insides, too. "Me too."

She lifted her gaze and the wind ruffled her golden hair.

"This isn't going to be easy for you, is it?" she asked. "Your brother is going to demand that you never speak to me again."

"Probably. But that doesn't mean I'll go along with it. It won't be easy for you, either. However this goes down."

She nodded. "Guaranteed. At this point, all I have is my personal integrity to lean on."

"A clear conscience is priceless," he said.

"So much for serious journalism," she said. "But that's my problem. Not yours."

"We aren't going to see too much of each other after this, are we?" he asked.

She shook her head. "No, probably not."

"In another life where I was the son of a hardworking tradesman, and you were an accountant or something, you and I would have had beautiful kids," he said.

She started to laugh and shook her head. "Brett, you think of the strangest things."

"Tell me I'm wrong," he said.

She shook her head more slowly this time. "You aren't wrong. We do have a connection that I haven't experienced before."

"Too bad we're star-crossed, huh?" he said.

"Yeah."

He knew why she was wrong for him. She

was the enemy when it came to his family. She was the observant, bright, articulate threat to all the peace and serenity that his family tried to maintain. She'd never be accepted by his family, and he'd never be able to seamlessly slip into her life, either. They were like a fox and chicken, and she was the fox!

"Before everything gets even crazier," he said softly and stepped closer. He put a finger under her chin, tipping her face upward.

"Do you mind?" he asked.

"You'd better do it fast," she whispered. "Real life is closing in."

He dipped his head down and caught her lips with his. Her breath was warm against his face, and he stepped closer as his lips moved over hers. He pulled her in and let the scent of her fruity perfume fill him right up.

This had to be the most ill-timed kiss of his life. He pulled back from it and dropped his arms. She smiled shakily.

"Wow…" she breathed.

"And that's what we're missing out on," he whispered back.

She laughed softly. "You like to toe that line, don't you?"

"Sure do."

And right now, she had no idea how much self-control it was taking for him to stay on the right side of the line. She was everything he longed for in that soft, unsullied part of his heart that the politics and the partying and the family pressures had never touched.

"I really am sorry they published that article," she said.

"Not your fault," he said gruffly.

"I'm sorry all the same."

The side door opened, and Brett looked to see Belinda in the doorway. She had a bright smile on her face.

"I have a fresh cherry pie!" she called. "If you'd like a piece, it's the perfect warm temperature. It doesn't get better than this!"

Brett looked down at Emaline.

"It's a whole different world here…" she murmured. "Let's go get pie. This is the most wholesome thing we'll ever eat, guaranteed."

They headed toward the house and Brett looked back at the yard. There were boot prints going in a few different lines toward Eli's farm and more footprints tramping through the backyard. What had started out as a pristine expanse of clean snow was now flattened, kicked up and trampled over.

That hadn't taken long, had it?

Inside, the house was fragrant from baking. Brett took off his boots and coat, and then took Emaline's to hang next to his own…

again. He wished he would have more opportunities to hang her coat next to his. It was the kind of luxury that money couldn't afford.

Damian was at the table, a piece of pie in front of him and some red custard from the filling smeared around his mouth. He held the fork like a shovel and hunched over his plate.

"That must be good pie," Brett said.

"A healthy appetite is a compliment to the cook," Belinda said. She had a piece of pie set aside on the counter.

"Is that for me?" he asked.

"No, that's for Eli." Belinda dished up another piece and handed it to him. "That's for you."

"Is he coming by?" Emaline asked.

"If he doesn't, then I'll bring it to him." Belinda handed another piece to Emaline. "That's what neighbors and friends do, even if they…have a falling-out. They eat pie."

Brett's heart went out to her. She wasn't going to be able to unring that bell. Eli had declared his love for her. There was no putting things back to the way they used to be, but it was obvious she'd try.

Heck, Brett was preaching to himself now. He'd changed things between him and Emaline, too. Who was he to offer advice about relationships? He bumbled along just like anyone else, and when he looked over at Emaline, she smiled and dropped her gaze. He wished her sweet, bashful expression didn't soften his heart the way it did. Nothing was going to be easy about this, was it?

Brett's phone rang again, and he looked down to see his brother's number. If it were just about him, he'd let the call go to voice mail, but this was about Damian. He put his plate down on the table and turned toward the sitting room as he picked up the call.

"Hi," he said.

The sound of Damian chattering to Belinda, asking what other kinds of pies she had, melted into the background.

"Are you alone?" Dean asked.

"Yeah, I just came into another room," Brett replied. "We can talk."

"Look, I'm sorry you're in the middle of all this. I shouldn't have agreed to those holiday public appearances in the first place. It was stupid and shortsighted on my part. How is Damian doing?"

"He's fine," Brett said. "He's stuffing his face with the best cherry pie you've ever seen."

"So, he's still having a good time?" Dean asked.

"Yes, he'll be okay," Brett replied. "Cards

on the table, he likes Emaline a lot. She's been very kind to him."

Dean sighed. "I hate this job sometimes. If the media didn't care about us, the kids would have less complicated lives."

"Pennsylvania needs a guy who hates the job sometimes," Brett replied.

"I guess so. Anyway, I called to tell you I just got off the phone with the lawyer. They read the article and said that we can sue the paper for slander, sloppy investigation and outright lying."

"Or…" Brett swallowed. "We could just tell people the truth. The story is out there. There are voters who will believe the worst of us if you simply deny it all. But if we told them the truth, that I'm Damian's—"

"Quiet." Dean's voice was commanding. "Don't even say that over the phone."

"But you know what I mean."

"Or, I could sue the paper and the journalists for everything they've got," Dean said. "There have to be consequences for these things. You can't have a newspaper that just slices into a person's life, gets it wrong, ruins their public image, and then waltzes off with no consequences. I want to make an example of this one, and I won't be pressured into revealing personal information to the world at large. That's extortion."

"Can you leave Emaline out of it, at least? Dean, she tried to stop the story from coming out."

"I don't believe that. She stands to gain the most from this. She just made her career."

"When this hits the fan, this will do more harm than good for her career. It wasn't true, and it'll come out that it wasn't true. Her name is all over it."

"A retraction on page six, so to speak," his brother replied. "If they force us to expose all our personal information, then they win. I won't do it."

"You don't have to sue the journalists, either," Brett said.

"One journalist in particular, you mean," Dean said dryly. "She's good, I'll give her that. But she's not the innocent you think she is."

"I'll put it to you this way, I won't cooperate with any lawsuit."

"I don't need you to. It's a false story plastered on all the major news networks. That's on her. I want these media professionals to think twice before they go after a family for no good reason."

Brett's blood simmered in anger. Wasn't this the way it always was?

"She's not what you think she is," Brett hissed.

"Brett, I'm looking out for you, too," Dean said. "Now let's not fight about this. I'll take care of things with the lawyers, and you take Damian to your place. I've got…let's see… three hours until the chopper takes me into the military base for a carol singing thing, and I need to get a bit of sleep first. I look haggard."

"That'll never do," Brett said dryly.

"I know, I know…" There was a smile in Dean's voice. "Look, Brett. I need you in order to keep my feet on the ground. You're part of the success here. And Damian needs his uncle, this Christmas more than ever."

That was the soft spot that Dean always hit, and it worked.

"I know. I'll get him to the ranch. Oh, and remind me that we need to talk about that school he's attending."

"Woodhaven? That's a great school."

"He's pretty miserable there. Also, he needs a horse. I'm happy to keep it on the ranch for him, but it has to be his, and he needs time with it on the regular."

There was a noticeable pause. Brett hadn't

done this before—insisted upon anything for his son. He'd always trusted Dean to know better than he would, anyway. But Dean was missing a few things.

"I'll talk to Bobbie and see what she thinks," Dean said. "We'll talk about it later."

Back off. That was the message.

"Look, I'll talk to you later," Dean said. "And thank you for everything you're doing here, Brett. I really appreciate you."

There was a time not so long ago when Brett had been the family problem. Now he was appreciated for all he contributed. It had been a tough climb from the gutter up to respectability. How much longer was that going to last now that Dean had figured out that Brett had fallen for that problematic vlogger?

CHAPTER FOURTEEN

EMALINE WENT UPSTAIRS and shut her bedroom door behind her. Below, she could hear the thump and scrape of Belinda adding more wood to the fire. She rubbed her hands over her face and sank onto the side of the bed. She just needed a few minutes to herself to process all of this...

Her article had come out, her friend had ignored her warning and they were both in a great deal of trouble. The story was wrong, and Dean Rockwell was litigious. Here was hoping the senator let this one go, but it was personal, and she didn't think he would.

And add to that, she'd just kissed Brett. Again.

"What are you doing?" she whispered to herself.

This B&B made it feel like the real world and its consequences were very far away, but that wasn't true. There were much bigger problems right now than runaway donkeys and an elderly woman who didn't know how she felt about her suitor.

But that kiss was burning in her mind more than anything else right now. He'd kissed her…and she'd kissed him back. It was like their lips were meant for each other, and she wanted a chance to slip into his arms again.

Which was utter foolishness, of course. She'd never been the type to be attracted to the wrong kind of guy. She'd always been careful that way—her family history made her unwilling to take romantic risks of any kind. And yet here she was thinking about kissing Brett Rockwell again!

It was more than attraction. She'd caught feelings for the man.

Damian wasn't supposed to talk to her, and Emaline just didn't have it in her to sit downstairs with a little boy who'd very obediently remain silent and an old woman who'd likely ask questions. So she stayed on the edge of the bed for a few more minutes, trying to find some sense of calm.

After a short time, she realized that the house was silent. She went down to the kitchen to investigate.

"Oh, there you are," Belinda said, turning with a smile. "Are you hungry?"

"Not really," Emaline said. "But thanks."

"How are you doing?" Belinda asked.

"Fine." Because that was the only answer she could politely give.

"I didn't mean to spy on you, but I looked out the window and...I saw that kiss." Belinda's eyes sparkled.

"Oh, that..." Emaline felt her cheeks heat. "That was wildly inappropriate."

"Did you know I'm a matchmaker?" Belinda said. "I have to tell you, when I introduce two people who have a spark like I witnessed out that window, I consider myself a wild success."

"It was only a kiss," Emaline hedged.

"Was it?" Belinda's voice softened.

Emaline sighed. "Maybe it was more than that. The thing is, there's a pretty intense connection between me and Brett, and he has surprisingly strong character. That's what makes me...feel what I do." How could she say that to an elderly Amish woman? "But we can't get involved. Not seriously. It's better not to start anything if we know there's no future."

"I agree," Belinda replied soberly. "We don't play with romance here. We believe in deep, abiding love and lasting marriages. And our young people marry early. But I've noticed that the best couples are the ones who were once convinced it could never work."

"I imagine the worst couples didn't listen to their better instincts," Emaline said.

Belinda chuckled. "True enough. Hindsight is clearest. But if it helps you at all, if you and Brett were an Amish couple, I'd say you had a good chance of working out."

"Except that he comes from a political family, and I'm aiming at becoming a reporter," Emaline said. "His family would never support this relationship, and I'm not sure I could continue with my goal if I am with him—not in good conscience, at least."

"Hmm." Belinda nodded. "That does complicate it."

"So, you see..." Emaline wasn't sure if she wanted the old woman to see her point of view on this or not. There was something comforting in determined Amish optimism.

"It would require sacrifice," Belinda finished for her.

Too much sacrifice. She'd been silly to let herself feel anything more for Brett. She'd known exactly where this stood from the start. The frustrating part was that Emaline was supposed to be emotionally tougher than this, and she hated proving George's previous instincts about her right, that she didn't have a thick enough skin.

"Is Damian hungry?" Belinda asked suddenly.

Emaline looked around and then went to the window. She scanned the empty yard.

"I don't know. Where is he?" Emaline asked.

She went to the sitting room next and poked her head inside. It was empty. Footsteps knocked against the stairs outside, and she heard someone come inside with a rush of cold air. She glanced into the mudroom, and it was Brett. He shot her a rueful smile.

"Hi," he said.

"Is Damian with you?" Emaline asked.

Brett's smile dropped. "No. He was inside."

"Maybe he's somewhere in the house," Belinda offered. "*Kinner* do love to explore the rooms upstairs."

"Damian!" Brett's voice boomed. "Where are you?"

They all froze and waited, but there was no response, no shuffle of feet to betray where the boy was.

"I'll go look upstairs," Emaline said.

"I'll come with you," Belinda added.

They went together, and between the two of them, they searched each room quickly. Amish furniture tended to be solid and sparse, leaving few places for a child to hide. They went back downstairs just as Brett came up from the basement.

"Did you find him?" Brett asked.

"No." Emaline's stomach knotted. That child had been told to be wary of her by his father…and maybe he'd overheard more of the truth, too. How would a five-year-old process it if he found out his uncle was really his birth father? Would he understand that? Or would it just be the incredible tension that had suddenly erupted that spooked the kid?

"Oh, he must have gone back outside to play," Belinda said, poking her head into the mudroom. "His boots and coat are gone."

"He must have," Brett said. "I'll just go find him."

Brett headed back outside. Emaline waited for about five minutes, listening to the distant sound of Brett calling Damian's name. She took another look upstairs, poked her head into the sitting room, into the hallway closet. Where was he?

After another few minutes, Emaline decided to help look outside. She put on her winter clothes and headed around the side of the house, past an empty garden plot, all the way over to the edge of the property. She followed a sagging fence and saw a frozen-over pond beyond. There were a few footprints this far, but they looked like men's boots. When she came back to the front of the house, Brett was just returning from the property next door, Eli in tow and Hund loping along ahead of them.

"Any luck?" Emaline called.

"No," Brett replied, picking up his pace.

"A boy that size couldn't get too far," Eli said. "He's probably playing with something or found an animal. I once worried my family sick when I discovered a little nest of hibernating mice in a field. I watched them sleeping for hours, apparently. My mother threatened to put a bell around my neck."

Emaline smiled faintly. It would be a funny story if they weren't facing their own missing kid.

"Where could he have gone?" Brett asked. "I mean, there's plenty of undisturbed snow, so we know which ways he didn't go. And we've checked everywhere else."

Emaline shook her head. "Doesn't he like to hide if he's upset about something?"

Brett bit his lip. "You're right, he hides from his teaching assistant at school sometimes."

Hund sniffed along the drive, and Emaline looked hopefully in that direction, but then the dog stopped to pee, and she sighed.

"Damian!" Brett called.

"Damian?" Emaline echoed. "We're getting worried, kiddo! Your uncle needs you to answer him!"

"It's getting late," Eli said. "The sun will set in a couple of hours."

There wasn't too much trouble the boy could get into now, but when the sun set, he'd be alone and in the dark. Anything could happen.

"Shoot…" Brett said, squeezing his eyes shut for a moment. Then he opened them.

"I'll check the barn again," Eli said, heading off with Hund.

"And I've got to call Dean. He might have a better idea than I do about where he might hide."

Brett deflated just a little bit.

"It takes a team sometimes," Emaline said.

"Yeah." She heard the defeat in his voice. He'd tried—she knew how hard he'd tried to step up this Christmas and be the dad he could never admit he was.

And he opened his phone.

BRETT'S CONVERSATION WITH his brother was short. Once Brett explained that after the talk about Emaline, Damian had disappeared, Dean had gone into general mode. He barked the pertinent details to Bobbie whose response was a terse, "What? Again?"

"I'm canceling tonight's meet and greet," Dean said. "We'll get our pilot to take the helicopter there. Is there a field or something by the house?"

"Of course," Brett said.

"Good. It'll take us probably an hour and a half to rustle up the pilot and get down there, but we'll be there soon enough. The more eyes looking for Damian, the better."

"Any idea of where he'd go?" Brett asked. "He hides sometimes, right?"

"Yes. One time, he left school property and tried to come home," Bobbie said. The call was obviously now on speaker. "We found him three miles down the road."

"We're still snowed in. I can't get the truck out over a massive snow bank in front of the drive, so I can't imagine he's made it to the road," Brett said.

"We'll see more from the sky anyway," Dean said. "I'm on my way. My pilot will get us there. Call me if there are any updates, and it would help if you could put something bright and colorful into a tree for us to spot from the air."

"Will do. And Dean, I'm sorry. This is my fault."

"Placing blame wastes time," Dean said.

"Let's just be thankful I've got the chopper so we can get Damian home where he belongs."

Home. Brett could tell that didn't mean his ranch. The pre-Christmas visit with Uncle Brett was canceled, it would seem, and Brett couldn't blame his brother. He was blaming himself. Brett should have kept a closer eye on the kid. He should have known that his brother's heavy-handed insistence that Damian not say another word to Emaline would be too much. And he shouldn't have been outside kissing her instead of watching Damian.

That had been stupid on his part, and selfish. Getting her into his arms had been a wild and strange relief. It wasn't smart, and his entire family would give him a tongue lashing for it. And...it might have been what had spooked Damian, too. What exactly had upset the boy? There were several excellent options to choose from, and Brett felt responsible for all of them.

"Where is that blasted donkey?" Eli shouted, and Brett and Emaline both looked over in surprise to where Eli stood in the stable doorway.

"Eli?" Belinda's voice from the doorway sounded scandalized. "That language!"

"He's gone, too!" Eli said.

"Do you think Damian is with Eeyore?" Emaline asked, and Brett looked down at her.

"If he's with the donkey, I'll actually feel better," Brett replied. "A donkey can't hide quite as well as a kid can."

"You'd think," Eli retorted. "But that donkey has a knack for it. All the same, if they're together, Eeyore will protect him. Donkeys are incredible guard animals. Most farmers get a donkey for that job, exactly."

It did make Brett feel a little better.

"We'd better not waste daylight," Eli said. "I'm going to go up the road past my place and see if I can't see him. I'll get some neighbors to take their buggies up the roads, too."

"Thank you," Brett said.

"Not a problem," Eli replied. "This is what community is for."

Belinda stood in the doorway of the house, a shawl pulled tightly around her shoulders.

"I'm going to stay here in case he comes back," Belinda called. "I'll take another couple of turns around the outside of the house, too."

"Where should I go?" Emaline asked.

"My brother said he's run off before," Brett said. "He stuck to a road that time and just kept walking, so maybe if you could go down the road in the other direction? If there are footprints, they might be his."

"The road ends about a mile that way," Eli said. "But he wouldn't know that."

"I'll go that way," Emaline said, and she met Brett's gaze worriedly. "We'll find him, Brett."

"Where will you go?" Eli asked.

Brett let out a slow breath. "If I was a five-year-old kid, I'd head for the next farm. It's something to aim for. If you don't mind, Eli, I'm going to take another look around your place."

"Feel free," Eli replied.

They'd already gone over it—the stable, the barn, the house, the chicken coop... It wasn't a big farm, but there were enough sheds and shelters over there.

"But first I have to see if Belinda will put something brightly colored over those apple trees. Something that will stand out in the snow."

Belinda was happy to oblige with a basket of brightly colored, knitted scarves. For the better part of the next hour, Brett searched the outbuildings around the ranch. There was a covered area where large bales of hay were stored, and he searched around those to no avail. Then there was an outhouse, an old chicken coop, a new chicken coop, and Brett went into the house, and even down into the musty, unfinished basement that was dim and creepy.

"Damian? It's me, buddy!"

Nothing. But Brett knew in his gut that if it were him, he'd have angled for this farm. And if there was any link between Brett and his son, maybe Damian would, too.

Brett headed back out of the house and stood in the snowy farmyard listening to the soft cluck of poultry. His gaze swung over the now familiar structures, shadows stretching long. It was then he spotted the stable door open just a crack. They certainly hadn't left it that way.

Brett picked up his pace and headed over in that direction. He pulled open the squeaking door and squinted, looking inside. Eeyore stood in the aisle between the two rows of stalls. He was munching out of another animal's manger.

"Damian," Brett said quietly. "I know you're here."

Damian's small pale face emerged from behind the donkey. Brett blinked back a mist of tears.

"Hi, Uncle Brett."

"There you are..." he said. "Why are you over here? You worried us sick."

Damian didn't answer.

"Did you take Eeyore out of the stable?"

The boy nodded.

"Did you think you'd be in trouble for that?"

Still silent. Brett hadn't hit on the reason he'd run yet. "Come here, kiddo." He held out a hand, and Damian came past the donkey, stopping behind Eeyore's back flank, and Brett instinctively grabbed Damian's arm and tugged him to a safe distance.

"You can't stand behind a donkey like that," Brett said. "You'll get kicked."

Damian looked back at Eeyore. "No, he won't kick me."

Forget it. That was an argument for another day. "Your parents are on their way."

Damian stared at him.

"I'd better call them and tell them I found you. They took the chopper, you know."

"Uh-oh," Damian said. "I'm in trouble."

"No, *I'm* in trouble," Brett replied. "Hold on."

He dialed his brother's number, and when he picked up, Brett could hear chopper blades in the background.

"I found him!" Brett said loudly into the phone.

"You found him?" his brother shouted back. "We're almost there anyway. See you soon!"

That had been loud enough for Damian to hear, and he looked worried.

"Damian, we all love you very much. We were really scared something bad might happen to you. You can't just run off like that."

"My dad is mad at me..." Damian whispered, and tears welled up in his eyes.

"He's mad at *me*, not you."

"No, he's mad at me," Damian said. "He was mad I talked to Emaline. And he was mad at Emaline, too. And he said I need to grow up and learn to obey." His voice shook and tears slipped down his cheeks.

"Oh..." Brett sighed. This was it—the trigger that had sent Damian running. "Look, sometimes when a guy gets scared, he sounds really mad, and that's what happened with your dad. He said something without thinking. He doesn't really think that you need to grow up. You're five! He knows that. He was just scared because stuff felt like it was getting out of control."

"But he yelled at me!" Damian hiccupped.

Brett doubted he'd yelled, but he'd probably raised his voice a bit. Brett said, "And he'll say he's sorry for that. You know him. He always says he's sorry if he raises his voice, doesn't he?"

Damian nodded.

"He knows how much you hate that and how hard that is for you. In fact, your dad was so scared something happened to you that he jumped in the helicopter to come look for you. He loves you. You know that."

"Is everyone mad at me now?"

"Come here…" Brett pulled the boy into his arms and gave him a long hug. "You are not replaceable, okay? We only have one of you."

Damian smiled tearily at the old joke. "Okay."

"Now, let me text Emaline and tell her to stop looking. We'll have to go find old Eli and the neighbors he roped in to help look for you."

"Eli, too?" Damian's eyes widened.

"More people than you will ever know really care about you," Brett said softly. "People who have never met you would want to help find you. You're very special."

Brett shot a text to Emaline.

I found him. He was in the stable.

Thank you for looking, and for helping out with this, for…everything.

He wasn't eloquent at the best of times, and typing on a phone didn't help much. A moment later, a text from her came back.

Oh, thank God.

There were three dots indicating that she was typing again, and he waited, but then they disappeared. Maybe she wasn't at her best with texting, either. Then another message popped up.

For you, anything.

He couldn't help the smile that toyed at his lips. He felt the same way.

"Come on," Brett said. "We'd better get back to the B&B. But first, I'm just going to lock Eeyore into a stall here. He's got a bit of an escape artist reputation around here, and I'd hate to lose the donkey after all of this."

Brett put Eeyore into a stall, and overhead he heard the whooshing blades of the chopper. Dean was here.

Brett led Damian outside, and they both shaded their eyes against the last of the sunlight on the horizon as a helicopter landed out on the field just beyond the house.

"Daddy's here," Damian said softly, and when Brett looked down at the boy, he had a hopeful little smile on his face.

It was almost Christmas, and Damian was going to spend this time with his parents, after all. Brett was never going to be enough, was he? He shouldn't be surprised. Dean and Bobbie had raised Damian, and good old Uncle Brett, a pile of gifts and a sincere belief in Santa Claus was never going to be enough to fill that little heart on Christmas morning.

It had been Dean and Bobbie for this kid from the start.

CHAPTER FIFTEEN

THE CHOPPING SOUND of helicopter blades roared through the house, and Belinda put her hands over her ears.

"What is that?" Eli exclaimed, clomping over to the window, his boots still on his feet, and little bits of snow melting on the floor around him.

Emaline and Belinda joined him at the window, watching as a man and a woman ducked out of the helicopter while the blades still spun overhead, whipping up the snow in the low rosy sunset light. She recognized the senator, looking cool and photogenic in a bomber jacket. He reached back to the woman behind him—Emaline recognized Bobbie, too—and she caught his hand as they jogged clear of the helicopter. They were here. Thank goodness Brett had found Damian.

There was a small nagging part of Emaline's heart that longed to get video of this. The senator and his wife flying in to see their young son. Not only would the clip be phenomenal in this lighting, but there would be the heart element, too. There'd be the breaking story of the senator's missing son and how he was found, maybe a little sound bite of Damian describing what it felt like to be lost and how glad he was to see his parents again. It would top the news channels for the next cycle, and it was guaranteed to go viral.

Emaline pulled out her phone and centered the shot—the rosy sunset in the background, the helicopter silhouetted, the senator and his wife marching forward with their heads down against the whirling snow, but something kept her from pressing Record. She slipped her phone back into her pocket. No, it felt wrong.

And there was the matter of that article that came out today—the article that the senator and his wife knew about. Her stomach knotted.

A tougher reporter than her would be silently celebrating her position right in the middle of this senator's family drama, but this was about more than news. Brett and Damian came marching from the other direction, and Emaline felt a rush of relief. The boy broke free of Brett and ran for his mother's arms.

"I'm so glad Brett was able to find him," Belinda murmured. "That poor boy."

"That little rascal," Eli countered with a

shake of his head. "He should have been taught better than to run off like that. I did that as a child, and I was lectured within an inch of my life and given all the dishwashing to do for a month! That's what I'd do if I was raising him."

"Then he should be glad you aren't raising him," Belinda said ruefully.

Eli muttered something in Pennsylvania Dutch, but Belinda only chuckled.

Outside the window, Bobbie sank to her knees and gathered Damian up in a hug. Even from this distance, Emaline could see the relief, the love, the parental protectiveness in that embrace, and her throat tightened with emotion.

"My, my, my…" Belinda murmured. "I've never in my life had a helicopter land on my property, and I don't believe I'll see it again."

"And a senator on your property, to boot," Eli said.

"We don't bother about those titles and positions, Eli," Belinda said.

"No, we don't…" Eli agreed, but Emaline could hear the wistfulness in his tone all the same. Eli was impressed.

"They're just like us," Belinda added. She must have heard his tone, too. "We all breathe the same air, require the same amount of food, water and exercise. We all need love and affection."

"Indeed, we do," Eli said meaningfully.

Outside the window, Dean, Bobbie, Brett and Damian were coming toward the house now, and Emaline's heartbeat stuttered in her chest.

"Oh, they're coming in," Belinda said, and she bustled over to the kitchen, opening cupboards and pulling down plates. "They'll be hungry, I'm sure. Eli, help me get the pies on the table, would you?"

The two old people seemed to work well together—almost instinctively. Eli went to the counter and uncovered two pies. He mutely accepted the serving utensils and carried the first pie to the table.

The side door opened then, and there was the stomp of boots and the murmur of voices, and Damian's piping chatter about Eeyore the donkey, who he loved more than anything.

"Where is the donkey?" Eli asked as Brett came into the room first.

"In your stable," Brett replied. "Locked up tight." He looked over his shoulder. Damian was now at his mother's side. The senator came into the room next, his gaze sweeping over the kitchen and landing on Emaline. His eyes narrowed just a little. He knew exactly who she was, she could tell.

"Mrs. Wickey, we'd like to pay you for the trouble these last few days," Bobbie said. "And for your discretion, please, if anyone wants to make a news story out of this."

Bobbie's icy gaze fell on Emaline next.

"Oh, it's not a bother, dear," Belinda said. "Damian has been a real delight, and the storms come when they come, don't they? There's not much that can be done but settle in and wait it out. I've got pie if you're all hungry."

"Thank you, Mrs. Wickey." Bobbie smiled warmly, shook the old woman's hand. "I'd love some pie. I haven't eaten in hours."

Emaline looked mutely at Brett where he stood apart from his brother and sister-in-law just a little bit. The political couple seemed to emanate energy, and she could see a change in Brett's dark eyes. He looked sadder, a little more distant. Damian was now plastered to Dean's side, and Brett had fallen into the background in some unexplainable way. He wasn't part of that bond.

She noticed that Brett didn't move toward her, either. He stood alone, like an island.

"But first," Bobbie said, turning to face Emaline. "I'd like a word with Miss Piper."

Emaline swallowed. "All right."

"In the other room, if you don't mind." Bobbie angled her head toward the sitting room, and Emaline looked at Belinda for permission. Half of her wished the old woman would deny it.

"*Yah*, of course," Belinda murmured.

Emaline was about to be lectured, and she led the way into the other room. It was the only upper hand she'd likely get, and when she turned, she found Bobbie Rockwell eyeing her in much the same way an eagle eyed a mouse.

"Emaline Piper," Bobbie said softly. "I'm Roberta Rockwell."

"Yes, I know," Emaline said.

"You wrote a vicious story about my family," Bobbie went on quietly. "One with no truth to it."

"That was a mistake," Emaline said.

"Ah." Bobbie pressed her lips together, her tone mild. "Was it, now?"

"It was released by accident," Emaline said. "It was only supposed to be a writing sample."

"No news story is released by accident. There are too many eyes that go over it, too many signatures needed before it sees daylight."

What was she supposed to tell this woman?

"There will be a retraction," Emaline said. "I'll write it myself."

"So, you knew it was false."

"I know *now*," Emaline clarified.

"My husband wants to sue you for everything you own and your paper, too," Bobbie said. "I dare say we'd win."

Emaline licked at her dry lips. Again, what could she say? The Rockwells would be within their rights to do just that.

"Brett pleaded for you, you should know," Bobbie went on. "He wants us to leave you alone."

"I'd be grateful for that," Emaline said with a weak smile.

"So, despite what you wrote, what you had published for the world to read, you now know that my husband did not cheat on me?" Bobbie said. "That he did not father a child with an aide, that he did not threaten a woman into giving up her newborn baby, and he did not hide some lurid secret from the public."

"Yes, ma'am," Emaline said. "I know that. Brett explained."

"I thought so…" She sighed, as if this was some confirmation she was looking for. "If it matters at all to you, we kept this private for our own reasons."

"Brett told me," Emaline said. "The full truth. What you did for him."

Bobbie took that in, surprise flickering over

her face for just a moment. "Well then. You know it's his story to tell, his son who needed a home and his personal addictions that kept him from being able to step up. And we didn't want the press running wild with that."

"I can see why," Emaline replied. "But you have to understand that all the signs seemed to point to something else, and no one would say anything, even in your defense!"

"And if you discovered that my husband had cheated on me, that would be the business of the people of Pennsylvania?" Bobbie asked.

"It would show them who they were voting for," Emaline replied.

"Because his personal life—*my* personal life—is more important than how he does the job?" she asked. "My privacy, my family, my marriage, my children...all of that is more important than how Dean runs the state? We're talking schools, roads, emergency response, laws..."

"It isn't personal," Emaline said.

"It never is—not to you," Bobbie snapped. "But it is to *me*! My husband runs the state, but there are people who have much more personal access to your life. Your accountant, for example. That is a person who looks into the minute details of your finances. Do you do this kind of careful vetting of your accountant or your investment specialist? Do you ask if that person has been faithful to their spouse, if they're kind to their children?"

Emaline swallowed. "No."

"No, you don't," Bobbie said. "Because it doesn't matter. If the banker knows how to invest your money or how to arrange your finances for your success—that's all that matters!"

"Mrs. Rockwell, I am deeply sorry for my mistake," Emaline said. "I know that your husband did nothing wrong, and I will write a retraction. I want to be the one to do that not just to atone here but because it's got to be worded carefully. I have to say that I know I was wrong but that I will not divulge the reason why I know it to be false. That's going to attract attention. Other reporters aren't going to leave this alone. I wasn't the only one on the scent there. But I won't be the one to tell your story. I can promise you that. If you and your husband decide to tell the truth about Damian's birth, or not, that will be up to you."

Bobbie looked over her shoulder toward the kitchen, and her eyes misted. She clenched her jaw and then turned back to Emaline.

"You've already done the damage," Bobbie said. "Do you know who this will hurt in the end? My son. Damian. He didn't ask for any of this. None of our kids did. They're just children growing up in a complicated world like everyone else's kids. But my kids are targeted."

Emaline had thought she'd been chasing down the truth, when all she'd really been running after was a story. It had been a mistake. The world was a bitter place where powerful men got away with all sorts of travesties. And yet this time, that hadn't been the case.

"What do you want me to do?" Emaline asked.

"I don't know yet," Bobbie said. "Maybe I just wanted you to look me in the face."

Emaline sucked in a wavering breath. Was Emaline about to be crushed under the Rockwell machine? She wouldn't be the first, or the last, she was sure...

But she also felt terrible for the damage she'd inadvertently done.

Brett had defended her, though, and that thought was a small consolation. At least Brett knew that she'd done her best. He seemed to recognize the real her—principled, honest, determined—just like she saw the real him underneath the armor of his family.

Maybe Emaline just wanted to be seen, too.

BRETT LOOKED TOWARD the sitting room. The women were in there, and he wondered if Emaline needed his help. But if he went in there, it wouldn't make things better. Bobbie was angry—he knew that—but she was also fair. If she thought Brett was under Emaline's sway, she'd go for the jugular. But if Bobbie just saw the Emaline he'd gotten to know, she'd see what he had. She might have some mercy, too.

"I should go bring Eeyore back," Eli said. "It's getting late. I like to leave things in order."

"I can do that," Brett said.

"I'll come with you," Dean replied.

"Forgive me, Senator, but are you used to farm life?" Eli asked. "It's bitterly cold out there, and you might be better by the fire for now."

"Sir, I just about grew up on a farm." Dean's drawl got more pronounced when he talked about his salt-of-the-earth experiences in childhood. "Our family owns a ranch."

"I own a ranch," Brett clarified, his voice low.

"The family ranch, yes." Dean met his gaze. *Very nice, Dean*, Brett thought. *Rub in that everything I have is from the family coffers.*

Brett was in no mood to bicker with his brother, no matter how much tension filled this room. He headed for the mudroom to get ready, his brother right behind him. Dean's boots were expensive leather hiking boots, not exactly right for a farm, but he'd stay warm enough out there.

"You'll need this," Eli said, handing over a kerosene lantern. "You two seem determined. I'll leave you to it."

"Thanks, Eli," Brett said, and the old man gave him a knowing nod. Maybe Eli knew a thing or two about brotherly dynamics, too.

Brett headed outside, the soft glow of the lantern shedding a circle of light around him in the twilight. His brother came out behind him and slammed the door solidly shut.

"Damian was talking about that donkey," Dean said. "I wonder if these people would sell him to us."

"I don't think so," Brett replied. "Belinda is very attached to him. Besides, he's a real escape artist. More than you could handle, I'm sure."

"I wouldn't be handling him. I'd have him boarded somewhere."

"He's an emotionally complicated donkey. I don't think he'd like it." Brett's boots crunched through the snow. "You don't just buy an animal like that and stick him in some boarding barn."

"You're the one who said Damian could use a horse."

"A horse! Not a donkey that belongs to someone else!" Brett shook his head and tried not to grit his teeth as they headed past Belinda's stable.

"What exactly is the problem here?" Dean demanded. "I'm trying to see things from your perspective, but I fail to see how I'm the bad guy here."

"You aren't."

"Then why are you ready to spit nails?"

Brett headed through the gate that joined the two properties—a new addition by the looks of things. The problem was that Dean hadn't done anything wrong. Not more than usual. Was he frustrating sometimes? Sure, but that wasn't it.

"I'm tired of being Uncle Brett." His voice was low, but it carried.

"What do you mean?" Dean asked.

"To my son."

The only sound was boots in snow for the next few beats, then Dean said, "This was your idea."

"Yeah. And five years ago, I couldn't be a dad."

"You can't just change your mind after a legal adoption," Dean said. "We've raised him and loved him from the beginning. That boy is every bit our son in every way that matters."

"I'm not suggesting I take him away," Brett said, stealing a look at his brother from the corner of his eye. Dean looked grim. "I'm saying that just being an uncle who comes by once in a while is getting…painful."

"What do you suggest?" Dean demanded.

"I don't know!" Brett stopped and turned to face his brother. "But I'm not the same guy I was five years ago. I'm not just hanging out on the family land, I'm running the ranch, and Mom signed it over to me. I'm not just some guy who can't get his act together enough to raise a child anymore. I think you need to acknowledge that."

"You think I don't?" Dean demanded. "I sent my son to stay with you for the week before Christmas. If that isn't a vote of confidence, I don't know what is! You're not the same guy. You help me out in a myriad of ways. We're very much a team."

"A team for your career," Brett said. "I'm on the train for your success."

"Our family's success," his brother countered.

"Yours, Dean." Brett sighed. "Look, it's been getting harder for me. I want to stay away from politics, I want to get to know my son better. Damian is a good kid, but I can't just stand back anymore. You're his dad, Dean. You're the one he knows, but it doesn't negate that I'm his father. Biology counts, too."

"You asked me to adopt your son," Dean said, his voice low. "You asked me to raise him as my own and never tell him otherwise. Bobbie and I stayed up nights with him, walked the living room with him when he was colicky and let him chew on our fingers when he was teething. We raised him and loved him and provided for him and sacrificed for him. He's our son now."

"But every adopted kid comes with bio parents," Brett said. "I think Damian's heart will be big enough to hold the both of us. I really do."

Dean shook his head. "I don't think he'll understand this."

"The longer we wait, the harder it'll be on him," Brett said. "He looks just like us, Dean. He's a Rockwell, and people are already piecing that together. He looks like a Rockwell, and it wasn't Emaline's fault for digging into that. When your adopted son looks just like you, people ask questions, and not just journalists. How long until Damian's old enough that his classmates start googling pictures of you when you were younger? How are you going to explain that to him when he's twelve or thirteen? At that age, kids hold grudges."

"Bobbie will never agree," Dean said.

"She might," Brett replied. "She's logical, and she's smarter than the two of us put together. I think she'll see that a lot of this is unavoidable."

They started across Eli's farmyard, past the coop with the low comfortable chortle of hens inside and past the dark house. The light from the lantern cut through the growing darkness toward the stable.

"What changed?" Dean asked.

"Me," Brett replied. "A little bit at a time, but it was me who changed. I grew. I healed. I stayed clean. This isn't a sign of weakness on my part, Dean. I'm capable of being a dad now. I'm not saying I can be like you to Damian. I'm not asking to take him away from you. I just need to have a truer relationship with him. I'm just saying…'Hey, it's Uncle Brett!' isn't going to be enough anymore. I'd rather have Damian know that I'm his father than have him question his entire life why the details don't quite add up."

"And if he's angry at you for giving him up?" Dean asked. "That's a possibility, you know. This could be a minefield. He's already struggling with school. This would be one more confusing thing he'd have to deal with."

"I know it's been tough for him—"

"Then why make it harder for him?" Dean asked. "You asked me to raise him. Am I letting you down in any way? Am I doing a bad job? Is Damian unloved? Is he missing out on anything?"

"You're a great dad," Brett said.

"Then?"

"Maybe I'd be great, too, as a biological father who still cares, and who might be able to give Damian a little more support on the side. Maybe it would confuse him a bit, but what if it didn't? What if it made him stronger?"

Dean was silent.

"We only have so much time until he's grown up, Dean. This is uncomfortable—I get that. But time slips away, and kids grow up. He'll find out about me eventually—there's no avoiding that when he looks just like us. We can't mess this up."

And for the first time in a really long time, Brett felt ready for it. Maybe his brother wasn't. Maybe his brother's career wasn't ready for it! Maybe Bobbie wasn't going to be ready, but Brett was. And that was going to have to change things around here. Because at the heart of this family was a little boy who needed support, stability and a whole lot of love.

For a long time, Brett had felt like he could only provide the love part of Damian's needs, but he could give all of it now—in an appropriate way that honored Dean and Bobbie's family with him, too. But at long last, Brett wasn't looking at his son through the lens of his own limitations.

Brett and Dean led Eeyore back through the snow to his familiar stable on Belinda's property, where Eli met them. The old man took over and got Eeyore settled in his stall next to the big quarter horse. Bobbie and Damian came outside, both dressed in their winter gear, and Damian with his headphones in one hand.

"Are you going somewhere?" Brett asked.

"We're taking him home," Bobbie said. "We were wrong to do those meet and greets over the holidays. Dean can finish it up if he feels he needs to, but I'll be taking Damian home."

"Santa will know where to find me," Damian said.

"He sure will." Bobbie smiled tenderly down at him.

Brett felt a lump rise in his throat, and he

gave Damian a sympathetic look. "It was a weird trip, huh?"

"I had fun," Damian said. "We had the donkey indoors!"

"Yeah, that was something."

But Brett could see Damian leaning toward Bobbie, one thin shoulder resting against her hip.

"Since we flew all the way out here, I don't think I could leave without my son," Dean said, then he flashed Brett an apologetic look. "Bobbie and I will talk, okay?"

"Thanks."

It was something.

"Go give Uncle Brett a hug goodbye," Bobbie said, and Damian came for a quick hug and then pulled away again, putting his headphones back on. Then the side door opened and Belinda came outside. The wind tugged at the shawl she'd wrapped around herself, but she tramped through the snow toward them anyway.

"Miss Belinda?" Damian said, going over to the old woman. He tugged on her shawl and she bent down a little. "I need to tell you that I tried to be very good this year. I did try."

"I know, little one," she said with a sparkle in her eye, and she tapped the side of her nose.

"I've taken note. And you not only tried, you succeeded. Don't you worry."

Damian beamed, and he pulled his headphones back up again.

Brett looked toward the little house, and he could see Emaline in the kitchen window. Their eyes met and a sweet smile touched her lips making him suddenly feel a well of hope.

A lot had transpired between them. Could any of it last?

"I'll talk to you later," Dean said, clapping Brett on the shoulder. "Thank you for taking Damian for a few days. Don't worry about him running away, okay? It was my own fault for even trying this. I guess it was too soon."

Right. Dean was closing that circle. He didn't want to start filling Damian in on his parentage just yet. But just because Dean wasn't ready didn't mean that the rest of the world wouldn't keep digging.

Maybe for the first time in a long time, Brett would stop dreading what they'd dig up.

Dean, Bobbie and Damian climbed into the helicopter, and the pilot slammed the doors shut, checked them twice and then headed for his own seat. The engine started and the blades started to turn.

"He thinks you're Mrs. Claus, Belinda,"

Brett said, raising his voice above the sound of the engine.

"I know, dear," Belinda said with a smile. "I didn't want to disappoint him."

Brett could have hugged her. She had a depth of compassion that they all needed right now. But instead, he stood there and watched as the helicopter took off and rose up into the sky. So much for a Christmas with his son.

CHAPTER SIXTEEN

THAT EVENING, Belinda and Eli went over to his property to check on the chickens. That was what they said, at least. Emaline had to wonder if they weren't leaving her and Brett alone to give them a bit of privacy.

The night was dark, and the kitchen was cozily warm with a newly stoked blaze in the potbellied stove. Brett had been quiet ever since Damian left with his parents, and Emaline had trouble reading what he was feeling. He'd put up a wall between them that felt personal, somehow. He stood by the window, his face reflected back at her in the glass.

"I'm sorry it turned out this way," she said. "I know you miss your son."

"My nephew."

"Your *son*," she said firmly. "Yes, your brother adopted him, but that doesn't make him any less yours."

Brett scrubbed a hand through his hair. "My brother was drawing a line tonight. I asked him if we could tell Damian who I really am, and he balked. He obviously has to discuss it with Bobbie, but I can tell he doesn't want to get into it with Damian."

"So, conversation over?" Emaline asked.

"What Dean wants, Dean gets. That's how our family works. He's the one who calls the shots."

Brett left the window and joined her at the stove. He held out his hands toward the black surface, and then he reached over and took her hand in his chilly fingers.

"I'm going to miss you," he said.

Her heart skipped a heavy beat, and she squeezed his hand in response. Whatever had developed here between them had been a surprise to them both. She'd have to leave all of this behind her, and she wondered if she'd ever be able to see Brett Rockwell in the papers again without feeling a stab of regret for how all of this had gone down.

"When are you leaving?" she asked.

"In the morning," he said. "I need to get back to the ranch. When are you going?"

"I'm leaving in the morning, too…" Maybe by the time she got back, the Rockwell legal team would have served her with papers already. She had no idea what to expect, but she knew she had to face it. "Real life awaits, huh?"

"Yeah…"

"Brett, if you're going to spend Christmas alone, why don't you come with me?" she asked.

"Where, to your mom's place?" A small smile tickled his lips.

"Yes. Why not?"

"I've got plans."

"Oh…"

"That came out more confidently than I meant," he said. "I have plans to sit alone and face reality. I think I need to do it. I need to figure out how I'm going to do things going forward."

"With Damian, you mean?"

He nodded. "He's not my legal son, but he's my kid, you know? I don't know if I can keep being good-time Uncle Brett. I'm not even sure it's good for Damian. But I did realize something—what Damian needs is going to have to come first. This isn't about how I feel."

"I think your feelings factor in," she countered.

"No, they don't." He sighed. "I saw him with Dean and Bobbie getting into the chopper. He needs his parents—and maybe Dean needs to have a few people he can lean on right now. What Damian needed this Christmas wasn't Uncle Brett. He needed his mom and dad here with him, celebrating with him, making him their priority, not the election."

"I think he needs you, too," she said.

Brett shook his head. "Less than I'd hoped."

"The truth matters, you know!" she said. "I know this isn't my business, but you are his biological father. You're the one who asked your brother to adopt him. You're the one who loved him enough to make sure he got everything he could possibly need and then stayed in close so that you'd make sure of it. At any point, you could have walked away, but you didn't! And that's all fact. It matters!"

Brett looked over at her, his eyes shining. "You think I'm a good guy."

"I do," she said. "I think you did the best you could and that your heart was in the right place all this time. I think you're a good man."

He lifted her fingers to his lips and pressed a soft kiss against them. "Thanks." He lowered her hand again. "You know what I used to tell Santa when I was Damian's age? That I'd done my best. And even when I wasn't like Dean, my grades weren't high, I couldn't charm a room like he could by the age of ten... Even when I was just living in my older brother's shadow, I told Santa that I'd done my best to be good." There were tears in his eyes when he looked up again. "Damian told

Belinda he'd been a good boy this year…" His voice caught.

"He thinks she's got Santa connections," she said softly.

"Yeah, but he needed someone to know he'd tried. That was important to him—the effort, how hard he tried. No one else really understands that. The world isn't easy for him. A guy never really grows out of needing someone to see that."

"I see it…" she whispered. He stepped a little closer and ran a finger down the side of her face.

He didn't say anything, but he dipped his head down, and his lips hovered over hers. Her heart hovered in anticipation, too. Then he closed the distance, and his mouth met hers. He kissed her with aching, heartbreaking slowness, and she leaned into his warm, gentle arms. She'd never been kissed like this before—like the entire universe spun on the axis of this one kiss… When he pulled back, her knees felt shaky.

"I wish this was only about what I wanted." His voice was husky.

"What do you want?" she whispered.

"You."

She smiled at that. "If only it were that simple."

"I know." He released her. "The thing is, Damian needs a solid, secure home with Dean and Bobbie. He needs to stay out of the papers, and he needs his parents to be focused on him. He needs—" he swallowed "—he needs less of me, and I've got to stop drawing attention to him."

"What are you trying to say?" she asked.

"I have to go back to my ranch and stay there. I need to keep my head down. For his sake."

Brett dropped his gaze.

"Do you want…company over there once in a while?" she asked.

"I can't, Em. I can't just keep doing this, no matter how much I want to. Dean and Bobbie aren't going to let Damian anywhere near me if I'm with you. That's just a fact. And when they travel, I need to be there for Damian. More than that, I have to keep my brother's trust. He runs the show. I might not like it, but it's how this works. I thought I was past attracting media attention, but clearly I'm not. I can't make my son's life harder. Right now, I have to disappear onto my ranch…alone."

"Is that what you want?" she whispered.

"No! It's not what I want! It's never about what I want!" he retorted. "It doesn't matter how I feel! It doesn't matter that I want my son to know me as his father. It doesn't matter that I've developed feelings for you!"

Emaline stared at him, her breath trapped in her throat.

Brett shook his head and heaved a sigh. "I didn't mean to say that part out loud."

"But you did…"

She'd been feeling this, too. She'd been feeling drawn to this stubborn, tough rancher with his playboy past, and she'd been trying to talk herself out of it. This couldn't work; they were from different worlds! Was that what this was…this pull toward him, this empathy for his heartbreak, this longing to see the man happy, this determination to make the world see him for who he really was?

"Look, Em, I don't know what this is, but I do feel it." He caught her hand again. "I'm not normally like this, and I'm still hoping if I go sit alone on my ranch that I'll become the same stonehearted stallion I used to be. So, yeah, I think I fell for you. I'm sorry if that's uncomfortable to hear."

"I fell, too." It came out before she could even think better of it.

"Yeah?" He searched her face, his gaze so bare and vulnerable that she could almost cry.

She nodded. "Yeah. You aren't the only one feeling this."

He pulled her back into his arms, and his lips came down over hers in a more passionate kiss this time—a kiss that she had to stop just to catch her breath. Looking up into his eyes, she wished more than anything that they could follow these feelings and see where they'd lead.

"Look, with that story, my hopes for getting into journalism are over," she breathed. "It's not going to happen for me. I need to focus on my vlogging and probably find a good defense lawyer for when your brother sues me. I need to protect myself, too."

And that was the problem. They were caught in this tangle of emotion, but she had to keep herself safe. The Rockwells were a powerful family, and she was in a dangerous position. A romance wasn't even feasible.

EMALINE'S WORDS STOPPED him short, and Brett straightened, pulling in a ragged breath. Her lips had felt so perfect against his. It was like she was made for him…in almost every way except perhaps the most important one. He couldn't be the reason she gave up her dreams. And he couldn't be with someone who'd tear his family apart, either. Real, intimate relationships meant opening up everything—the good, the bad, the ugly—and she lived her life online. He needed to retreat.

There was a reason why wealthy men courted wealthy women. They all moved in similar circles. They all understood the rules and what it took to keep those families protected. And while he no longer felt like he needed to protect his brother, Dean was a part of Damian's world. And Dean had helped Brett out when he had nowhere else to turn. He owed his brother.

How was Brett supposed to know that having his son so close was going to end up hurting this much? All the same, his brother had done what he'd asked, even at a risk to his own political career. He'd done it...

And now, Brett owed them all. This wasn't about his feelings.

"Any chance you could see yourself living on a ranch and leaving all of this behind you?" he asked, but even as the words came out, they felt wrong. Emaline wasn't part of this world of obligations, hidden strings and hidden triggers all over the place. She had the luxury of being a regular woman—an extraordinary woman—but someone free of all those demands.

"I have a whole life..." She shook her head, and he understood, maybe even better than she did.

"Yeah." He swallowed past a lump in his throat. "And I'm a Rockwell. There's no changing who you are. You'll be telling important stories, Emaline Piper. Whether it's in print or online."

"I wish that was more comforting." Tears misted her eyes.

"I'm going to see you rise," he said quietly. "And I'm going to be super proud of you."

"I hope so, but—" Her chin trembled.

"I'll do what I can to keep Dean and Bobbie from suing you," he said. "I've already talked to my brother about it once, and I'll bring it up again. They can go after the newspaper, but I'll make it a personal favor to me if they leave you and George alone."

"Can you stop them?" she asked.

"They'll owe me if I go away and quit asking for more with their son."

"You shouldn't have to—" she began.

"I was already planning on it," he said. "And I'll make a few deals with my brother. I still have some favors he owes me, too. I'll call them in. Every last one."

"You'd do that for me?"

"Emaline, I'd do pretty much anything for you," he said.

He wanted to kiss her, to hold her, to show her the depth of what he was feeling, but he couldn't do that now. He was supposed to be the strong one, and he was barely holding it together as it was.

"They'll have to publish a retraction," she said. "I have the proof of the text I sent that I tried to stop the story from coming out. George will have to face the music on that one. He didn't trust my instinct. He thought I was caving in."

"Don't back off on that one. I can recommend a good lawyer if that helps."

She didn't answer.

"Forgive me for wanting to take care of you a little bit," he said. "Someone should. That wasn't fair."

"I don't know if I can afford a good lawyer," she said.

Sometimes he forgot that most people had financial limits that he didn't have to worry about. He felt a little foolish for not thinking of it before.

"I'll pay for it," he replied. "Your dignity and your reputation matter. I don't want you to take a hit for this. But you might have to tell them how you knew that story was wrong. You might have to say that I'm Damian's biological father."

"Nope." She met his gaze. "I'll protect my source to the end."

He couldn't help but smile at that. "You think you can get away with that?"

"If I want to be a journalist, I'm nothing if my source can't trust me." She smiled sadly. "If *you* can't trust me."

"At least I'll always be your source. That's something, right?"

He was trying to joke a little bit, but his heart was breaking. He wanted to be so much more to her. He wanted to be her hero, her comfort, the rock she came back to.

"Always." She squeezed his hand.

Outside, he could hear the sound of the plows making another pass down their side road. Everything would be clear by morning. The bob of a lantern was visible coming back toward the house. Two lanterns this time. Eli must be walking Belinda home. He envied the simplicity of their problems.

"If we didn't have an old Amish lady coming back, I'd ask you to sit up with me tonight," he said softly.

"I don't think I dare…"

He could see the pain in her eyes, and a tear spilled down her cheek.

"I'm sorry," he said.

"It isn't your fault, Brett."

Yet he felt like it was. Brett pulled her into his arms and held her close. He could feel the rise and fall of her chest as she tried to hold back her tears. He wished they had more time, more privacy, but would it even help? His feelings would only get more complicated, and the goodbye would be more painful.

Footsteps sounded outside on the stairs, and then the door opened. Brett released Emaline, and she looked up at him once, then fled for the staircase. As she disappeared at the top, Belinda came into the kitchen, shaking out her snowy shawl. She went to the window and waved.

"He walked you home," Brett said.

"Of course." Belinda turned back and gave Brett a smile. "Eli always walks me home."

Maybe one day he'd be equally cocooned on his ranch, forgotten by the people who stirred political pots and left to simply live his life. Maybe then he could find Emaline again...

But he knew better than to even hope for that.

"Are you all right, dear?" Belinda asked gently. "You look wrung out."

That summed it up. "It's been a tough day."

Belinda nodded. "I could tell. Would pie help?"

For the life of him, Belinda Wickey standing there in her cranberry red dress, her white hair pulled back and covered in her *kapp* and those twinkling blue eyes made him think of Mrs. Claus. Damian hadn't been wrong. If he were thirty years younger, he might tell her that he'd been a good boy, too.

"Yeah, pie might help," he said.

She smiled and headed for the counter.

Brett didn't want to be alone tonight. Not yet. He needed to sit here in a warm kitchen with a kind old woman and remind himself that there was good reason for his broken heart and that a man's obligations and sacrifices were what made him into the good person he wanted to be.

Being good hurt sometimes. He wouldn't talk about it, but he had a feeling that Belinda would understand. And tonight, that would be enough.

CHAPTER SEVENTEEN

EMALINE LAY AWAKE that night for a long time. She cried until she had no more tears, and then she sat by the window watching the moon move slowly across the sky. She heard Brett go to bed, heard the springs on his bed creak as he tossed and turned, and she held herself back from going next door. He knew what he needed to do, and no matter what they felt, no matter how much they felt in this short time, this relationship wasn't possible.

Emaline managed to sleep for about three hours, and then she woke up to the sound of Belinda working in the kitchen. Last night, she'd thought she'd wait to see Brett once more before she left, but this morning, still feeling a little teary, she didn't think she'd be able to face him with any dignity. The last thing she wanted to do was cry on Brett's shoulder in front of a very confused and very sweet old lady.

So, as quietly as she could, she made her bed, packed her bag and opened her bedroom door. She stopped and listened. There was no sound coming from the other room. Maybe she was hoping he'd be up, too, taking the choice out of her hands. But he wasn't. All was quiet except for the scrape of the wood stove's damper. She carried her bag downstairs to the kitchen, where Belinda turned and smiled.

"Good morning, dear," she said. "You're up early."

"I need to head home," Emaline said. "But I wanted to thank you for my stay. It was lovely—even the storm. Here, for the cost of my stay."

She handed Belinda a check. The old woman frowned at it. "This is too much."

"I added the extra days up. I insist upon paying for it."

"That's very kind," Belinda said. "If you're sure it's not a hardship."

"It's not," Emaline said. At least, she'd work it out. "Get your niece to look up the name of your bed-and-breakfast in a few days, and you'll see all the posts. I think you'll like them. There'll be no faces, and I hope they'll help you drum up all sorts of business."

"I do appreciate it, dear," Belinda said. "I might not understand everything you do, but Jill will explain it to me."

"Tell Eli goodbye for me, would you? And give Eeyore a scratch from me, too."

"Will you stay for breakfast?" Belinda asked. "I was just about to start cooking."

"No..." Emaline swallowed. "I don't think I could eat this early."

She didn't think she could eat at all, quite frankly. Her stomach was in knots, and she felt weakened from her tears the night before and her poor sleep.

"Well, thank you for coming," Belinda said. "And I do hope you'll come again."

Emaline nodded quickly. She was feeling emotional again already. The thought of coming back and not seeing Brett would be too hard, though. Her heart had gotten entangled here, and that was too painful to be simply pushed into the past. At least for a long while.

"Would you like me to say anything to Brett?" Belinda asked.

"Tell him—" Emaline swallowed. "I don't know. Tell him goodbye."

That was a loaded word, but they needed to go their separate ways, and there was no point in dragging that out.

"It's the matchmaker in me," Belinda said softly, "but I really thought I sensed something special between the two of you."

"It's complicated," Emaline said. "And if I

talk about it right now, I'll just start crying. I need to get going." She swallowed and turned toward the door. "Thank you for everything, Belinda. I appreciate it."

Emaline's car was covered in snow. She started the engine to warm it up, stowed her things and cleared the accumulation off the car.

The drive was plowed, and that big bank of snow had been cleared from the front of the driveway. The roads were clear once more. She looked up at the second-floor windows. Her room had open curtains the way she'd left them. Brett's window had curtains drawn. She didn't blame him for sleeping. It was early, and the last few days had been tiring ones.

But then Emaline looked over toward Eli's property and did a double take. Brett wasn't in the house, after all. He was with Eli by the fence, the dog bouncing through the snow next to the old man. Brett's gaze was locked on her, and she lifted one gloved hand in a wave.

Brett waved back, but he didn't move toward her. If she stopped now, she might not drive away, and that wouldn't be helpful for either of them. So she got into the car and drove away.

The Butternut Amish B&B was not real life. There was no future here for her—just some hopes and dreams and a piece of her heart—but there was no way to integrate that into the rest of her life…or into the rest of his.

As Emaline turned onto the road, she wiped a tear off her cheek. It took a solid half hour of driving before she pulled over to the side of the road and gave herself up to the tears that she couldn't hold back anymore.

She'd fallen in love with him. That was the problem. This wasn't just catching feelings. She'd gone and fallen in love with the rebellious Rockwell. It had been reckless and stupid and unavoidable. She'd fallen for him, and there was no way out of it, no shortcut to the pain. But a good cry did help, and when she blew her nose and wiped her eyes, her phone pinged. She looked over to see a new text message from her half sister.

I'm sorry about how emotional I got before. Maybe I'm starting to get angry, after all. But I'd like to talk again, if you're up to it.

Sitting in her car with cold toes and a soggy tissue in one hand, she couldn't help but think about all the things that had gone wrong. Yet here she had a sister who just wanted to talk.

Ironically, Maggie wouldn't care a bit if Emaline got a job with a newspaper or not. She wouldn't be embarrassed if Emaline ended up being sued by the Rockwells. She didn't really want anything out of Emaline except…to be seen. Bobbie's words came back like a slap: *Maybe I just want you to look me in the face.*

It was probably time that Emaline faced the family who'd won in the competition over their father. Maybe she wasn't quite so over her father's betrayal after all. His lies had crushed her. And she'd still seen everything through that traumatic lens, even Dean Rockwell. Her article that was supposed to kick-start her career in real, hard-hitting journalism had been completely false, and the truest things she'd worked on all this time had been vlog posts about a donkey who went missing in a snowstorm, the simple Christmas decorations on an Amish windowsill and a sensitive little boy who'd found a friend. She'd post the full vlogs over the next few days, but she already felt very good about them.

They had been true! And the ironic thing was that truth had been about the beautiful, simple, easy things in the world. It had been about friendship and hope, and a connection

to animals and Christmas miracles. *Fluffy*—
that's what people called it. She preferred *uplifting*. And the cynical look at a wealthy man
who everyone believed was using his clout to
get his way hadn't been true at all…

She picked up her phone to text back, and
her finger hovered over the phone number. Her
sister deserved more than a text. It rang once
and her sister picked up.

"Hello?"

"Hi, Maggie."

"Hi," Maggie said. "I wanted to apologize."

"Forget it," Emaline said. "I need to apologize, too. I haven't been at my best. Let's just
call it even and let it go."

Emaline watched as a horse and buggy trot-
ted past, going at a pretty quick pace. The
buggy was boxy and only had a small window,
but a child's face was plastered there, looking
outside. The vehicle whisked past.

"Look, the thing you should know about
me is that I'm always trying to keep the peace
around here," Maggie said. "Maybe you got
off easy—your mom moved on. Mine didn't!
And I always feel somewhat responsible to
keep Dad and Mom at peace with each other,
to keep Dad happy in our home…" There was
a pause. "This is going to sound awful, but
that's why I messaged you this Christmas.

Dad had been complaining that he lost his other kids, and Mom was defending herself, and…I was doing what I always do. I was trying to fix it so he'd stick around."

"So, that's what was going on," Emaline murmured.

"I'm sorry. It isn't that I don't want to know you, because I do. But, yeah, that's what pushed me to contact you this Christmas."

"I'm not upset," Emaline said. "It's nice to hear the honest truth."

"I seem to try and keep the peace like that a lot," Maggie said.

"Well, stop it," Emaline joked. "Sometimes people need to just duke it out."

Maggie laughed softly. "Easier said than done."

"I know…" Emaline's mind went back over these last few days. Was she really so different from her sister? "You're not the only one who's got issues because of what Dad did. For me, Dad leaving made me feel like I wasn't good enough for him to stay. So I'm always trying to prove I'm worthy enough…for everything. I may even have a few more trust issues than I thought."

"I'm sorry for that…"

"It's not on you, Maggie," Emaline said. "That's on Dad. You aren't the only one who works too hard to fix things and prove herself. I've got the same problem. I'm just coming at it from a different angle."

"So, what do we do?" Maggie asked.

Emaline was silent for a moment. "How busy is your Christmas? Maybe we could get together."

"Do you really want to drag our parents into this?" Maggie asked. "I'm not sure I want to face your mother, and if you wanted to come to my parents' place, I'm sure—"

"No, no! I don't want that at all!" Emaline said. "I know a Chinese food place that's open Christmas Day, and I wanted to know if you wanted to—I don't know—split some chow mein or something. Just us sisters."

"Just us?"

"Yeah. I know I gave you a hard time before, but I want my sister in my life."

"Yeah. I'd like that a lot."

"Perfect." Emaline couldn't help but smile. "And we've got nothing to prove, okay? We share DNA. That's enough."

Maggie laughed softly. "What a relief."

"I need to get driving," Emaline said. "I have to focus on the road. It's pretty slippery out here. I'll text you the address to the restaurant when I get back, and you can tell me what time you can be there."

"That sounds good. We'll talk later."

Emaline hung up the call and pulled out onto the snowy road once more. Sun sparkled on the unbroken snow that covered the field next to her, and she felt a surge of hope.

She'd been so determined to mitigate the damage her father's choices had caused in her own psyche that it was oddly relieving to just admit to herself that she hadn't gotten over it yet. Maybe she never would... Maybe she'd always be a little too vigilant, and maybe Maggie would always be a little too quick to try and fix everything around her, but they'd get through it. Maybe they didn't have to be over it in order to be happy or successful in life.

And Emaline had a feeling that she'd be better for having her sister in her life.

BRETT AND ELI finished with the last of the stalls in the barn, and Brett's boots felt heavy. He was tired—physically and emotionally. His chest was tight, too, as if even getting his heart to beat was taking extra effort. Watching Emaline drive away had just about crushed him.

He'd thought for a split second that she might turn off the car and...stay. But she hadn't. She'd just pulled out and driven off.

He'd almost texted her a hundred times since then, but he hadn't. She was right—they knew where this stood. She'd just been stronger than him.

Eli had let the cows back outside to the field, the feeder filled with fresh hay. The stalls were now clean, and their boots echoed on the cement floor.

"So, what happened between you and the young lady?" Eli asked.

"Nothing."

"That's not true. Obviously, it was something."

"Nothing that will last, so it doesn't matter," Brett clarified.

"Hmm." Eli sighed. "I'm not sure about that. If you feel like this—"

"I'm fine."

"That's not true, either," Eli said, and this time he looked genuinely hurt. "Look, Brett, I know we men tend to bury our feelings, but an outright lie hurts you on the inside. You're better off telling me to leave you alone than to lie about it."

Right—Amish sensibilities. They didn't fib about these things, it would seem.

"All right," Brett said. "I respect you, Eli, and I'm sorry I lied. The truth is, I'm not okay.

I fell for Emaline, but it can't work. There's no possible way. So I need to just get over it."

"Did you know that Belinda is a matchmaker?" Eli asked. "She's very good, you know. She's matched many couples over the years, some even as poorly matched as you and that young *Englisher* lady."

Brett sighed. "I'm not Amish, Eli."

"I know, but…you are in love."

Brett blinked at him. "I mean, I feel something for her. I feel a lot for her. I…I want to see her and protect her and be the man who makes her happy. And I…miss her a lot. Already."

Eli raised his bushy eyebrows. "And?"

And… Brett's heart skipped a beat as he strung it all together. "It's too soon to fall in love with her. That would be really…impetuous on my part."

"So?" Eli shrugged. "It is what it is."

Maybe Eli was right. Because this did definitely feel like love. That only made him a bigger fool right now.

"Eli, you're probably the only one who'd understand this," Brett said, "but sometimes you can fall for a woman so hard it makes your teeth rattle, but there just isn't a way forward. Like you and Belinda. You love her— you have for decades—and it just won't work.

Sometimes we don't get the woman we love. That's just a brutal fact."

"Well, as it turns out," Eli said quietly, "Belinda and I are getting married."

"What?" Brett spun around.

"Yah."

"I thought—"

"Last night, we went out to do chores together," Eli said. "And I took one more shot at it. I told her I loved her and that I knew she was worried about a life with me but that I'd spend the rest of my days making her days easier. I asked her to take a chance on me."

"And she…did?" Brett asked.

"First, she told me I was a rather large risk, and then she said she'd miss me desperately if I left." Eli shrugged. "And after a very quiet, very honest conversation, she didn't think I was such a risk after all, and she agreed to marry me."

"Congratulations," Brett said.

"Thank you." Eli's eyes misted. "At long last, I've got my girl."

"When is the wedding?" Brett asked.

"Oh, our *banns* have to be read at church first, and then we have to issue invitations to our friends and families. We have to figure out who will host the wedding for us—she thinks her son will—and I have to go have a sit-down with her children and tell them that I'll do well by their mother."

"So, there's a lot of preparation," Brett said.

"I've waited a long time for this day, and I want to do it right," the old man replied. "I'll finally be able to grow out a beard. Only married men can wear beards. I don't even know if I'll have a nice full beard or a little scrappy one." Eli chuckled. "But I'll wear it with pride, however it grows."

"I'm really happy for you, Eli," Brett said. "At least one of us should get the girl, right?"

"You could, too," Eli said.

"I'm not sure how."

"I don't know the ins and outs of your situation," Eli said. "You've assured me that it's very complicated. But I know human nature, and I know that pride is usually what gets between us and our heart's desire."

"It's not my pride," he said.

"You think your family is very important," Eli said. "Rockwells. You think your people are worth protecting more than her people. You think your brother's needs are more important than anyone else's, including your own. You think your family's claim to your future is stronger than what you want for yourself. Because they are such an important and wealthy family."

"You know a bit more than you let on," Brett said.

"I listen." The old man smiled ruefully. "What I just described was pride. Family stands by each other. They help each other. They lift each other up. And they accept help when they need it. They open up their ranks and welcome in a new in-law. They're there when hard times hit and when something good needs celebrating. And let me tell you something—every family matters. Every last one. Not just the Rockwells."

Brett looked at the old man in surprise. No one had ever spoken to him quite that directly before. His family's strings had tied him down for as long as he could remember. But they'd been there for him, too. Was it possible that he didn't need to give Emaline up for their sake? Was there some way this might actually work?

"I'm sorry if I overstepped," Eli added, dropping his gaze, "but it needed saying."

"Damian is my son," Brett said. He explained the situation briefly.

"Ah...that explains a lot." Eli nodded.

"Damian needs stability—" Brett started.

"He needs the truth," Eli interrupted.

"Yeah...well, I mentioned that to my brother, and he wasn't so keen on the idea."

Eli shrugged. "So insist. I don't think brothers are that different between our people and yours. Sometimes brothers in Amish families will go so far as to have a fight out in the barn to settle things."

Brett started to laugh. "Are you serious? I thought you were peace-loving people."

"We don't tend to advertise that, but..." Eli shrugged meekly. "The thing is, peace is the goal, but sometimes—between brothers, at least—it takes a headlock to get there."

Brett couldn't help but laugh. Out here in the barn, it all seemed like it could be simple, easily handled. His complicated problems felt a little less impossible out here in Amish Country.

They were the Rockwells, and maybe they'd gotten a little too high of an opinion about themselves. Damian needed stability, but he'd need the truth eventually. Damian needed his parents, but he'd also need Brett—a relationship they'd sort out over time. The Rockwells had secrets, but what was the worst that could happen? Dean might not get elected, and their family might actually get to settle and give everyone else a chance to matter, too. Things would change, sure, but the worst-case scenario suddenly didn't feel so terrible.

"I don't think I can just fight my brother in the barn, but you're right about the rest. You Amish have your ways of doing things right, making sure everyone understands and appreciates what's going on when you get married," Brett said. "I might need to figure that out for us—if Emaline will have me."

"Oh, bop him in the nose and be done with it," Eli said. "And forget the complicated paths—tell her you love her and ask her to marry you. Anything less is wasting your time." Eli shot him a grin. "Trust me, I know about wasted time. Learn from an old man. If I had to do it over, I'd have marched over here twenty years ago and made Belinda see me. But better late than never. When a woman is the right one, you'll never forget her anyway. Just accept that." Eli rubbed a gloved hand under his nose. "And after all that bravado, maybe the best piece of advice I have is this: the most important conversations are the private, quiet ones. Those are the talks that change everything. That was the talk that made Belinda agree to be my wife."

A private, quiet talk.

That sounded pretty perfect, but Brett had other things to sort out first.

Starting with Dean.

CHAPTER EIGHTEEN

EMALINE DROPPED HER bag off at her apartment and then spent the next couple of hours cleaning up and making her apartment look festive. She pulled out her little artificial Christmas tree and decorated it with her mix of old ornaments she'd brought from her mom's place and newer ones she'd collected over the years. She liked the result.

Mom would decorate and cook like crazy, but Emaline needed a little Christmas spirit here in her own home.

But she also felt guilty. She might not have wanted to hurt the Rockwell family the way she had, but she'd done damage. She knew what it felt like to be on the receiving end of someone else's behavior. She wanted to make this better…even if she couldn't make it exactly right.

She opened her laptop and searched the senator's office. She found a phone number and dialed it. Predictably, she was shunted off to voice mail.

"This is Emaline Piper, and I was hoping to speak with Mrs. Rockwell. I know she's pretty upset with me right now, but I wanted to try and make things right, if I can."

She left her number, and a few minutes later her phone rang. The number was private, and she picked up.

"Hello?"

"Hello, Emaline." Bobbie's firm voice came through.

"Mrs. Rockwell, thank you for calling me back," Emaline said.

"My assistant passed along your message." Her tone was chilly. "I was curious to hear what you have to say."

This didn't seem promising, but she'd gotten a return call, and that was better than simply being ignored.

"I know I really messed things up for you, and it wasn't my intent," Emaline said. "I sent in a writing sample based on my hunch and someone else's research. I didn't think it would be published, but that was naive of me. I want you to know that I warned the other journalist off the story when I learned from Brett that Dean isn't Damian's dad."

Silence hung on the other end of the phone, but she could tell Bobbie was still there.

So she went on, "But it was too late. He

thought he had evidence—obviously, it's misleading, but he really thought he did. He's not a bad guy, either. He was just so convinced that your husband was that kind of man, and... Sometimes we jump to unfair conclusions, and I'm really, really sorry that we did that to you. And I understand how writing a correction notice doesn't do much after something that juicy is out there, so I had an idea..."

"What's that?" Bobbie sounded cautious.

"I have a pretty big following online, and if you've seen my vlog posts, you can see the kind of stories I do. I'd like to offer my services to you. Let me go with you to some local spot and get some video of you with Damian—mother and son. Let's put a visual out there of what your relationship with your boy looks like. Let them see the love there, the truth of the kind of family you really are."

"You'd do that?" Bobbie asked.

"I would."

"How much would you charge?"

"Nothing. This is my olive branch. I don't have much I can offer a family like yours, Mrs. Rockwell, but I do have some talent up my sleeve. It's the best I've got."

"You have some integrity," Bobbie said quietly. "I'm actually rather impressed by that. Most journalists would lawyer up, not reach out."

Maybe she was being foolish by not doing just that, she realized.

"I'm not actually a journalist yet," Emaline said. "I'm more of a storyteller who is trying to be a decent person."

"Well, let me discuss it with the team and get back to you," Bobbie replied. "Brett seems to think you're worth fighting for, and I can see why."

"He does?" Her stomach suddenly flipped.

Bobbie laughed softly. "I'll let him speak for himself. I'll get back to you about your offer. Take care, Miss Piper."

Emaline hung up, her heartbeat galloping in her chest. What was Brett saying about her? And fighting for her how?

BOBBIE DID GET back to her, and they agreed to a local riding facility that catered to special needs kids two days after Christmas. It was an opportunity to spotlight a worthy nonprofit organization as well as show Bobbie as the caring mother she was.

It took a few tries, but Emaline managed to get Bobbie to stop using her election smile and just relax with her boy. That wasn't easy to do on camera, and Emaline knew it, but she'd also seen Bobbie with Damian, and that special bond was one she wanted to capture.

People could vote any way they wanted, but Bobbie deserved to be seen fairly for once. She was more than Dean's wife.

Damian loved riding. He sat ramrod straight on the back of a gentle mare, his riding helmet shining in the afternoon sunlight, and Emaline got a shot of Bobbie leaning against a rail as she watched him pass, and then how she called after him, "Squeeze with your knees, Damian! There you go!"

"I'm good at this, Mom!" Damian hollered back over his shoulder.

"Face front!" Bobbie called back with that maternal panic about safety, and Emaline couldn't help but grin. This was perfect.

Her phone vibrated with a text, and she stopped the recording and flicked over to read it.

I miss you. So much.

It was from Brett, and she felt tears mist her eyes.

I miss you, too, she texted back.

Because she did—desperately.

Good. I'm glad, he texted. I want to see you. I have it on good authority that the quiet conversations are the ones that change everything. So come talk quietly with me...

Her heart skipped a beat. Every fiber of her being wanted to hop back in the car, but she couldn't.

I'm spending the day with your sister-in-law, putting together a vlog post about a riding center just outside of Pittsburgh, she texted to Brett.

I'm at the Chronicle, he replied.

What are you doing there? she asked.

Apparently putting everyone into a tizzy. Let me buy you dinner tonight, and I'll explain.

He was in town? Just the senator's younger brother hanging out in the reception area at the newspaper that was hell-bent on taking his brother down. Everyone probably was in a tizzy! She didn't even know if she was getting sued yet!

Dinner would be great.

Seeing him would be a relief. Brett Rockwell was like no man she'd ever met before... But he was still a member of one of the most powerful families in the state. None of that had changed. What on earth did he have in mind?

BRETT CHOSE A table in the back of the Scoop, away from windows and within sight of the front door. He'd caused a tornado of excitement at the *Chronicle* that afternoon. He had a meeting with the editor, where he promised an interview—but only with Emaline Piper. He suggested that he could get his family to back off the lawsuit they were threatening, and it might get Emaline another chance at a spot at the paper, telling the kinds of in-depth stories she was good at. Who knew?

The booth was cozily lit and was far enough from everyone else for them to have some privacy. Brett fiddled with a napkin, his eye on the door. He had an idea, but it was one that would require a whole lot of bravery from both of them.

Emaline arrived a few minutes later, and Brett stood up to show her where he was. She smiled and wove her way through the tables to the booth he'd chosen. He didn't wait for her to say a word. He pulled her into his arms and into a kiss, relief flooding through him to have her close again. She melted into his arms and held his sides with handfuls of his shirt. When he pulled back, she blinked up at him.

"That was…public," she said.

He felt his face heat. "I actually forgot."

"You probably shouldn't," she whispered, but her cheeks were pink. She slid into the booth across from him.

"So, as I said, I miss you," he said, coming right to the point.

She smiled. "Me too."

"And I thought my feelings for you might lessen given a few days, but…that didn't happen."

"Good." She grinned at him.

"I love you," he said softly.

"I love you, too, Brett."

"Yeah?" It felt like a vice around his chest had suddenly released.

She nodded, a smile sparkling in her eyes. "It's wildly inconvenient, but yes. I really do."

He reached across the table and caught her hand. "I know this was fast. I've never gotten serious this quickly before. I don't want you thinking this is the way I usually am. You're special."

Emaline squeezed his fingers. "You're saying everything I want to hear, but do you have a solution to our obvious problem?"

"I do. I say we ignore it."

She chuckled. "Ignore that I ruined your family's life…"

"Yes." He met her gaze seriously. "Here's the thing. I talked to my brother over Christmas. We all got together at Dean and Bobbie's place, after all. And they're going to tell Damian who I am."

Her eyebrows went up. "Wow."

"Yeah, and for New Year's Eve, we're all going to be at my ranch—all of us, Dean and his family, my mother, me—and we'll start something new. We'll be telling the truth, even when it's uncomfortable."

"Publicly?" she asked softly.

"Yes, publicly."

He could feel her held breath.

"If you want the exclusive interview about my rehab, turning my life around, having my brother adopt my son—all of it—it's yours," he said.

"Are you serious?"

"I don't joke about airing family secrets." He smiled faintly. "But I was hoping it might be a conflict of interest."

"How so?" she asked.

"If you're marrying me." She blinked twice and he couldn't help but chuckle. "Come on. We're both adults. You're absolutely amazing, and I want to spend the rest of my life with you. No secrets. No hiding. I just need to know…can you be there for Damian? We have to meet him where he's at, and that can be a lot of work. He also comes with a complicated history. Can you have a stepson like Damian and just love him?"

Emaline started to nod, and tears welled in

her eyes. "I know a thing or two about complicated histories…" her voice got tight with emotion "…and, yes, I sure can."

A waitress swept up to their table, a pad of paper in her hand. She smiled at them brightly.

"Hi, there. Welcome to the Scoop. I'm Tiffany, and I'll be your waitress today."

Brett looked up at a bright-eyed teenager in mild surprise.

"Tiffany, could we have a minute?" he asked.

"Oh, sure. I'll get you some water to start."

"Thanks."

Tiffany headed back to the kitchen, and Brett caught Emaline's hand again.

"I don't think we have much time. Tiffany seems like a go-getter. I need to know your answer. Marry me."

"When?" she asked. Still not a yes, but this was moving in the right direction.

Brett cast around in his head for an appropriate time. "This spring? Summer? Fall?"

"How about next Christmas at the Butternut Amish B&B?" Her eyes sparkled, and for the life of him, he wished there wasn't a table between them. He wanted her closer, in his arms, and he never wanted to let go of her again.

"That sounds perfect. You want to be engaged for a full year?"

"I need a full year!" she said. "A woman doesn't become a Rockwell in a snap. Besides…I want to enjoy it a little bit. And get to know your family. You need to get to know mine, too. There are a few…tensions…that need ironing out. But I'm telling you, I think I made some progress with Bobbie today."

"I can't wait to hear more about that, but first, is that an official yes?" He grinned.

Tiffany bustled up to the table again with two ice waters on a tray. She placed little cocktail napkins in front of each of them, then put down the waters. She gave them each a bright smile.

"We have some specials today," Tiffany said. "There's lemon chicken couscous with a—"

Brett put a hand up and Tiffany paused. He locked his gaze on Emaline.

"Say yes," he said, his voice low. "For the love of all that's good, just say yes!"

"Yes, Brett," she said, a smile breaking out across her face. She seemed to be enjoying his agony, and Brett slipped out of his side of the booth, went behind Tiffany and slid into Emaline's side. He touched her chin to turn her toward him and kissed her tenderly.

"I love you," he whispered.

"I love you, too!"

Eli was right about those quiet conversations. He'd have to tell his family and deal with their frustration around his choice in a bride. But they'd survive. He'd tell them on New Year's Eve. They all needed to meet Emaline properly, get to know her a bit. It sounded like Bobbie had already started to.

He looked back up at Tiffany, who looked wide-eyed and mildly confused.

"Sorry," he said. "You were telling us the specials."

"There's lemon chicken couscous with a broccoli and cheddar baked soup. We've got honey garlic shredded pork..."

And he listened to the specials, watched Emaline's eyes sparkle as she ordered, and then he just said he'd have whatever she was having.

They'd have dinner, and then he planned to take her ring shopping at Tiffany's. He knew the manager, and even if it was closed, he'd reopen for Brett, especially considering the amount of money Brett was planning on dropping on a ring for Emaline. By the time he left her side tonight, he wanted an engagement ring on her finger.

Strange how freeing it was to just go with his heart! But it felt right. For the first time in a long time, he could see his whole future rolling out in front of him with this woman at his side. She didn't come family-approved, but he didn't care a bit.

She wasn't perfect for the Rockwells. She was perfect for *him*. The Rockwells would catch up!

EPILOGUE

THE NEXT YEAR was filled with wedding plans and career growth for Emaline. Dean and Bobbie decided not to sue the paper, but they did offer to push for a job for Emaline, if she wanted it. She asked them not to bother. She had her own plans that involved growing her vlogging career. This was how doors opened when a woman had a powerful family behind her. It was eye-opening! But all the same, she wanted to make it on her own.

Brett gave George his tell-all interview, since Emaline agreed it would be a conflict of interest. George used the opportunity to make sure he told a balanced and fair story. His editor thought he hadn't been tough enough on Brett, but George stuck to his guns. Sometimes the truth wasn't scandalous or shocking. Sometimes, it was just the story of a guy who did his best and was recovering from addiction.

Emaline's vlog became more and more animal and agriculture focused as she spent more time with Brett at his ranch, and her viewership started growing again, even with the pivot in content. There was interest in how ranches functioned and a close-up view into the world of beef production.

Belinda and Eli Lapp were more than happy to have their B&B chosen as Emaline and Brett's wedding venue. Belinda and Eli had had a small Amish wedding that spring, and they'd settled in to run the B&B together. Eli's farm next door had been sold, and it was now being run by the young Amish couple who'd purchased it. Eli's hens had come with him, and a new large coop was set up in the backyard. His cows had been sold to a hobby farm where they'd be mollycoddled, just like Eli hoped.

There was no electricity, but the Amish community had a few solutions for an outdoor wedding in the middle of winter. They put up a large tent and warmed it with some rented heaters that were plugged into generators—apparently this would be acceptable since the generators ran on gasoline and since Emaline and Brett weren't Amish. Belinda let them use the bedrooms upstairs to get ready for the ceremony.

The day of the wedding was bright and sunny—just a couple of days before Christmas. The horse and Eeyore were out in their paddock watching all the excitement, and the photographer even got a few pictures of Emaline in her white fur-trimmed wrap, with Eeyore putting his nose forward for a pet.

Brett's best man was his brother Dean, and he had another little groomsman in his son. Damian had adjusted surprisingly well to the news of his biological father. He already knew he was adopted, so having his biological dad so close and already someone who loved him had made the emotional transition easier than they'd feared. Damian had replaced his big headphones with some ear plugs for the wedding, and Brett had been proud of him for that step forward.

Emaline asked Maggie to stand as her maid of honor, and everyone commented on how alike Emaline and Maggie looked. They were certainly sisters, and Maggie had thoroughly enjoyed getting to know her half brothers over the last year, too. Of course, they were all at the wedding with their mother, too. Emaline had invited her father in a moment of grave maturity, but some sort of drama had prevented him from attending, and he'd sent a card and a gift. That relationship was in process.

They kept the wedding small, with fifty

guests between them, most of whom were family—plus Eli and Belinda, of course. It was their way of keeping the wedding under the radar of the newspapers. They'd release a few photos later, when they were ready. The old Amish couple was mildly scandalized when they found out they'd be sitting side by side during the wedding. Amish weddings had men on one side and women on the other, and Emaline couldn't help but chuckle when she saw Eli touch Belinda's hand and Belinda's face blaze into a blush.

The wedding ceremony was short and sweet. The minister talked about love, commitment and family. When it was time to exchange rings and make their vows, Emaline felt her stomach flutter with nerves. But she'd never seen Brett look more confident.

Their "I dos" were from the heart, and when Brett and Emaline Rockwell were announced as officially married, Brett stepped closer and dipped his head down to catch her lips with his. She leaned into his embrace, and her heart overflowed with happiness.

But as they pulled back, someone suddenly said, "Where is that donkey going?"

And then there was a bustle of attention as Eeyore went trotting past the opening of the tent, and Eli jumped up and started climbing over people's knees to go after him. The younger people got the idea that the donkey had to be caught, and everything turned into a flurry of activity.

"Let them chase Eeyore down," Brett said, tugging Emaline back against him. "We're busy, Mrs. Rockwell."

Emaline looked up into his eyes laughingly. "Oh, are we?"

And he lowered his lips to hers again, pulling her in close. Emaline could hear the chatter and shouting as people went off in pursuit of the donkey, and she pulled back from the kiss when she felt a tug on her skirt.

She looked down at Damian, who hooked a thumb over his shoulder. "The wedding is done now. You can stop kissing."

Emaline laughed and bent down to smile at Damian. On his wrist was a little braided yarn friendship bracelet, and a lump rose in her throat when she recognized it.

"Damian, you wore our bracelet?"

"Yep," Damian said. "Uncle Brett saved it for me."

"You want to see something?" Emaline said, and she lowered her flowers so that he could see the handle of the bouquet where she'd wound the little straw bracelet that he'd made for her a year earlier.

"You have yours, too." Damian's eyes widened, and he touched the earplug in one ear, cocking his head to one side as he inspected the braided straw.

She looked up to see Dean and Bobbie standing behind their son, Dean's arm around his wife's waist.

"Always," Emaline said. "I had to have it on my wedding day."

Damian smiled up at her, and her heart blossomed open for this little boy and for her husband at her side, and the whole tangled family that came with them. Brett blinked a couple of times against the tears glistening in his eyes, and she felt the same way.

This was it—their family, their beginning. And as Brett's hand caught hers, she felt with absolute certainty that everything was going to be okay.

This wasn't a story she was telling anymore; it was their story together that was about to begin.

* * * * *

Don't miss the next
Harlequin Heartwarming book
from Patricia Johns,
coming July 2024